Time After Time

J.P. BOWIE

MLR PRESS AUTHORS

Featuring a roll call of some of the best writers of gay erotica and mysteries today!

Maura Anderson
Victor J. Banis
Jeanne Barrack
Laura Baumbach
Alex Beecroft
Sarah Black
Ally Blue
J.P. Bowie
P.A. Brown
James Buchanan
Jordan Castillo Price
Kirby Crow
Dick D.
Jason Edding
Angela Fiddler
Dakota Flint
Kimberly Gardner
Storm Grant
Amber Green
LB Gregg
Drewey Wayne Gunn

Samantha Kane
Kiernan Kelly
JL Langley
Josh Lanyon
Clare London
William Maltese
Gary Martine
Z.A. Maxfield
Jet Mykles
L. Picaro
Neil Plakcy
Luisa Prieto
Rick R. Reed
AM Riley
George Seaton
Jardonn Smith
Caro Soles
Richard Stevenson
Claire Thompson
Kit Zheng

Check out titles, both available and forthcoming, at
www.mlrpress.com

Time After Time

J.P. BOWIE

mlrpress

Copyright 2009 by J.P. Bowie

All rights reserved, including the right of reproduction in whole or in part in any form.

Published by
MLR Press, LLC
3052 Gaines Waterport Rd.
Albion, NY 14411

Visit ManLoveRomance Press, LLC on the Internet:
www.mlrpress.com

Cover Art by Deana C. Jamroz
Editing by Kris Jacen
Printed in the United States of America.

ISBN# 978-1-60820-056-6

First Edition 2009

For Phil, Always

CHAPTER ONE

For the umpteenth time in twenty minutes, Michael Ballantyne glanced toward the diner entrance to see if his brother Brad had yet deigned to arrive for their lunch date. "Where in hell is he?" he muttered to himself, sucking up half his iced tea in frustration. He caught the waiter's eye and ordered a burger. No point in waiting any longer—looked like Brad was a no show.

He tried to shuck off the feeling of disappointment that his brother hadn't even bothered to call him to say he couldn't make it, but just as the waiter took his order, Michael saw a red-faced Brad dash into the diner and scan the crowded room. On seeing Michael wave at him, he hurried over to the booth.

"Shit, sorry," he said, sliding onto the seat opposite Michael. "Had a client who just wouldn't get off the phone. What're you having?"

"Cheeseburger…"

"I'll have the same," Brad told the waiter, "and a beer."

"Drinking at lunch time?"

"I'm taking the afternoon off. I've been working way too hard lately."

Michael chuckled. "Who told you that?"

"I told me that, my boy, and it's the truth. Five closings in one month, two of 'em utter bastards—I'm exhausted." Brad slumped in his seat to emphasize his words.

"You should be pleased; everyone else I know in real estate is bitching about how slow it is."

"That's 'cause they don't know how to play a bad market." Brad grinned at his brother. "So, how're you doin'?"

"Okay."

"Still seeing Steve?"

"I guess…"

"You *guess?*"

Michael gazed at his brother's handsome face, his forehead now creased by a frown. "Well, he's out of town right now on a business trip trying to find new clients. I haven't seen very much of him lately. I think he's losing interest."

Brad raised an eyebrow. "What a clown. Losing interest in a good looking dude like you—if you weren't my brother, I'd be putting the make on you myself."

Michael laughed softly. "You'd have to turn gay too. I don't think Miranda would approve, do you?"

"Probably not." Brad touched Michael's hand. "He's not good enough for you, bro. Miranda and I both agree on that."

Michael shrugged. "Steve's all right. He's just a businessman first."

"Huh…" Brad fell silent as the waiter delivered their burgers and his beer. "So, you said you hadn't been sleeping too well lately. What's up with that?"

Michael hesitated. Did he really want to tell his brother about the strangely erotic dreams he'd been having? Dreams that would wake him in the middle of the night and keep him awake with the memory of how incredible they were—how incredible the man in his dreams was. He felt his face flush as he remembered.

"What's wrong?" Brad was staring at him with concern.

"Nothing.   It's just that I've been having these strange dreams for the last three weeks or so. It's a bit embarrassing…"

"How so?"

Michael shifted in his seat and couldn't meet his brother's eyes as he answered. "Um… they're kind of erotic…" He cleared his throat. "You don't want to hear this."

"Try me."

"Well, there's this guy, and he's making love to me."

"And it's not Steve, I take it," Brad said through a mouthful of burger.

Michael shook his head. "No, it's not anyone I know, or have ever known. I'd *like* to know him," he added with a shaky laugh. "He's English, and he's quite, uh… incredible."

"English, huh? So what's the problem?"

"There's no problem. I'm just a bit confused as to why I should have the same dream about the same guy night after night."

"Some kind of wish fulfillment maybe," Brad suggested. "I mean, it sounds like your relationship with Steve isn't going anywhere, so you're compensating by dreaming of a guy who'll love you unconditionally."

Michael stared at his brother. "Okay, when did you become a budding Freud?"

Brad chuckled and picked up a napkin to wipe his mouth. "Nothing very complicated there, Michael. You're horny, so getting off in your dreams works like a charm."

"Brad!"

"Well, doesn't it?"

"Trust you to take it to the lowest common denominator."

"And trust you to make more of it than it is," Brad said, grinning. "Every guy has a wet dream now and then, Michael—especially when they're not getting any."

Michael groaned and shook his head. "I knew I shouldn't have told you about this. Now you're going to give me shit about it every time we're together. *Don't* tell Miranda!"

"Are you kidding? She'll love this. She'll think it so romantic that her brother-in-law has a dream man in his life."

"That's the problem—he's not in my life."

"Nor is Steve by the sounds of things. You know what I think?"

"No, but I know you're about to tell me."

"I think you should tell Steve to go to hell. He keeps you dangling there for his own convenience. You know, Miranda and I have talked about this—"

"Oh great," Michael moaned. "My brother and sister-in-law sit around talking about my love life."

Brad chuckled. "Or lack of it. But seriously, I haven't said this before, but Steve's not the guy for you. He's just way too self-centered…"

"Well, he's got a lot on his mind. Running your own business is a full-time commitment…"

"Yeah, yeah," Brad made a dismissive gesture. "But that night we all had dinner together, I couldn't get over the fact that every time the conversation strayed to something that didn't directly concern him, his eyes sorta just glazed over, and he lost all interest in what we were saying. I mean, what d'you guys talk about when you're together? Is he remotely interested in what you do?"

"Of course he is." Michael looked away from his brother's searching gaze. "Well, I think he is…"

"Well, he should be. Graphic art is… is *art* for Chrissakes. You're a talented guy. What does he do? Sells computer parts—no talent needed for that, is there?"

"Brad, you're being very judgmental all of a sudden."

Brad's eyes narrowed as he stared at Michael. "I don't want to see my little brother get hurt, that's all. It doesn't take an analyst to see you're unhappy. Dreaming about getting laid instead of getting the real thing means you're compensating for what's lacking in your life."

Michael sighed. "Okay, I admit I'm a tad ticked off he doesn't seem to want to spend more time with me, but I really don't think the dreams have anything to do with Steve. They've just started recently…"

"Because you're frustrated…" Brad gave him a mischievous smile. "Tell me, how d'you feel when you wake up from one of these dreams? Are you, uh… damp?"

"*Brad!*" Michael felt his face grow hot. "You really are too much." He looked around the crowded diner, praying no one could hear their conversation, but the noise level was reassuringly high.

Brad laughed at his brother's embarrassment. "Michael, you and I have shared just about everything in our lives. There's not much you and I don't know about each other—we've slept in the same bed, shared the same tent on camping trips, skinny dipped together—and then there was that time when we…"

"Okay, now you're really embarrassing me," Michael hissed under his breath. But what Brad had said was true. Unlike a lot of siblings, he and Brad had always been close, with a bond that had grown even stronger after the unexpected death of their parents. Now he gazed fondly at his brother's smiling face, at the sparkle in his eyes, and knew he could tell him just about anything.

"All right, yes I'm… I'm…"

"Wet."

Michael groaned. "Yes."

"And the guy?"

"Incredible, like I said. He's like a god come to life. Dark hair that falls in curls over his forehead, eyes so dark blue they're almost cobalt, lips that… Jesus, why am I telling my straight brother all this?"

"Because you want to share, and we always share, remember? You listened to me when Miranda and I were having our problems; and despite the fact that I'm straight, I love my gay baby brother, and I want to see you happy—and *laid.*"

Michael's laugh was followed by a smile of real affection. "I love you too, big brother—and you'll be the first to know when it happens."

"Well, after you, hopefully," his brother kidded him.

§ § § §

Later, as he entered his apartment, Michael immediately noticed the flashing light on his answering machine. Steve? He could only hope. He hesitated before pressing the message button. What Brad had said about Steve still bothered him. Was he being blind to Steve's faults simply because he didn't want the relationship, such as it was, to fail?

"Oh, come on," he muttered. "Get a grip." He pressed the button and sighed with disappointment as a voice rasped in his ears. It wasn't Steve.

"This message is for Mr. Michael Ballantyne. My name is Ronald Fortescue of Fortescue, Reynolds and Haversham, Solicitors. My office is located in London, England, and we represent the estate of Mr. Lionel Burroughs. Mr. Burroughs, I regret to say, passed away quite recently and has left a will that names you, Mr. Ballantyne, as his sole beneficiary."

Michael stared at the answering machine in disbelief. "What the hell? Is this some kind of joke?"

"If you would care to phone my office as soon as possible, I will make arrangements to inform you of the exact details of Mr. Burroughs will, along with the conditions of your inheritance. Here is my number…"

Michael had to play the message twice more before his shaking fingers could write the number down. This had to be some kind of a hoax, like one of those emails he got now and then telling him he'd won a million dollars on a lottery he'd never entered. But the man had left a phone number… He glanced at his watch. Six o'clock. London was what… eight hours ahead? No point in calling right then. He'd do it first thing in the morning. Should he call Brad and tell him? No, he'd wait until he'd spoken to this Fortescue guy. Maybe the whole thing was one big mistake; they'd gotten the wrong Michael Ballantyne. Yeah, that was it… there had to be a hundred Michael Ballantynes in the Los Angeles phone book. They'd just picked the wrong one.

Maybe he should call Brad after all. Quickly, he punched in his brother's number. "Hi Brad, it's Michael."

"No kidding. I do have caller ID y'know."

"Right. Listen, I just got a weird message on my answering machine."

"Well, this is L.A., Michael."

"Be serious. Some guy from England is telling me I've been left an inheritance or something…"

"Sweet. How much?"

"I don't know that—but Brad, I've never heard of this guy, a Lionel Burroughs. Have you?"

"Burroughs? Nope, can't say I have."

"You think he might have been a friend of Mom and Dad's?"

"I have no idea, Michael. I don't recall them ever mentioning a Lionel Burroughs. They were only in England that one time, remember?"

Michael remembered only too well. It was shortly after that trip that his parents had been killed in a deadly freeway accident involving multiple vehicles. The memory of that terrible time sent an involuntary shudder through Michael's body.

"Yes," he said quietly. "I remember… Anyway," he continued after clearing his throat, "I have to call this solicitor guy in London tomorrow. I guess he'll be able to tell me what the connection is."

"Can't wait to hear more, bro. Call me soon as you've talked to him."

"Will do… I'll talk to you later. Tell Miranda I said 'hi.'"

With another glance at the phone number he'd written on the notepad he kept by the phone, Michael walked through his bedroom and into the bathroom to undress. He had no plans for the evening and was looking forward to lounging in sweats in front of the television with a pizza and beer. He stood for a moment in front of the mirror as he removed his shirt and gazed at himself critically.

What was it about him that Steve found so easy to resist?

He wasn't bad looking. Even Brad said he was good looking. He kept himself in shape, and he always made sure he smelled nice. *But it wasn't enough obviously*, he thought despondently. Sighing, he ran a hand through his chestnut-brown hair and threw his shirt into the laundry basket. As he met his own green-eyed gaze in the mirror, he wondered if Brad had been right about those dreams. Was he simply dreaming this beautiful guy to replace the man he could tell was slipping away from him?

Wow, that's really pathetic, he thought, grimacing at his reflection. Yet, those dreams seemed so real—the *man* felt real, warm and hard bodied under Michael's hands, his skin so smooth, his lips so soft, his kiss a sweet hunger…

Jesus! Michael stepped back from the mirror. He was hard as a rock. "Pull yourself together," he muttered. The phone's strident ring brought him back to reality. He picked it up in the bedroom.

"Michael Ballantyne."

"Mikey, how are you?"

Steve. He was the only one who called him Mikey and got away with it. Michael hated that particular abbreviation, but from Steve he'd grin and bear it.

"Hey, it's good to hear your voice." Michael sat down heavily on the bed. "Where are you?"

"Still in Vancouver, but I'll be back in a couple of days. Wanna get together?"

"That'd be great…" He paused, then said quietly, "I miss you."

"Yeah… miss you too, Mikey."

"What are you doing?"

"Right now I'm lying in bed watching Canadian television. It's even worse than the dreck they serve up in the States. What are you doing?"

"I just got home. Going to kick back and watch some dreck on TV, too." Michael had a vision of Steve lying on the hotel bed, his muscled, quarterback physique stretched out in all its glory, his blond hair rumpled by the pillow. He was hard again.

"Well, you have a good evening," Steve said. "I'll call you when I get back."

No, don't hang up yet. Talk to me some more. "Oh, okay, Steve. Look forward to seeing you when you get back."

"Right... Take it easy. See ya, Mikey." And he was gone.

"Damn," Michael muttered, putting the phone down. Why couldn't he have thought of something to keep Steve talking on the phone longer? Why hadn't he told him about the call from England? Surely that would have intrigued Steve. His hand strayed to his crotch, gripping the hard flesh through his slacks. He lay back on the bed, but the face that swam before his closed eyes wasn't Steve's... it was the man in his dreams.

CHAPTER TWO

"Michael, my love..."

Michael gazed up at the beautiful face that hovered over him. He reached up to slip his hand through the black curls that crowned the man's head, to draw him nearer, to touch those luscious lips with his own, to hold them pressed to his in a long, lingering kiss.

"Jonathan," Michael whispered when at last the man drew back slightly but kept his lips lightly touching Michael's. He didn't know how he knew the man's name—he was so strangely familiar, yet he remained a mystery, as if perhaps they had known one another a long time ago. Any further thoughts vanished from Michael's mind as Jonathan took his lips again in another long, searing kiss. Their hands roamed over one another's bodies, stroking, caressing, bringing to Michael a tumult of sensations he'd never known before.

Under Michael's hands, Jonathan's body felt sleek and strong, hard muscle covered by warm, smooth skin. His lips on Michael's were soft yet demanding, tenderness mixed with passion, the blue of his eyes darkened by desire.

Eagerly Michael wound his legs around Jonathan's slim waist, shivering with anticipation. He raised his hips to let the man's hot, throbbing flesh slip between his buttocks and push against the ring of muscle that guarded his tight hole.

His breath hissed through his teeth as Jonathan pushed forward, driving his rock hard erection deep inside Michael, filling him completely. Michael wrapped his arms around Jonathan's neck, bringing their mouths together in another rapturous kiss while their bodies rocked together, and Jonathan fucked Michael with long, exquisitely pleasurable strokes. Michael slid his hands down the length of Jonathan's smooth, muscular back, cupping the round swell of his buttocks, letting his fingers stray into the moist cleft, probing gently at his opening before slipping his middle finger all the way in. Jonathan's body bucked, and he growled as Michael found his sweet spot, stroking it tenderly, knowing he was bringing his lover the same powerfully sweet sensations he felt coursing through his own body.

Their rhythm increased, Jonathan plunging in and out of Michael, thrusting so hard it should have brought pain, but there was only pleasure in their union—pleasure and wonder combined with a complete and steadfast fulfillment. Jonathan's breathing became harsh, and Michael knew he was about to explode inside him.

"Yes," Michael moaned in a long and whispered breath. "Come inside me, my love. I love you…"

Jonathan's body shuddered as his climax overtook him. He cried out, "Michael, oh Michael," then released a torrent of semen, the scorching heat of which caused Michael to rear in ecstasy, his own orgasm showering them both with his hot seed. They held each other until their spasming bodies calmed, and they lay quietly savoring the sweet afterglow of their love making.

"Michael…" Jonathan's eyes held a sadness Michael had not seen before. Gently Jonathan caressed his face, kissed his lips, then whispered, "Michael, my love—avenge us, and set us free…"

Michael moaned as he opened his eyes and realized he'd been dreaming—again. He must have fallen asleep, still half dressed, and oh, but now he was thoroughly *wet*. He rolled off the bed, unbuckled his slacks, and let them slip to his ankles. Yuck, he'd come inside his briefs. He slipped those off too and walked into the bathroom, throwing his soiled clothes into the laundry basket.

Man, but that guy in my dream is totally incredible, he thought, turning on the shower and stepping inside. *And now I know his name—Jonathan.* As he soaped himself, he wondered why the dream had suddenly taken a darker turn. What had Jonathan meant by 'avenge us'?

"Wait a minute," he growled under his breath as he rinsed off. "It was just a dream, that's all—just my vivid imagination."

But the memory of those words haunted him even after he'd toweled himself dry and slipped on a sweatshirt and pants. Microwaving a couple of pizza slices, then pulling a beer from the fridge, he plunked himself down in front of the TV and surfed the channels, looking for *Frasier* or another comedy to free his mind of the foreboding feeling that had suddenly settled on him. For some strange reason he wondered if maybe tomorrow, after he'd talked to this solicitor guy, Fortescue, things would be clearer.

§ § § §

The alarm grating in Michael's ear woke him from a deep and restless sleep. He sat up in bed, trying to ignore the dull headache that throbbed in his skull. Six o'clock—that meant it was afternoon in England. Time to call and find out if this was all just a hoax—but first, coffee.

Later, sipping on his java, he punched in the number Fortescue had left and was slightly surprised to hear a woman's voice with a cool and very English accent announce, "Fortescue, Reynolds, and Shapiro, how may I help you?"

"Oh, uh… is Mr. Fortescue there?"

"Whom shall I say is calling?"

"Uh… Michael Ballantyne."

"One moment, please."

A moment or two with music passed, then, "Mr. Ballantyne. Thank you for phoning so promptly."

"Oh, hi, Mr. Fortescue. Your call took me by surprise."

"No doubt," Fortescue chuckled. "I take it you had no knowledge of Mr. Burroughs prior to my call."

"Right—I'm thinking there must be some mistake."

"No mistake, I can assure you. We are quite certain that you are the Michael Ballantyne mentioned in Mr. Burroughs' will."

"Okay… so what did he leave me?"

"Unfortunately, I cannot disclose that to you over the phone. The will cannot be read until you are in my office, seated in front of me."

"But how are we going to do that?"

"You will get on a plane and fly to London."

Funny guy. "Fly to London?" Michael croaked. "But that's crazy—I have a job and… and I have a friend who's coming into town tomorrow expecting to see me and…"

"Then I am sorry, Mr. Ballantyne, you will forfeit your right to benefit from Mr. Burroughs' will. Unless you are seated in my office within twenty-four hours from the time we first speak—which is now—you will not be entitled to know the contents of the will. The terms are quite specific on that matter."

"But I can't just drop everything and take off like that…"

"Again, I am sorry, Mr. Ballantyne. You must therefore relinquish your rights to the inheritance. My regrets…"

"Just a minute, buster!" Michael snapped.

"I *beg* your pardon?"

"You sound mighty eager to dump me all of a sudden."

"I can assure you that such a thing never entered my mind, Mr. Ballantyne. I am merely following the instructions I was given by the deceased."

"Okay, I guess I can be there."

"Do you have a valid passport, Mr. Ballantyne?"

"Uh, yeah…" Mentally he thanked his brother and Miranda for taking him on that cruise to the Caribbean for his twenty-fourth birthday. "I got it a couple of years ago for a cruise."

"Very good. I will arrange for a first-class ticket to be waiting for you at Los Angeles Airport. There is a British Airways flight leaving at four this afternoon. It will get you to my office in time to satisfy the deadline."

Jesus. Four this afternoon, Michael groaned. *What in hell can I tell Joe?* His boss was definitely not going to take this news well. Michael had been working on the graphics for a new client's advertising campaign due to be completed by the end of the week.

"Shit," he muttered as he put the phone down. "This had better be worth it!"

He dialed Joe's home number, his stomach sinking as he heard his boss's grumpy voice asking, "What in hell are you calling me for at this time of the morning?"

"Uh, Joe… I need some time off to fly to London today. It's kinda important…"

"What are you, nuts?" Joe barked. "You have a deadline this week, so *no*, you can't have the time off."

"But this is important."

"And your job isn't? You show up and finish that project or you're fired." The loud click on Joe's end told Michael their conversation was over.

"That son-of-a-*bitch*," Michael seethed. "Fire me, would he? I'll show him—I'll quit! No, I won't," he groaned. "I need that job. Damn!"

He punched in his brother's phone number. "Brad, listen, that solicitor guy wants me to fly to London this afternoon. What am I going to do?"

"Get on the plane, of course," Brad said, chuckling. "If he needs you there that fast it must be really big."

"But Joe said he'd fire me if I don't show up at the office."

"He won't fire you, Michael. You're the best he's got."

"Uh… I've never heard him say that…"

"Well, you'll get another job easy enough. Go to London and call me soon as you know what it's all about."

"You sure I should do this?"

"Michael…" Brad sounded exasperated. "This might be the chance of a lifetime for you—and when you're rolling in money, don't forget your big brother loves you very much."

Michael laughed softly. "I knew you'd have an ulterior motive. Okay, I'll call you with the news—good or bad."

"Think *positive*, Michael. Why would they drag you five thousand miles to give you bad news from someone you don't even know? Now go, enjoy, and let me know when I can call you Michael Rockefeller!"

§§§§

Michael settled back into his ultra-comfortable seat aboard the Boeing 777 that was taking him to London. Their departure had been delayed by more than two hours due to landing gear problems, a fact that made Michael somewhat nervous, despite being treated like royalty in the first class lounge. He'd been nervous too about the deadline Mr. Fortescue had given him, but a quick call to the solicitor had put his mind at ease.

"Don't worry, Mr. Ballantyne," Fortescue had said smoothly. "As long as you're on your way, I can extend the deadline to suit us both."

Michael smiled to himself, remembering that right up until the moment when the British Airways receptionist had handed him his first-class ticket, he'd been unable to completely dispel the feeling that all this just might be a hoax—that he'd jeopardized his job for the sake of some malicious prank. But now, here he was, having just finished a delicious meal of filet mignon washed down with fine champagne, and feeling mighty contented.

The first class compartment was virtually empty. Because there was no one in a nearby seat to talk to, Michael closed his eyes and let himself be lulled to sleep by the gentle drone of the plane's engines.

"Michael…" The voice came so close to Michael's ear that he could almost feel the warmth of Jonathan's lips.

"Jonathan…"

"Yes, my love, I'm here."

Michael could see him now standing before him, his beautiful face clouded by an expression of sadness.

"What is it, Jonathan? Tell me what's wrong."

"Come back to me, my love."

"But I'm here," Michael murmured. "I'll never leave you…"

His words were stilled by Jonathan gathering him in his arms, his mouth crushing Michael's with a kiss that set his blood on fire. Michael moaned as Jonathan's tongue slipped between his parted lips, swirled inside his mouth, and set every fiber of his nerves alive with erotic desire. They fell upon the ground, their bodies writhing together, hands tearing at each other's clothes.

Michael gasped with exhilaration and the sensation of his lover's smooth, hard body covering his own, the warm flesh sending rivers of ecstasy coursing through his blood. Their kiss deepened, tongues tussling, probing each and every part of one another's mouths.

"Jonathan," Michael moaned as he felt his lover's hard flesh slip between his thighs...

"Mr. Ballantyne?"

"Ooooh," Michael moaned again, but this time with a complaining note. "Go away, don't wake me..."

"Mr. Ballantyne, are you all right, sir?"

"Huh?" Michael sat bolt upright in his seat and stared into the concerned eyes of a young flight attendant.

"Are you all right?" he repeated, his boyish face slightly flushed with seeming embarrassment. "You were moaning in your sleep."

Jesus. "Yeah, sorry, yeah, I'm fine," Michael mumbled, his face reddening as he looked down at the obvious tent in his jeans. *Shit.* "Sorry," he moved the blanket over his crotch. "I must have been dreaming."

"Can I get you anything?"

"No, no, I'm fine, thanks." Michael watched as the flight attendant made his way back to the galley. *Lord,* he thought, *what on earth must he have been thinking? Some first class passenger I make, moaning and writhing in my seat and sporting a stiffie the flight attendant couldn't have missed.*

Despite himself, Michael chuckled. Then he remembered just what he'd been dreaming and *who* he'd been dreaming about. Not for the first time he wondered just what all this was about. Why was he dreaming about a man he'd never met—and what had Jonathan meant? *Come back to me...* Those words spun in his brain, but what did they mean? When had they ever been together? In another life, perhaps? But that was just foolish fancy. He didn't believe in ghosts or reincarnation. Yet, when he closed his eyes as he now did, he could still see his dream lover's face, and he knew without a doubt that even if he never met Jonathan, he would never forget him.

CHAPTER THREE

As tired as he was by the long flight, Michael took a moment to admire Mr. Fortescue's efficiency. No sooner had he stepped into the arrival hall at Heathrow airport than he spotted a tall, uniformed chauffeur holding up a placard with 'Mr. Michael Ballantyne' emblazoned on it in large letters. The chauffeur smiled and nodded as Michael approached him. He had a kind face, revealing a sprinkling of salt and pepper in his hair as he removed his cap.

"I'm Matthew, Mr. Ballantyne."

"Pleased to meet you, Matthew," Michael said, smiling as held out his hand to shake.

"Nice flight, sir?"

"Very nice... Just a bit tiring."

"No trouble with Customs?"

"No. I just have this carry-on, and they waved me right through."

"Shall I take that for you, sir?"

"No, I'm good." They chatted politely as Matthew guided him through the arrival hall to the parking garage; and Michael let out a low whistle of surprise when Matthew opened the door of a very sleek, silver-gray Rolls Royce.

"There are some refreshments inside, sir, if you care for something," Matthew murmured, indicating the built-in bar.

"Maybe some water for now—but I'd really love some coffee."

"I'll arrange that when we arrive at Mr. Fortescue's office. We'll be there in a jiffy."

"Great," Michael sighed as he sank back into the luxurious leather seat. He was asleep before the car left the parking garage.

He heard music carried on a summer breeze from the large house he could see through the trees that surrounded him. He stood at the base of a large oak, looking up through its branches at the smiling face above him.

"Come on," Jonathan called down. "Get yourself up here." Jonathan's eyes twinkled with mischief—but it was a much younger Jonathan, just a boy.

"I can't," Michael yelled. "I've got on my new suit for the party. Mother would box my ears if I got it dirty."

"You are such a bore today," Jonathan groused, swinging down from the tree branch and landing in front of Michael. He put his hands on Michael's shoulders to steady himself. "Why do we have to go to that silly party anyway?"

"It's not a silly party—it's your birthday party." Michael couldn't tear his eyes away from the smoothness of Jonathan's chest that his open shirt revealed, slick with sweat from his exertions. "Are... aren't you going to get ready? Your parents will be looking for you..."

Jonathan sighed. "I'd much rather spend the day with you. All those old fogies in there will be no fun at all."

"But it can't be your birthday party if you're not there, and your mother will be so upset if you disappoint everyone."

"You're right." He shrugged, then put his arm around Michael's shoulder. "Come on then, you can give me a hand changing."

Michael leaned in close and slipped an arm around Jonathan's waist. He inhaled the scent of his clean sweat and the warmth of his body pressed to his own. He found himself wishing that there was no party to attend, just an afternoon spent with Jonathan—the two of them, alone together.

He followed Jonathan up the grand staircase to his bedroom, a sunny room, its walls lined with pictures of aeroplanes. He sat on the bed and watched Jonathan strip off his shirt, then splash his face and chest with cool water. Jonathan grinned at him over the top of his towel.

"Hand me that blue shirt from the wardrobe there, would you?"

Michael handed him the shirt, resisting the urge to run his hands over Jonathan's supple torso as his friend raised his arms to pull the shirt over his head. Jonathan's smile was still in place when his head poked through the collar of the shirt, and he leaned forward to kiss Michael's cheek.

"You're my best friend. Did you know that?"

Michael felt his cheeks redden, especially where Jonathan's warm lips had touched him. "And you're my *best friend," he whispered, his heart bursting with happiness.*

"Here we are, sir." Matthew's cheerful announcement woke Michael from his doze. He looked around him with dull eyes, trying to remember where he was—and where he'd just been. "Mr. Fortescue's office," Matthew added as if he'd realized Michael wasn't quite with it.

"Oh, right." Michael struggled out of the car and paused to look at the imposing edifice that housed the solicitor's office. Following Matthew through the carved wood and glass door, he thought that what he'd really like about now was a good hot shower and a cup of coffee.

"Any chance of that coffee, Matthew?"

"I'll see to it right away, sir, soon as I get you to Mr. Fortescue." Matthew tapped on a door marked *Lionel Fortescue, Esq.,* and Michael was suddenly seized by a feeling of quiet excitement. Instinctively he knew that whatever Fortescue was about to disclose to him would change his life forever. He shivered as Matthew stepped aside to allow him to step into the cavernous room beyond.

"Ah, Mr. Ballantyne." From behind a huge mahogany desk, Mr. Fortescue, a tall, reed-thin gentleman with a mane of white hair greeted Michael with what seemed to be genuine warmth. "Come and sit down, you must be tired after that long journey." He held out his hand, and Michael grasped it firmly.

"I could use a cup of coffee," Michael said, grinning. "Sorry, I look a bit rumpled," he added, sitting down on the big leather chair opposite Fortescue's desk.

"Quite understandable. Matthew, please arrange for some coffee."

As Matthew left the room, Fortescue pulled a large envelope from his desk drawer. "I think we should begin right away while we wait for your coffee." He held up the envelope for Michael to see. "You will notice that this envelope has been sealed with wax and has not been opened since Mr. Burroughs signed the documents. With your permission, I will now break the seal."

Michael nodded, his throat suddenly dry. Fortescue slid a paperknife under the wax seal and pried the envelope open. Briefly he scanned the documents he withdrew from the envelope, then smiled at Michael.

"You may recall when we spoke yesterday that I told you it was imperative you be here for the reading of Mr. Burroughs' will. I stressed the importance of your presence because it was relayed to me by Mr. Burroughs himself that no one but you, and myself of course, should be privy to the contents of this will. Mr. Burroughs was unmarried and an only child, so he had no living relatives." A tap on the door made him pause. "Come in."

Matthew appeared carrying a silver tray, a silver coffeepot, and some delicate-looking china cups and saucers.

"Cream and sugar, sir?"

"No, just black will be great," Michael replied, inhaling the rich coffee aroma. "Just what I need. Thank you Matthew."

"You're welcome, sir." Matthew turned and left the room.

Michael took a long sip of his coffee, then asked, "So, does it say anywhere in there just why I'm in Mr. Burroughs'will?"

"No, but there is a letter that is addressed to you personally. I rather think that you may find an explanation from Mr. Burroughs himself in the letter."

"Okay... good..."

"Now to the content of the will itself..." Fortescue slipped on a pair of rimless glasses and began to read. "I, Lionel Edward Burroughs, being of sound mind and body, do hereby bequeath to Mr. Michael Adam Ballantyne, currently residing in the city of Los Angeles in the United States of America, my home in Hertfordshire known as Bedford Park and all its contents, including my collection of rare books and coins. In addition—"

"There's more?" Michael croaked. His head was already swimming from what Fortescue had just told him. *A home named after a park? Jesus. And where the hell is Hertfordshire?*

"Oh, yes." The solicitor smiled benignly at Michael. "A rather large sum of money—um… after all taxes were satisfied, just a little over five million pounds has been deposited in your name, in Barclay's Bank."

"*What?*" Michael thought he might just pass out.

Fortescue leaned forward with concern. "My dear Mr. Ballantyne, are you all right? You look a little pale."

"No, I'm fine, I'm fine," Michael replied shakily. "It's just that it's all so much—a house, rare books, *five million pounds*. I never, for one moment, thought it would be anything like this."

"Of course." Fortescue nodded his head in understanding. "Relax for a moment, drink your coffee—there are some… um… *conditions* to be met…"

"Conditions?" Michael felt a momentary unease. Was all this too good to be true after all?

"Yes, in order to benefit from all of this, you must take up residence in Bedford Park for a minimum of one year…"

"One *year*," Michael gasped. "But my job—it's hanging on a thread as it is."

"That condition is irrevocable, I'm afraid, but really, Mr. Ballantyne, with five million pounds in the bank, isn't your concern for your job a little redundant?"

Michael chuckled. "Right, what was I thinking?" What *had* he been thinking? Joe had been ready to fire him—just wait 'til he told the old so-and-so this bit of news. And just wait 'til he told Brad about this. He'd bust a gut! Michael could send him and Miranda first-class air tickets so they could come stay for as long as they liked. *Woohoo!*

"And in order that you will have no financial problems during your first year at Bedford Park," Fortescue continued, "I have been instructed to put the sum of five hundred thousand pounds at your immediate disposal."

"That is amazingly generous," Michael said,

"I understand Mr. Burroughs was indeed a generous man," Fortescue agreed.

"So, any other conditions?" Michael asked.

"Only that you keep on the staff at Bedford Park. Matthew MacDonald, your chauffeur and butler, Mrs. Macdonald, his wife who is the housekeeper and cook, and I believe there's a housemaid named Emily—oh, and two gardeners—but you'll meet all of them when you arrive at Bedford Park tomorrow."

Staff? He was going to have staff? Oh, my God…

His stunned look caused Fortescue to smile. "Bedford Park is a rather large residence, Mr. Ballantyne. You will need help running it, and I believe the present staff is extremely efficient. Furthermore, their salaries are to be paid from a separate trust fund for as long as they are employed at Bedford Park." He paused for a moment, frowning. "There is one rather annoying problem."

Uh oh, Michael thought. *I figured this was all too good to be true.*

"Shortly after Mr. Burroughs died, a man moved into the lodge by the main gate. He said Mr. Burroughs had hired him to keep an eye on the estate, a sort of security person. I had no knowledge of this arrangement. Mr. Burroughs did not mention him to me, and I did try to explain that since Mr. Burroughs was deceased, any private verbal agreement they might have had was now null and void. He refused to vacate the lodge, showing me a letter signed by Mr. Burroughs stating that he had indeed employed him and granted him the residence. However, he is not included in the salary trust."

"So he's working there unpaid?"

"It would appear so. You will probably want to make it your business to ascertain just what he's doing there and if you want to keep him on."

Great! I get to be the axe man.

"Now…" Fortescue handed Michael an envelope. "Here is the letter Mr. Burroughs left for you to read at your leisure. I have arranged accommodation for you at the Mayfair Hotel for tonight. Matthew will drive you to your new home in the morning."

"That's very nice of you," Michael muttered, still slightly stunned. "Tell me, Mr. Fortescue, where exactly is Hertfordshire?"

Fortescue chuckled. "Just north of London, actually. I have a small map here for you." He pointed to a spot above the sprawling metropolis marked 'London.' "The estate is located near Abingdon, a smallish town outside the larger town of Royston. Royston is located near where Hertfordshire borders Cambridgeshire. Perhaps you've heard of Cambridge University?"

"Oh yeah, I've heard of Cambridge. Don't they have a famous boat race with uh…?"

"Oxford University," Fortescue prompted.

"That's it. I've seen it on TV—it usually rains that day."

Fortescue beamed at him. "Quite right; and now I'm sure you're anxious to get to the hotel and rest. As soon as you can, you should pay the bank manager a visit, let him meet his very valuable client, and set up a checking account." He held a key ring from which hung a bunch of keys. "Keys to the castle, if you will. I wish you all the best, Mr. Ballantyne, and hope your new home suits you well."

Michael took the keys and shook the proffered hand. "Thanks—and why don't you and Mrs. Fortescue visit me sometime? Anytime you're up Hertfordshire way!"

§ § § §

Michael's room at the Mayfair was the epitome of luxury, but all he could think of was showering, then hitting the sack. God, but he was tired, yet he wondered if he would sleep. So much to think about—an estate, millions of pounds, a chauffeur, a housekeeper—*Jeez*! He had to tell Brad… and Steve. Whoa, Steve would be getting into town tonight, and he hadn't even alerted him to the fact that he was in London, not LA. He glanced at his watch, almost one o'clock. That meant it wasn't even five in the morning in Los Angeles. It was way too early to call anyone. He'd shower and take a nap, then spread the good news. Pulling off his clothes he went into the bathroom.

Wow! This is impressive, he thought, looking round the large tiled room. *A shower* and *a tub. Maybe a long, soothing bath would be just the ticket.* There was a variety of toiletries displayed on the vanity, so he turned on the tub faucets and sniffed at a bottle marked *Pour Le Bain.* "Nice." He emptied the contents into the water, then slipped into the rapidly filling tub and lay back, luxuriating in the warm, soapy water, which he turned off when it reached his chin. He let out a long sigh of contentment. "Man, this is the life," he murmured, dozing off.

He was walking slowly through an orchard, the branches of the trees heavy with their autumn crop of apples. He knew he was being watched, and he smiled, affecting a nonchalant air, strolling even more slowly toward a thickly wooded part of the orchard. Behind him, he heard the crack of a twig, then a muttered curse followed by a chuckle. He turned to see a figure disappear behind a tree.

"I can see you, you know," he called out.

"Damn…" Jonathan appeared from behind the tree. "I'll be no use in an ambush." He was wearing an army uniform and looked devastatingly handsome. "You got my message then."

"Yes… You leave tonight?"

"Fraid so. They're shipping us off to France. I wanted to see you before I left." He opened his arms, and Michael walked into his embrace, his lips seeking Jonathan's for the kiss he prayed would not be their last.

"I love you," Michael gasped into his lover's mouth.

"I love you too… it's going to be hell away from you."

"My call-up papers are on the way," Michael said, nuzzling Jonathan's neck. "I might be joining you in France."

"I hope not." Jonathan held him tightly. "I'm praying they give you a nice desk job somewhere safe."

"*Safe—while you're on the frontline? I'd never live down the shame, Jonathan. I know it's unlikely that we would meet even if they posted me to France, but I couldn't bear to stay 'safe' behind a desk while you and everyone else we know is fighting the Jerries. We just have to keep in touch no matter what—and perhaps we'll get some leave at the same time.*"

Jonathan slipped his hands inside Michael's shirt and caressed the warm skin that covered his lover's lithe torso. "*I love you so much,*" he whispered. "*If anything happens to me, remember that, always.*"

Michael leaned back a little to gaze into Jonathan's eyes. "*We'll both come back safely,*" he said with a fierce determination. "*And when we do…*" His eyes twinkled as he smiled into Jonathan's. "*When we do, I promise you I will love you, each and every part of you, 'til you beg me to stop.*"

Jonathan gazed at him through glistening eyes. "*That would be never, my love, never.*"

By mutual consent and still in each other's arms, they sank onto the leafy ground beneath the trees, their bodies pressed together so tightly that Michael could scarcely breathe, but what did breathing matter when his beloved Jonathan was holding him, crushing him to his firm and perfect body? He writhed in ecstasy over the hard heat of Jonathan's erection that pushed against his own. Feverishly he pulled at the buttons of Jonathan's shirt, eager to feel the warm, smooth skin beneath the coarse uniform fabric.

A shuddering gasp escaped Jonathan's lips as Michael took each small nipple into his mouth and teased them with his tongue and teeth. Michael's hand slid down Jonathan's torso to grip the hard bulge behind the fly of his trousers. With a quiet desperation, his fingers fumbled with the buttons, then slipped inside, eager to explore the rigid heat that throbbed at his touch…

"Whoa!" Michael spat out the bath water he had almost swallowed. "Must have dozed off again," he muttered. And dreamed again… and was hard again. His hand slid down the length of his body to grasp the erection that ached between his thighs. The dreams were so powerful, so real each time, and this one had been no exception. He closed his eyes, giving in to the sensual memory of Jonathan's hot, hard body pressed to his, taking his parted lips in one long, searing kiss.

"*Jonathan*," he whispered, his breath shuddering in his chest. With a soft, needy moan, he let the sensation of his orgasm take over, his hips bucking under water, his cum erupting in gut-wrenching spasms, landing on the surface near his chin.

As he dried himself with one of the big, white, fluffy towels hanging on a heated rail, he thought about what this recent dream represented rather than the sensuality it had invoked. Whoever Jonathan was—and whoever he, Michael, was in these dreams—it was obvious they had been parted by a war. From the look of the uniform Jonathan was wearing, it could have been the Second World War. But what did it all mean, and what did it have to do with him? *Why* was he having these dreams? Could they in some way be connected with what was happening now? The inheritance, the estate in Hertfordshire... Lionel Burroughs?

Wait... the letter Mr. Fortescue had given him. What had he done with it? Slipping on a hotel robe and quickly combing his still-damp hair, he hurried back into the bedroom to check the inside pocket of the jacket he'd been wearing earlier. Right, still there. Maybe now he'd get some answers to all the questions bombarding his mind. Before he called Brad, he'd read the letter that might shed some light on just why Lionel Burroughs had left him all his worldly goods.

CHAPTER FOUR

Michael propped himself up against the bed pillows and tore open the envelope. A knock at the door had him sighing with impatience. Who the hell...?

"Who is it?"

"Room service, sir."

I didn't order any room service, he thought, rolling off the bed and padding over to the door. A perky-faced young man beamed at him as he opened the door.

"Compliments of Mr. Ronald Fortescue, sir," the young man chirped at Michael.

"Oh, great, come on in."

"Champagne, Scottish smoked salmon, and chicken salad." He removed the white linen cloth with a flourish. "Can I get you anything else, sir?" he asked, uncorking the champagne.

Michael suddenly felt very hungry. "No, that all looks terrific, thanks. Here, let me get you something."

"No thanks, sir, that's all been taken care of." He handed Michael a glass of champagne. "Cheers, sir." And with another smile he was gone.

"Wow," Michael murmured, savoring the champagne. "Not bad."

Not bad? It was the best he'd ever tasted. He made himself a plate of salmon on crackers with cream cheese and some chicken salad, then retreated back to the bed. "Man, this *is* the life!" *Okay... let's see what old Lionel has to say.* He set down his champagne glass and unfolded the letter.

My dear Michael,

If you are reading this, it means you have accepted the terms of my will and are soon to be Master of Bedford Park. I hope you will not regret your decision, and that you will be happy in my old home—your new home. Feel free to make any changes you might consider more to your liking—it belongs to you now.

I'm sure you are wondering just why I left my estate and sundry possessions to you. Let me try to explain the reasons. You see, I need you to solve a mystery. Shortly after I purchased Bedford Park thirty years ago, my partner William and I were convinced that the house was haunted—but not in a frightening way, let me be quick to point that out in case you feel like taking the next plane back to America! No, our ghost was a benign one—and very handsome—a young man such as yourself with an achingly sad expression.

Naturally, William and I were intrigued. We did some research and discovered that the previous owner's son, Jonathan Harcourt, mysteriously disappeared two years after he had returned from active duty abroad. This would have been after the Second World War.

"Jonathan…" Michael shivered as he remembered the dream he'd had while in the bath. Jonathan had been wearing a soldier's uniform, and they had talked about the war. Now, after reading this part of the letter, he began to wonder if these dreams were not dreams at all, but some form of latent memory. But how could that be possible? His hand shook a little as he resumed reading.

William and I presumed that our ghost was Jonathan Harcourt. He lived in Cambridge, but his disappearance occurred while he was visiting his parents at Bedford Park. Of course, search parties scoured the grounds of Bedford Park and the nearby countryside for days afterward, but no trace of him was found. Now here's the intriguing part. He had a friend named Michael Thornton, slightly younger than himself.

'Wow…' Michael's eyes widened. Was this just a coincidence? He'd been dreaming for several days and nights about a guy named Jonathan, and now, according to Lionel

Burroughs, it so happened he had a friend with the name Michael. "Don't jump to conclusions," he muttered, but kept on reading.

Michael and Jonathan, after returning home from the war, were employed as teachers at Cambridge. The two men must have been devoted to one another, for Michael committed suicide a year to the day that Jonathan disappeared. It seems that he had moved heaven and earth to try to find Jonathan, never giving up the search, and even hired private detectives, but all to no avail. It was rumoured that Jonathan had been murdered and his body buried by a man named Henry Bryant, who owed Jonathan a substantial amount of money. Bryant apparently had an alibi and was never brought to trial.

William and I found the story of Jonathan and Michael wonderfully romantic, and for many years left it at that, quite unfazed by our resident ghost who seemed to appear mostly to myself, and on occasion to William. I'm afraid our friends thought we were quite barmy—that's an English expression for someone who's not quite all there.

William died two years ago, and I'm afraid I took it very badly, turning to the bottle for comfort and alienating several friends in the process. I even began talking out loud to our ghost whenever I saw him, calling to him by name—Jonathan. If anyone had seen or heard me, they would have taken me off to an asylum.

And then one day, something extraordinary happened. On my desk in the study I found a photograph of two young men in army uniforms. How it got there, I could only guess. The staff denied putting it on my desk, and although I told myself it was impossible, I came to believe that Jonathan had placed it there. I sat and stared at the photograph of these two handsome young men—and I cried for them, that their lives should have been cut off so cruelly while so young, and so very much in love with one another.

So now, you are probably asking, what in the world has all this got to do with you? It's quite simple really. I'm the nosy type, always asking questions. I used to drive William mad with my inquisitiveness. Lucy Ballard, a librarian friend who had actually known both men personally, told me that Michael Thornton's parents left England to live in America after their son's death. Although they were by this time both in their late forties, they had a daughter, Angela, who married a certain Andrew Ballantyne, and subsequently had two sons, Bradley and you, Michael.

Michael exhaled a long breath of shock—and disbelief. If this were true, why wouldn't his mom and dad have mentioned that he had an uncle who had committed suicide years ago? Of course his mom wouldn't have known her brother. He'd died long before she was born—was that the reason she and his dad had gone on that trip to England shortly before their car accident? Did Brad know anything about this, and in his big brother way thought it best his little brother didn't need to know he'd had a gay uncle who'd committed suicide? He turned to the next page of the letter.

My friend lost touch with the Thortons, and it was not until much later that she discovered your parents had been killed in a terrible motor accident.

We never met Jonathan's parents, from whom we purchased Bedford Park. The entire real estate transaction was done through our mutual solicitors. I wanted to know more about their son, but William suggested they might not want to know he was haunting their old home, and in any case, our solicitors informed me that Mr. and Mrs. Harcourt had instructed them not to divulge their new address to anyone.

When my doctors told me I had terminal cancer and only had three months to live, I wasn't very upset. To me, it meant that I would soon be with William again.

Now, you might find this quite hard to believe, but one night not so long ago, Jonathan came and sat with me as if to comfort me. It was then, almost as if he had willed it, that I decided to leave everything to you, Michael. I have no family; there is no one to contest the will. All I ask is that you do your best to find out just what happened to Jonathan—who killed him and why. Perhaps then he will find rest.

Well, all this writing has quite exhausted me, so I will close now, wishing you a good and fulfilled life, with every happiness.

Sincerely,

Lionel E. Burroughs.

Michael put the letter down on the comforter beside him and stared into space, his mind churning with the information he'd just read. So, the man he'd been dreaming about for the past several weeks, Jonathan, was now haunting the house he was about to live in. How was he going to feel when a ghostly Jonathan appeared in front of him—if, of course, he ever did? There was still the distinct possibility that Lionel Burroughs had simply been hallucinating, and that all of this was just the product of a desperate old man's imagination grasping at anything to ease his loneliness.

He was just about to put the letter back in the envelope when he noticed there was something else inside it—a photograph. Michael's eyes widened with shock as he stared at the two young men pictured there.

"Oh my God," he whispered. He grabbed his cell phone and punched in his brother's number. "Brad, it's me."

"Yes, Michael, I know it's you," Brad said patiently. "So, how's it goin' over there in 'Jolly Old'? You find out anything yet?"

"Boy, have I ever. How does a country estate and five million pounds in the bank sound?"

There was a prolonged silence at the other end then Brad croaked, "Are you shittin' me?"

"No, I'm not. I own an estate called Bedford Park in Hertfordshire, and the previous owner, Lionel Burroughs, left me five million pounds on top of everything else."

"Jesus, Michael, that's incredible!"

"I know, but there are one or two things we need to talk about."

"Oh, yeah?" Brad chuckled. "Like you're not going to share?"

"Silly, no, there's a letter Lionel Burroughs left for me, and I just got through reading it—and Brad, there's some weird stuff here."

"Like what?"

"Well, remember I told you I was having these strange dreams about a guy making love to me?"

"Yeah—don't tell me it was this Lionel guy—"

"No!" Michael managed a laugh. "His name is Jonathan, and it appears he actually existed, but he disappeared, possibly murdered just after the Second World War—"

"Whoa, wait a minute. Where did you hear this?"

"In the letter Lionel wrote me. He bought the house from Jonathan's parents after their son disappeared, but here's the thing, Brad. Jonathan had a friend named Michael, and it sounds like they were lovers. He committed suicide a year after Jonathan's disappearance. His parents went to the States and had a daughter—*our mother*, Brad. Michael was our uncle. Did you know we had a gay uncle who committed suicide?"

"Uh, well…"

"*Brad,* why didn't you tell me about him? Why keep me in the dark about something like that?"

"Well, I didn't know all the facts. Mom mentioned it only once, and Dad kinda stopped her from saying too much. I can only think they didn't want you to know, seeing as how you're…"

"Seeing as how I'm gay? We're not all suicidal, Brad."

"I know that."

"Well, why didn't you tell me?"

"I don't know!" Brad sounded defensive. "Mom said he died long before she was born, and Grandma took a long time to ever tell her she'd had a brother—and that he'd committed suicide. It just wasn't something people talked about back then,

I guess. Anyway, when she and Dad went to England, they visited his grave."

"Jesus," Michael whispered. "Brad, I'm looking at a photograph Lionel left me of two guys in army uniforms. One of them could be me, Brad. It's Michael, our uncle, and I look exactly like him. The other guy is Jonathan, the man I've been dreaming about. What in hell does all this mean?"

"I don't know, Michael, but it's kinda exciting, isn't it? Like our uncle and this guy Jonathan had a secret love affair and maybe someone was jealous, murdered Jonathan, and..."

"Brad, I don't think it's exciting, I think it's sad that these two men never lived long enough to really enjoy a life together. I mean, gay guys didn't exactly have the best of times in those days, and then to have your lover murdered and his body never found. It's just depressing is what it is!"

"D'you want Miranda and me to come over and be with you?" Brad asked.

"Yes, but wait 'til I've gotten to the house and taken a good look around. One thing I didn't mention is that according to Lionel, it's haunted—by Jonathan's ghost."

"Oh, for cryin' out loud..."

"Will Miranda freak?"

"No, she loves all that stuff, but *I'll* freak," Brad said, chuckling. "Okay, listen, I've got a couple of tricky escrows to close before I can get away, so it'll be a week or two. Is that OK?"

"Yeah, don't worry," Michael assured him. "If it gets too hairy, I can always check into a hotel. After all, I'm quite wealthy now."

CHAPTER FIVE

The next day, Matthew called Michael's room from the hotel lobby to tell him it was time to leave for his new home. Michael felt a quiet sense of excitement as he took the elevator down to where Matthew was waiting. Even if Lionel hadn't been hallucinating about the house being haunted, there had been nothing in his letter to make him feel that Jonathan's ghost was some kind of threat. On the contrary, he had even tried to comfort Lionel; not a scary ghost at all.

Matthew was all smiles as he greeted Michael politely and took his bag. "Sleep well, sir?" he asked as they walked briskly through the parking garage to where the Rolls sat in all of its gleaming splendor.

"Yes thanks, Matthew, and please don't call me 'sir.' It's too stuffy. My name is Michael."

"And that's too familiar for a member of your staff to be calling you, I'm afraid," Matthew said, shaking his head. "There's a certain protocol in life that must still be observed."

"Not by me, Matthew."

"Well, we're a bit old fashioned here, sir... uh... Mr. Ballantyne."

"Michael."

"Well, what if we settle for *Mr.* Michael?"

"That's a start, I guess."

Chuckling, Matthew opened the car door. "You'll give old Tom the gardener a fit if you tell him to call you anything but 'sir.' He's one of the old school; still touches his cap and all that."

"Lord," Michael groaned, getting in the car. As Matthew settled himself in the driver's seat, he asked, "By the way, Matthew, d'you know anything about the house being haunted?"

"Oh, yes, but I've never clapped eyes on it. Mr. Burroughs saw it all the time—Mr. Samuels too, or so he said—but none of the rest of us ever saw or heard it. Between you and me, and without sounding too disrespectful, I think they were a mite tipsy and seeing things."

"Both of them at the same time?"

"Well, I think Mr. Samuels just went along with it, if you know what I mean."

"Ah…" So the ghostly part of Lionel's story might have been his imagination after all, and his partner William simply put up with it. Still, there was the fact that they had both researched the story of Jonathan's disappearance. Then there was that photograph, along with the fact that his uncle, Michael Thornton, had been gay and had committed suicide. All that had been confirmed by Brad. The rest of the story he had to unravel as Lionel had requested. He owed the old guy at least that much!

Despite the heavy traffic leaving London, the ride to Abingdon took only a couple of hours, and Michael had his first chance to view and admire the English countryside, the rolling fields and wooded areas that seemed to stretch for miles on either side of the road. England didn't seem that small when you were actually there, he reflected, staring out of the car window. He smiled as they passed through some small villages with quaint names such as Puckeridge and Chipping.

"Only in England," he murmured.

"We'll be there just in time for a spot of lunch," Matthew informed him as they passed through the larger town of Royston and headed east towards Abingdon. "We're just on this side of Abingdon."

"Great, I am feeling quite hungry."

"My wife Annie is a wonderful cook—shouldn't be surprised if you put some meat on those bones of yours in no time. She'll take one look at you and decide you're too skinny."

"Skinny, me?" Michael exclaimed, slightly miffed. The members of the staff might balk at calling him by his first name, but at least Matthew wasn't above saying what he thought!

"Oh, sorry sir, I mean, Mr. Michael, didn't mean to be rude."

"That's okay… I just don't consider myself skinny." Michael laughed lightly. "I prefer the word 'lithe.'"

"Ah yes, well, you would, wouldn't you?"

Eh? Michael decided to drop the matter, especially as he'd just seen a sign that read 'Great and Little Chishill,' another that read Abingdon, and under it an arrow pointing left to '*Bedford Park.*'

"We're here?"

"Yes," Matthew said as he pulled in through enormous wrought iron gates and headed up the driveway. Michael glanced at the small house just inside the gates.

"Who lives in there?" he asked, wondering how Matthew would explain Jack Trenton.

Matthew's snort of derision said it all. "Bloody upstart is who lives there, sir, I mean Mr. Michael, Jack Trenton by name. No one knows where he came from, but he says Mr. Burroughs hired him, and he won't budge. Fortunately he keeps to himself. You might never see him, if you're lucky."

Hmm, Michael mused with some discomfort, *but I might just have to see him, if I'm going to terminate his employment.*

And then, there it was, the house that in his wildest imaginings, Michael could never have believed he would ever call 'home.' It was simply magnificent. Built entirely of red brick, its tall, elegant windows were framed by rich, dark green ivy that climbed in profusion to the eaves.

"Wait 'til Brad and Miranda see this," he gasped, his breath fogging the window glass. "Wow, it's beautiful…"

"Yes, that it is, Mr. Michael. Built in Queen Victoria's day, and said to have been visited by Her Majesty herself on several occasions for parties and the like."

"Really? I didn't figure the Queen as a party girl."

"She was, in her younger days, so they say," Matthew assured him, pulling up in front of an impressive set of steps that led to an ornately carved front door. As Matthew opened the door for him, Michael hopped out and stared at the gabled building that towered over him. *Doesn't look haunted*, he thought with a degree of disappointment that surprised him. Had he really wanted to encounter Jonathan in ghostly form?

No, much rather meet him in the flesh!

"Oh, Mr. Ballantyne, sir…!"

Michael stared at the plump figure descending the steps at an alarming rate.

The woman spoke again. "Ever so sorry I wasn't outside for your arrival, and Emily's upstairs still dusting, but your room is quite ready, thank goodness."

"Mr. Michael," Matthew said with a smile. "This is my wife Annie MacDonald, the woman who's in charge of everything at Bedford Park."

Michael held out his hand. "Pleased to meet you, Mrs. MacDonald."

The lady grasped Michael's hand and bobbed a small curtsey. *Oh, please don't do that*, Michael groaned mentally.

"Oh, Mr. Ballantyne, sir…" Mrs. MacDonald's beaming smile and cheerful manner were contagious, and Michael found himself relaxing and smiling back at the buxom lady. "It's a joy to have you here," she said warmly. "The house has been so gloomy since Mr. Burroughs passed away. I hope you'll find everything to your liking."

"I'm sure I will," Michael told her as she and Matthew accompanied him into the house. The interior vestibule was high ceilinged, light and airy. Michael paused to admire the paintings of landscapes that lined the walls.

"Local artist, Mr. Michael," Matthew murmured. "Mr. Burroughs bought up nearly everything the man painted. You can visit all of that scenery within walking distance. This one here is of the house itself."

"It's great," Michael said, gazing at the finely detailed painting of Bedford Park. They walked into a spacious room, one wall of which consisted entirely of French doors and windows, beyond which Michael could see rolling lawns and trees.

"Wow," he breathed. "This is beautiful."

"Mr. Burroughs and Mr. Samuels did all their entertaining in this room," Mrs. MacDonald remarked. "Here, and in the dining room next door. They had some very nice dinner parties when Mr. Samuels was still alive." She pointed to the first chair to the right of the head of the table. "Sir Ian McKellan sat right there one night, and over here..."

"All right, Annie," Matthew said, chuckling. "You can drop all the names you want later. Mr. Michael's hungry."

"I guess Mr. Burroughs lived a quiet life after his partner died." Michael stared through the windows at the landscaping, which obviously required a lot of maintenance.

"Yes..." There was a moment or two of awkward silence, then Matthew said, "Would you care to see your room and then have some lunch?"

"That'd be great," Michael replied, turning to smile at them both. "Lead the way, Matthew."

"Would you prefer lunch in the dining room or the study, Mr. Ballantyne?" Mrs. MacDonald asked.

"How about if we all have lunch in the kitchen? That'll save you having to go to any extra trouble."

"Oh... all... in the kitchen? Well, if you don't mind the mess..."

Matthew laughed. "Mess? There's never a mess in your kitchen. I've always said you could eat off the floor in there."

"The kitchen will do just fine," Michael assured her, as Matthew picked up his bag and headed for the vestibule. "Give me ten minutes to wash up." He followed Matthew up the curved staircase that led to the upper floor. A young girl appeared on the landing. She stared at Michael, her mouth slightly open.

"Emily," Matthew boomed. "Come and meet the new Master of the house."

"Matthew," Michael groaned. "I'm not anyone's master."

"Just a figure of speech, sir... I mean, Mr. Michael."

Michael grinned. "I bet I'll get you to drop that *Mister* bit soon." He held out his hand to greet Emily. "Hello, Emily, I'm Michael."

"Oh, sir... very pleased to meet you..." She appeared quite startled by Michael's friendly smile.

Michael watched her as she fled down the stairs. "Wasn't Mr. Burroughs friendly with the staff?"

"Emily's only been with us less than a year," Matthew explained. "Mr. Burroughs was... well, let's just say he wasn't in the best frame of mind the last year of his life." He opened the door to a large bedroom decorated in muted tones of beige and cream.

"Nice," Michael murmured.

"This is actually one of the guest rooms, Mr. Michael. Mr. Burroughs left instructions that the master bedroom should be redecorated and refurnished to your taste before you moved in, as it were. I'll show you the room if you wish?"

"That's okay." Michael took his bag from the older man and laid it on the bed. "I'll do some exploring on my own after lunch if that's all right with you."

"Very good. We'll see you downstairs in a few minutes then."

Left alone, Michael opened his case and stared at the few clothes he'd brought with him. "Need to find a clothes store pretty soon," he muttered. He hadn't reckoned on a year's stay when he'd packed. That reminded him, he'd better call his landlord, give a month's notice, and ask Brad to go over there and pick up his stuff. He checked out the bathroom, washed his hands and face, and then took a slow walk round the upper floor of the house. He counted six large bedrooms, all with their own bathrooms. The master bedroom, the one that Matthew had said was to be redecorated, was immense, bigger than Michael's whole apartment in LA. Somehow he just couldn't see himself sleeping in this room even after the dark wallpaper and heavy drapes had been removed. He gazed about the room, shivering slightly, and before he left he had the uncanny feeling that he was being watched. He shook himself and strode briskly across the landing toward the stairs.

Now there you go with your overactive imagination again, he told himself. *Get a grip.*

After prowling about downstairs, he found the kitchen by following his nose, sniffing at the delicious aroma of some kind of stew wafting into the corridor.

"Wow, that smells good," he said entering the kitchen. The three members of his staff that he'd met smiled back at him in various degrees of shyness and uncertainty. Okay, he was going to have to loosen up the atmosphere here, he thought as he sat down at the table. "So, what's cookin'?"

"Shepherd's Pie." Mrs. MacDonald placed a steaming plate in front of him.

"Thanks. Now, I hope you're all joining me." He looked up at her and indicated the empty seats at the table.

"Well, we don't normally eat with the master."

"I'm not the *master*, Mrs. MacDonald, and you must stop thinking of me in that way. This house was left to me by Mr. Burroughs, but I don't have any illusions of grandeur. I'm a graphic artist by trade. Until yesterday, I rented a small apartment in Los Angeles, and I'm very much in awe of what has happened to me recently. So, if you don't mind, I'd like to have lunch with all of you and get to know you better."

"Sounds good to me," Matthew said, sitting down opposite Michael.

"Come on, Emily," Michael coaxed the young girl. "You too..."

"Just a minute!" Annie MacDonald, hands on ample hips, glared at her husband. "Since when have I been the housemaid, Matthew MacDonald? If we're all to have lunch with Mr. Ballantyne, you and Emily can help yourselves, I'm sure."

Matthew guffawed and jumped to his feet. "Thought I'd try it once, Annie. Can't blame a man for tryin', now can you?"

"Oh, sit down. I'll throw some on a plate for you." She gave Michael a warm smile. "Mr. Burroughs was a nice man, and he'd sometimes have a cup of tea or coffee in here with me, but never lunch. This'll take some getting used to."

Michael waited until they'd all sat down with their lunch in front of them then said, "And while we're at it, I'd like all of you to call me by my first name, Michael."

All three stared at him like he was quite mad. "Oh, can't do that," Mrs. MacDonald all but whispered, shaking her head adamantly. "Not proper, it's not."

"I suggested we call him Mr. Michael, if he was all right with it," Matthew told the two women, after a mouthful of shepherd's pie. "And he agreed to that."

"For the time being," Michael said. "This is really delicious, Mrs. MacDonald. Okay, can we all agree then that things can be a bit more relaxed around here? I want to regard you as my friends rather than my 'staff.' No standing on ceremony, okay?"

"Suits me," Matthew said, stuffing his face with shepherd's pie.

"It'll take some getting used to," his wife remarked, sitting at the table. Emily said nothing. She was too busy enjoying her lunch.

"D'you have enough help here?' Michael asked. "Seems like a lot of work for just the three of you."

"Oh, we have two ladies from town come in twice a week to do the polishing and heavy chores," Mrs. MacDonald told him. "Emily does a nice job of keeping it clean in between. And of course I keep the kitchen spic and span, as you can see."

"Yes, indeed." Michael smiled across the table at her. There was no way he'd ever argue that point.

Later, strolling through the grounds, Michael wondered what his 'staff' made of him. *Probably think I'm some kind of weirdo not wanting them all to bow and scrape every time I come in the room.* He was surprised that this kind of attitude still existed, even in England. He supposed that old habits and traditions died hard.

He found himself heading toward a wooded part of the grounds. *Looks like an orchard*, he thought, and remembered the dream he'd had in the hotel where he and Jonathan had said goodbye before Jonathan reported for active duty. As he walked between the sheltering trees, he couldn't quite rid himself of the feeling he'd been here before—of course he had been, in his dream. Yet, it seemed even more familiar than that. Wasn't that the tree Jonathan had been hiding behind? He stopped, his heart pounding with anticipation. Again, he had the idea he was being watched.

"Jonathan?"

Michael practically jumped out of his skin and took a step back at the sight of a man emerging from behind the tree.

"Sorry, sir…" It was an old man wearing rough tweed pants, a checkered shirt open at the collar, and a cloth cap. The man touched his cap and gave Michael a nod that was almost a bow. "Tom Smithers, sir. I'm your gardener. Didn't mean to startle you, sir."

Feeling foolish, Michael gave a shaky laugh. "That's okay." He held out his hand. "Michael Ballantyne."

"Yes, sir." Tom touched his cap again, then took Michael's hand in a calloused grip. "Welcome to Bedford Park, sir."

"You do a great job here, Tom. Do you have some help?"

"Oh, yes. Son Dan's usually here, but he's down in London gallivantin' about with his girlfriend, on holiday like, then there's a couple of lads come three times a week to help out with the mowin' and the like."

"How long have you worked here?"

"Mr. Burroughs hired me when he bought the place."

"So you didn't know the previous owners?"

"Knew of 'em. Quiet folks though, 'specially after their son disappeared."

"You knew about that?"

"Whole town knew. It was in papers and the radio. Terrible sad…" Tom shifted his feet uncomfortably. "Well, I'll be off, sir. I were just makin' my rounds before dark."

"Right, nice talking with you, Tom."

"Mutual, sir. Hope you're happy here."

Michael stood under the trees and watched Tom walk away. He'd been hoping the old gardener might have been employed during Jonathan's lifetime, but that would have been too easy an avenue for information. Well, the library seemed as good a place as any to start his research into the mystery of Jonathan's disappearance. He'd have Matthew drive him into town in the morning, and he could do some clothes shopping at the same time.

He started back toward the house, then paused and turned to glance behind him. Once again he could swear he was being watched, and this time it was giving him the creeps.

"Tom?"

There was no reply; the old gardener must have moved out of earshot. From the shadowed trees that surrounded him he had a sense that someone, or something, was lurking nearby, watching him. His skin prickled as a feeling of menace swept over him, causing him to move swiftly out of the orchard and onto the open sward of the lawn in front of the house. He could see Matthew sweeping the terrace in front of the French doors, and it was that scene of normalcy that allowed him to slow his pace and catch his breath.

What the hell had that been about? he wondered. He could almost hear the furious pounding of his heart as he stood staring back into the orchard at the leafy branches swaying in the gentle breeze. *One day, my imagination is going to scare me to death*, he thought grimly, turning away and walking back to the house.

CHAPTER SIX

Mrs. MacDonald had prepared an excellent dinner of baked salmon, russet potatoes, and fresh spinach, and once again Michael insisted on eating in the kitchen in company with Matthew and the good cook herself. Emily had gone home earlier, not being a live-in maid, Annie informed him.

"Do we have some good wine handy?" Michael asked Matthew, who nodded and led him down into a fair-sized wine cellar located beneath the kitchen. Michael selected a promising dry white wine to have with the salmon and instructed Matthew to set out three glasses. He could tell he was surprising his chauffeur and cook at every turn, but in his mind it beat sitting alone in a vast dining room, staring down the length of a table that could seat twenty people or more.

"I bumped into Tom the gardener in the orchard this afternoon," he told them. "Nice old guy."

"Cantankerous is more like it," his housekeeper said with a sniff. "He's getting too old for the job if you ask me."

"Now Annie…" Matthew took a long sip of wine. "I'm sure he was respectful of Mr. Michael—wasn't he?"

"Oh yes, very. I asked him about the previous owners of Bedford Park, but he said he hadn't worked for them. Did either of you know the Harcourts?"

"Not really," Matthew replied. "I mean, we knew *of* them. You can't live in a place like this and not have people wonder about you."

"What about the son that disappeared?"

"Before my time," Mrs. MacDonald said, also taking a healthy swig of her wine. "Of course, it was talked about for a long while after. Only real mystery they'd had around here, so people remembered it."

"Well, you're probably wondering why Mr. Burroughs left me everything in his will." Michael felt it was only fair he should let them know the connection before rumors started. "Jonathan Harcourt had a friend named Michael Thornton—he was my uncle."

"Really?" Matthew stared at him wide-eyed. "You mean the young man that committed suicide?"

"You knew about that?"

"Read about it. Some chap from London wrote a magazine article after he'd interviewed Mr. Burroughs. Caused quite a stir, as he intimated that maybe is wasn't suicide after all." Matthew shook his head. "Mr. Burroughs… well, it was like an obsession with him, 'specially after Mr. Samuels died. He kept seeing this ghost, talking out loud to it, asking it questions. We thought we'd have to call in the doctor."

"You thought he was going nuts," Michael said. "He left me a letter, and I have to admit I thought he was too, but I verified the part about my uncle with my brother. Seems that after Michael died, his parents left for the States and had a daughter, she was my mother."

"Fancy that," Mrs. MacDonald murmured. "Small world, isn't it?"

Michael smiled. His housekeeper was already quite tipsy. "It certainly is," he remarked, pouring her and Matthew another glass of wine. "Mr. Burroughs said Jonathan's parents sort of disappeared after they sold the house. You wouldn't know where they moved to, would you?"

"No, like I said, it was all before my time," she replied after another sip of wine. "Never gave it a thought, really. But old Miss Ballard, a friend of Mr. Burroughs, works in the Royston library, she might know. There was a time when she knew everything about everybody!"

"She's not still at the library, is she?" Michael asked.

"Yes, she is. Must be eighty if she's a day, but she won't hear of retiring."

"Cool... Mr. Burroughs mentioned her in his letter. I intended checking out the library anyway. Now you've given me another reason. Can you drive me into town in the morning, Matthew?"

"Of course." Matthew squinted at Michael. "What is it you want to find out?"

"In his letter, Mr. Burroughs asked me to try and solve the mystery of Jonathan's disappearance. Most likely I won't, but I thought I'd give it my best shot."

"It happened so long ago, Mr. Michael," Matthew remarked. "Any clues would have long since vanished."

"I know, but as I'll have a lot of time on my hands, it's something to do." He paused, knowing he wasn't going to like the answer to his next question. "The guy that lives in the house by the gate, what's the story there?"

Mrs. MacDonald shook her head before she answered. "He just appeared one day out of the blue. Said Mr. Burroughs had hired him. We told him poor Mr. Burroughs had passed, but he said he had a letter of employment and he intended to stay. Even had the keys to the house. We see him sometimes prowling about."

"Prowling?"

"Well, he says he's keeping things in order as per Mr. Burroughs instructions."

"But we both think he's a big fat liar," Matthew interrupted. "Mr. Burroughs would have told us if he were hiring anyone. Even Tom the gardener didn't know about him coming. I reckon that letter's a forgery."

Michael sighed. "The solicitor Mr. Fortescue told me he'd asked the man to leave, but he refused."

"But *you* could give him the sack. You're the one in charge now."

"Yeah, I suppose I should confront him as soon as possible."

"I'll go with you, if you like," Matthew said, "just in case he gets nasty."

"There's safety in numbers," his wife added.

"Thanks, but I don't think he'll be much of a problem." Michael stood up and stretched. "Think I'll turn in. Still feeling a bit jet-lagged…"

Mrs. MacDonald yawned. "I'm feeling a bit sleepy myself. Don't know why, I'm sure."

Matthew chuckled. "It's called 'wine,' my dear."

"Well, good night to you both." Michael headed for the door. "Sweet dreams."

§ § § §

"Michael…"

Michael's eyes fluttered open, and he smiled, stretching his lithe, naked body sensuously under the lustful gaze of his lover. Jonathan's tongue slipped between Michael's parted lips, caressing the inside of his mouth and sending little jolts of excitement through his entire body. A long, low moan escaped him as their kiss went on and on, and he gave in to his desire. His hands stroked Jonathan's body. The exquisite feel of smooth skin under his hands, combined with the heat Jonathan's lips created, made Michael's head reel from an overload of emotion. He sighed with happiness, gazing up over Jonathan's head to see the gently swaying branches of the trees they lay under, and the azure blue of the sky beyond. They were in the orchard again—their favorite meeting place, their special place away from prying eyes and inquisitive stares.

Here they were free to enjoy each other for the short but precious time they had on leave.

"I thought I'd died and gone to heaven when you wrote and said you'd be home at the same time as me," Michael whispered, his lips on Jonathan's ear.

"I know, I couldn't believe it myself." Jonathan smiled into Michael's eyes, then traced a sensuous trail of kisses along the curve of his jaw. "I love you so much, Michael. I pray every day for this wretched war to be over, and for you and I to be together, forever."

His hand strayed over Michael's chest, teasing each nipple, then gliding over his torso to reach for the prize he sought. Michael's throbbing erection pulsed in Jonathan's hand as he gently squeezed and stroked the warm, hard flesh, bringing soft moans of pleasure from his lover's lips, lips he now claimed with a kiss that was sweet, yet demanding, tender but edged with a hunger neither man could ignore.

Jonathan moved over Michael's body, his kisses leaving a searing heat on Michael's skin. Michael's hips bucked as Jonathan's lips encircled the head of his cock, his tongue swirling over the velvety flesh, licking up the salty essence that spilled from the slit.

Michael moaned aloud, "Jonathan…"

"Jonathan!" Michael's eyes flew open and he sat upright in the bed. "Jeez…" He flopped back down on the pillow. "Another dream…" Just how much longer was this going to go on? He reached down and gripped his erection in his fist, ready to finish off what the dream had started. God, but that had been hot. Why the hell couldn't he meet someone like Jonathan in real life? Someone who actually cared about him? Not like Steve, who was only there when he wanted to get his rocks off. Or so it had seemed to Michael at times.

He groaned as the vision of Jonathan's beautiful face and body swam before his tightly shut eyes. He ran his thumb over the swollen head of his cock, lubricating the shaft with the precum that coated his fingers. He flung the sheet back and stared at his pulsing erection as he pumped it slowly at first, then faster as his hips bucked and his orgasm churned in his balls. He came in great jolting spasms, spraying his naked chest with his hot cream.

Oh, God… He lay still for a while, letting his breathing calm down and his body recover. Then he rose and padded into the bathroom to wash up. Staring at his reflection in the mirror, he was reminded again of just how closely he resembled his uncle in the photograph Lionel had left him. More and more these dreams seemed like memories rather than dreams—but whose memories? His, or his *uncle's*?

"Dear God…" Was he…? Could he even dare to think it possible that he might be his uncle reincarnated? No, no… it wasn't possible. He didn't even believe in such things—he didn't even believe in heaven or hell. There was no such thing as an *afterlife*… was there? Troubled by these thoughts, he walked back into the bedroom and lay down on the cool sheets. As crazy an idea as he'd just had, the more he thought about it, even if he still thought it crazy, there seemed to be a glimmer of credibility to it. After all, the dreams he had of Jonathan involved what he already knew of his and his uncle's relationship.

According to Lionel's letter, they had both served in the army overseas during the Second World War, and some of the dreams he'd had certainly bore that out, especially the one he'd just experienced. They'd both been on furlough.

Jonathan had disappeared, presumed murdered, and that might account for his asking Michael to *avenge* him. What Lionel hadn't told him in his letter was that Jonathan and Michael appeared to have known each other since childhood. That dream he'd had about Jonathan climbing trees and mentioning his birthday party, they'd been young boys then.

No doubt about it, they had been devoted to one another, and if his dreams were any indication, they had enjoyed some pretty hot sex! He couldn't wait to go to the library and talk to the old lady there, maybe even research some stuff about Bedford Park.

He yawned and glanced at the clock by his bed. Two in the morning—maybe he'd sleep now. Lots to do tomorrow… or rather, today…

§ § § §

Inside the house by the gates to Bedford Park, Jack Trenton sat by the fireside reading, as he had done over and over since his father's death. Always the same thing — the letter the old man had left him. When he'd first read it, he'd judged his father as daft as a cave full of bats, but now it seemed that what he'd foretold was coming to pass.

His father's name would be violated if the newcomer to Bedford Park ever found out the truth. Changing the family name would not be enough—the newcomer must be stopped from discovering what happened to Jonathan Harcourt, and under no circumstances must he ever find out just where the body was hidden. His father had gone to a lot of trouble to keep that secret, invoking powers he never should have called upon, and God alone knew what would happen if Michael Ballantyne stumbled upon the truth.

No, that must not happen. He, Jack Trenton, would not allow it, even if he went to hell for what he had to do to prevent it. What his father had begun all those years ago, he had vowed to uphold, no matter what the cost to himself—or anyone else.

CHAPTER SEVEN

The following morning, Michael woke later than he had intended. He lay on his back staring blearily up at the ceiling, contemplating dashing about the town of Royston to talk to the bank manager, buy new clothes, and visit the library, all of which had somehow lost their appeal. Maybe he'd just take it easy today, have lots of coffee, and ask Mrs. MacDonald to make him some breakfast. He glanced at his watch—almost noon. Make that lunch, Mrs. M.

Groaning, he swung his legs over the side of the bed, then padded into the bathroom. After he'd relieved himself and splashed his face with cold water, he began to feel a little more human. He threw on his favorite sweats, one of the few things he'd thought to pack, then ventured downstairs looking for Matthew or Mrs. MacDonald. Instead, he found Emily in the kitchen wiping down the counters.

"'Morning, Emily," he said, making the young girl jump. "Oh, sorry, didn't mean to startle you."

"Oh, Mr. Ballantyne, sir…" Emily stared at him with wide eyes. "They've gone out."

"Who's gone out?"

"Mr. and Mrs. MacDonald. They've gone to the shops in Abingdon for provisions. I'm ever so sorry."

Michael chuckled. "No need to be sorry. I slept in. Any chance of some coffee?"

"I'll make some for you straight away. Matthew said you was probably jet-lagged, so we was to leave you sleeping and not make any noise."

"That was nice of you." He sat at the kitchen table, watching while the young girl busied herself making his coffee. "So, how do you like working here, Emily?"

"I like it."

"Doesn't bother you that it's a haunted house?" he asked jokingly.

Emily shrugged. "Not really. He's a nice ghost."

Michael stared at her. "You've seen it? Uh, I mean him."

"Once, just after Mr. Burroughs passed. He was in the study. He smiled at me."

"Uh huh…" Michael wondered if Emily's imagination was as overactive as his own. "Did he do anything, or say anything?"

Emily giggled. "Everyone knows ghosts can't speak, sir. No, he just was standing by the window looking out at the orchard. When I came in, I sort of gave out with a little scream, not very loud, but he did give me quite a turn."

"I bet. Then what happened?"

"He just smiled, kind of sad like, and then he was gone."

"Did you tell Matthew or Mrs. MacDonald?"

"Oh yes, but they said I was seeing things. Said they'd been in the house for years and never, not once, had ever seen him." Emily brought a mug down from one of the cabinets. "You take milk, sir?"

"No, just black is fine. So, you're sure it was him, not a trick of the light or something?"

"It was definitely him. See, my mum and me, we have the sight. Only us with the sight can see a ghost, even if they don't want you to."

"Ah." Michael nodded politely, mentally humming the theme from the Twilight Zone. "Is he still in the house?"

"Oh, yes." Emily put a mug of coffee in front of Michael. "He'll be here 'til it's all sorted out."

"Sorted out?"

"Yes. Oh, here's Mr. and Mrs. MacDonald. I better help with the groceries. It was very nice talking with you, sir."

"Er, yes it was," Michael murmured, watching her hurry out the back door to where Matthew had just pulled up in the Rolls.

So Emily had seen Jonathan in the study.

Michael got up from the table and walked across the hall to the wood-paneled room that housed a large collection of books, along with some nice pieces of antique furniture that included a desk and leather-upholstered chairs. He stood in the doorway looking toward the window, wondering if maybe he waited long enough, Jonathan would appear as he had done for Emily.

Yeah, right…

He walked slowly into the study, looked around at the expensive furnishings and thought, *Wow, this is all mine now.* He sat down at the desk and ran his fingers over the rich wood, still not quite able to grasp all that had happened in the past seventy-two hours. That's all it had been. Such a short space of time to have your life turned totally upside down. The movement he caught from the corner of his eye made him jump, then laugh shakily. The fine silk drapes were waving in a breeze from the open window. Was that what Emily had seen, a moving drape, a trick of the light? But she'd said he'd smiled at her…

Come on, Jonathan, smile for me.

"Ah, you're up, Mr. Michael." Matthew was standing in the study doorway. "Did you have a good sleep?"

"Yes, eventually." Michael rose from his chair. "I think we'll skip the trip into Royston today. Is Mrs. MacDonald free to make some lunch?"

"Of course, I'll see to it straight away."

"Uh, Matthew, Emily told me she'd seen the ghost here."

Matthew chuckled. "Yes, she says she did. She might have seen *something*, but I bet it weren't no ghost. I'll just go and tell Mrs. MacDonald to get cracking with the lunch."

"Thanks, Matthew."

Michael walked over to the window and gazed out across the lawn to the orchard beyond. Somehow he couldn't quite get Emily's words out of his mind.

He'll be here 'til it's all sorted out…

Michael spent the afternoon exploring the house. The master bedroom which he was to have redecorated was going to be a challenge. For starters, it was immense, and badly needed brightening. *Maybe terracotta walls and white trim*, he thought, standing in the middle of the room. The bed could stay. It was a four poster, impressive in a rich mahogany. It just needed brighter colors for the comforter. He'd definitely get rid of the heavy drapes and replace them with shutters; and the bathroom needed some TLC. New tile, perhaps…

He stepped back to take it all in, his artist's eye already seeing the transformation. Suddenly, he felt warmth spread over his back and envelope him, as if someone was embracing him from behind. For a moment, he couldn't move. The short hairs on the back of his neck stood up, but he felt no fear. Instead, he found himself leaning back into this unreal embrace, turning his head to rest it on a phantom shoulder. His skin tingled with electricity, and he realized he'd stopped breathing. All he could hear was the pounding of his own heart—and then the gentlest of kisses was laid on his cheek.

"Jesus!" Michael whirled round, clutching at the empty space behind him. *Oh, now, what was that? What the fuck was that?* His imagination again… that was all, but *damn*, it had felt so real. The kiss… warm, soft lips… He could still feel the trace of them on his cheek. *Holy… I must be going nuts.*

"Oh terrific," he said aloud. "I get left a fortune, and have to settle for the loony bin!"

The guest room he was using until the master bedroom was refurbished seemed totally devoid of any kind of manifestation. *Thank you very much.* He hadn't mentioned his strange experience to Matthew or his wife at dinner for fear they might feel they'd better call the doctor.

No one gets to carry me away just yet, he thought grimly. Now more than ever, he was determined he would make the trip into Royston, visit the library, and hopefully get a chance to talk to the old lady whom Mrs. MacDonald had said "knew everyone and everything." He needed to talk to someone who had the skinny on just what might have happened at Bedford Park all those years ago.

Lying in the semi darkness of the bedroom, he gazed at the soft shafts of moonlight that filtered through the drapes and cast silvery shapes on the wall opposite his bed. It would be so easy to imagine a ghostly presence in a house like this. A house with a history. A home once filled with boyish laughter, and later with a man's longing for love and acceptance before tragedy changed his life, and that of the man he loved.

Lionel had found the story romantic, and yes, Michael could see the romance in it, but it was a bittersweet romance without the happy ever after it deserved. How terrible it must have been for his uncle Michael to have never known what had happened to his lover. They had been lovers since boyhood, separated by long years of war, finally reunited, ready to live their lives together, and then…

"*Jonathan!*"

He was in a place he'd never seen before, surrounded by walls of a strange grayish white. Walls strangely porous to the touch of his fingers as he felt his way along the dimly lit passage.

"*Jonathan! Where are you?*"

Up ahead, he could hear voices raised in anger, accusations and shouted retorts.

"*Jonathan!*" *He was screaming now, terrified that something terrible was about to happen. He could hear Jonathan's voice, and another he thought he recognized. The passage he was stumbling through seemed to never end. No matter how fast he ran, there was always another endless tunnel in front of him, and the voices he could hear remained in the distance, far from him, unreachable…*

"*Oh my God…*" *Sweat poured from his body, soaking his shirt and pants as he struggled to close the distance between him and the man he loved. The man whom he knew was in terrible danger. "Oh God, help me!" His shouted plea was muffled, sucked into the soft stone that enclosed him. The passageway was narrowing, closing in on him as he ran. Now he could barely squeeze his way past the walls. And then—NO—the passageway ended. He was staring at a blank wall, but from the other side he could still hear the voices. Frantically he began tearing at the wall with his bare hands.*

"Jonathan, Jonathan…"

"Michael…" His lover's voice came to him from behind this impenetrable barrier. "Go back, go back, Michael! Get away from here. Get away! Save yourself!" Jonathan's voice was suddenly cut off, and the passageway was plunged into darkness.

"No!"

Michael sat bolt upright in the bed, his naked body slick with sweat. He was breathing heavily as if he'd been running.

"Jesus…" He threw back the covers and sprang from the bed, turning on the bedside lamp as he did so. For a few moments he stood, waiting for his breathing to return to normal, shivering as a cool breeze from the window wrapped itself around his sweat-covered body.

What the hell had that been about? And why had his dreams, those sensuous erotic dreams, why had they now suddenly turned nightmarish? Was there a message in there, a clue to what had happened to Jonathan? As Michael hurried into the bathroom and turned on the shower, he knew without a doubt that in the morning, Matthew and he were going into town, and somehow he was going to get some answers.

CHAPTER EIGHT

Sitting up front with Matthew in the Rolls, Michael stared out the window as they cruised through the streets of Royston.

"Is this an old town?" he asked.

"Oh, yes." Matthew paused as he stopped at a red light. "Before Roman times, I think. One of the kings—can't remember which one—had a hunting lodge built here, just for his and his court's pleasure. There's the library," he added, pointing to a rather plain stone building. "Do you want to go there first?"

"Better make it the bank first."

"Right-o. The bank it is."

"You'd better come in, Matthew. It might take a while."

"No problem. I can read a newspaper." Matthew pulled up alongside the bank. He chuckled as he checked out the row of parking meters in front of the building. "Blimey, they want to take your money *before* you get inside."

"I have absolutely no change on me," Michael said, alarmed.

"Not to worry, I think I have a few pence."

Michael had to laugh at the irony of the moment. There he was with five million pounds in the bank, making his butler dig in his pockets for parking meter change.

"I'll buy you lunch after we're through here and at the library," he said.

"Lovely, there's a pub not far from there, *The Dogcatcher's Arms*. They do a bang-up lunch."

The bank was fairly busy, but once Michael had introduced himself to the receptionist, the manager descended on him, hand outstretched, a congenial smile lighting up his chubby features.

"Mr. Ballantyne, welcome. I am Harold Bennett, the bank manager. Mr. Fortescue told me you would be calling. May I congratulate you on your good fortune, sir?"

For the next hour, Michael had to make nice while listening to the manager try to sell him every kind of account and investment five million pounds could buy.

"Right now, I'd just like to have access to some of the money so I can buy a few new clothes and have some cash in my pocket for emergencies," Michael told Bennett. "Let's see how the economy's going to pan out before I decide on stock investments. But thanks for the information."

"Of course, any time," Bennett gushed. "How much would you like today?"

Feeling flush, Michael left the bank with a cash card, a handsome wad of British pound notes in his pocket, and for the first time since he'd arrived in England, the realization of just how rich he was. Not a bad feeling at all.

On the short drive over to the library, Michael noticed that the day was turning mild and humid. He was glad he'd decided to wear a short-sleeved shirt and cotton khaki pants, and he felt sorry for Matthew in his dark uniform.

"You can take that jacket off if you like, Matthew. It's a bit warm."

"I'm all right, Mr. Michael. Quite used to it."

The interior of the library was practically empty and hushed as they made their way across the lobby to the reception desk. Michael spotted Miss Ballard immediately. It could only be her, he thought. Small and spry with gray curls and a *pince-nez* parked on the tip of her nose, her gasp of surprise upon seeing the two men approach her seemed to echo through the high-ceilinged room.

"Well, I know you can't be him, but for a moment I was taken aback," she said, moving her glasses further up her nose and peering up at Michael.

"This is Mr. Michael Ballantyne, Miss Ballard," Matthew said formally. "He's the new owner of Bedford Park."

"Is he indeed?" The old lady gave Michael another long look up and down. "How appropriate."

Michael smiled at her. "Appropriate?"

"You look just like him—Michael Thornton, Jonathan's friend."

"He was my uncle," Michael told her.

"Of course, hence the resemblance. My word... and now, Mr. Ballantyne, you are the new owner." She beamed up at him. "Jonathan would be pleased."

"Please, call me Michael. I wondered if I could ask you about some of the history of Bedford Park. Mr. Burroughs left me a letter explaining some of it, but I feel there's more to know."

Miss Ballard stared up at Michael for so long that Matthew eventually cleared his throat, trying to attract her attention. "Uh, Miss Ballard, do you have a few minutes to spare Mr. Michael?"

The old lady started slightly before smiling at Michael. "Oh, yes. As you can see, we're not very busy right now. Miss Albright?" She gestured to another elderly lady. "I can take a break," she told Michael. "We can have tea in the back room."

"That would be very nice," Michael said.

"I'll just go find a paper," Matthew muttered.

"Miss Albright, will you take over for a little while?" Miss Ballard, not waiting for the lady to reply, was already shepherding Michael away from the reception desk. "I must say, your resemblance to Michael Thornton is quite extraordinary. You could almost be his twin."

"Yes, I noticed that in the photograph Mr. Burroughs left me."

"Quite extraordinary," Miss Ballard said again. She led him down a corridor and through a door into a small room set aside for the employees. "Oh, someone has already brewed some tea, how lovely. Take a seat anywhere."

"So you knew my uncle personally?" Michael asked, taking a seat at the table.

"Oh yes, and Jonathan Harcourt. I was rather in love with them both, but they didn't have much time for girls."

"You mean…?"

Miss Ballard turned and smiled at him. "Rather like yourself, I think. They were of the homosexual persuasion."

Michael grinned. "I've never heard it put quite like that before." *Wow, her gaydar must be pretty sharp*, he thought ruefully. *And here I thought I had my butch look goin' today.* He wiped the smile off his face as he listened to Miss Ballard.

"Well, of course the expression 'gay' wasn't used back then. Now, how do you take your tea; milk and sugar?"

"No thanks. Just the way it comes."

"So, Lionel left everything to you?" she asked, putting a cup of hot tea in front of Michael.

"Yes, it was a bit of a surprise, to say the least."

"I'm sure, but Lionel was always rather rash. Once he'd got hold of an idea, he couldn't be dissuaded."

"You were good friends?"

"Yes, and with his partner, William." Miss Ballard took a dainty sip of her tea. "You mentioned a photograph."

"Yes, I have it here." He fished it out of his back pocket and handed it to her.

"Oh yes, I remember taking this when they came back on leave." She glanced up at Michael. "Extraordinary likeness." She handed it back to Michael. "I suppose Lionel told you about the ghost?"

"Yes, he said it was Jonathan Harcourt's ghost."

"Mmm, that's what he told me."

"You sound doubtful."

"Well, I never saw the ghost—no one did except Lionel. William said he did, but I think he only said that to make Lionel feel better."

"Yes, Matthew suggested that too, but Emily the housemaid told me she's seen it—I mean, him."

Miss Ballard pursed her lips. "Young girls have romantic notions."

"She said he smiled at her."

"*Very* romantic notions at times. A ghost, smiling? I mean, you can see *through* them, so it would be hard to distinguish whether they were smiling or scowling, wouldn't you say?"

Michael nodded, deciding at that moment not to mention the strange experience he'd had in the master bedroom. "Do you have any ideas about Jonathan's disappearance?"

"Well, he certainly didn't run off," she said decisively. "He was devoted to your uncle, so there was no reason for him to leave on a whim. The popular consensus was that he had been murdered, and I have to admit I agree with that assumption."

"You must have spoken to my uncle after Jonathan went missing."

"Oh, of course, he came to see me on several occasions afterward." She looked away for a moment. "If anything, our mutual grief made our friendship even stronger. I think it was because I was the only one who knew what Michael and Jonathan had meant to each other."

"Did he seem suicidal to you?"

"Absolutely not, Michael; in fact, when I got the news of his death, I was shocked to hear it had been suicide. I could not believe it, but according to the police he'd left a note."

"A note? Lionel didn't mention that."

"Probably because it cast no light on his death. All it said was that he couldn't live without Jonathan."

"How did he die?"

"He hanged himself." Miss Ballard's eyes grew misty. "Something else I couldn't quite believe. They were both such beautiful men. It was just tragic that they should both have been taken so young."

"Matthew told me some reporter intimated that my uncle didn't commit suicide, that he'd also been murdered."

She nodded, her eyes glistening. "Yes, I read that article, and I must say that as much as I hate to think of it, I tend to agree. Your uncle was so determined to find out what happened to Jonathan. It didn't seem like him to give up by taking his own life. A pity that the police seemed reticent in pursuing the matter."

"Lionel's letter mentioned a Henry Bryant."

"*Henry…*" Miss Ballard rolled the name off her tongue as though it tasted bad. "A rotten egg if ever there was one—a complete cad, a devious man without scruples, and capable of murder if you ask me."

"But he had an alibi."

"Concocted, I'm sure, and corroborated by witnesses who refused to take a lie detector test. There again, the police were lax." She sighed sadly. "But of course it is of no consequence now. Henry Bryant died a year ago without having the decency to make a deathbed confession."

"So you think he did it?"

"I think he could have done it." Miss Ballard grimaced as she remembered. "He owed Jonathan a deal of money and couldn't, or wouldn't, pay it back. Michael told me that Jonathan and Henry had a row over it, but that Jonathan had more or less washed his hands of the affair."

"So, if he wasn't going to press for the loan to be repaid, there was no reason for Bryant to kill Jonathan."

"You'd think not," Miss Ballard said, then added slowly, "however, he was the jealous sort."

"Of Jonathan and my uncle, you mean?"

"Exactly. Michael mentioned to me that Henry had made, um… shall we say, *advances* toward him."

"Oh, wow…" Michael stared at the old lady. "Did you or my uncle mention that to the police?"

"Heavens no, such a thing would have smeared Jonathan's name, and Michael's too, of course. You have to remember this happened in 1947. The term, 'the love that dared not speak its name' certainly applied in those days, I'm afraid."

"Right… even though they'd both fought for their country," Michael said with some bitterness.

Miss Ballard smiled and touched Michael's hand. "People can be very cruel, back then just as much as today." She paused, then her fingers, tiny and brittle, interlaced with Michael's. "It's so strange," she said quietly, "but when I look at you, I feel as though I'm young again, holding hands with you and Jonathan, rambling through the grounds at Bedford Park, laughing at the silly jokes we made, trying to forget that you'd both soon be off to the war." Her eyes gleamed with unshed tears as she gazed into Michael's eyes. "You loved him so very much."

Michael felt a shiver run up his spine at her words, and before he could stop himself, he said, "Yes, I did love him. I still do."

Whoa! Where had that come from?

Michael sat back, breaking the spell that seemed to have enveloped them both for a brief moment. Miss Ballard wiped her eyes with a small handkerchief.

"My," she murmured. "What memories you have brought me."

"I'm sorry." Michael forced a smile to his face. "I seemed to have been caught up in those memories with you. Can you tell me where my uncle is buried? I think I'd like to visit his grave."

"West Park Cemetery, Matthew can take you there."

"You mentioned all three of you in the grounds at Bedford Park, but my uncle didn't live there."

"No, he and his parents lived next door to me, here in Royston. That's how we met," she said, smiling. "He was literally the boy next door."

"And how did he meet Jonathan?"

"At school. They were both on the rugby team, best friends in no time, almost inseparable from the day they met." Her eyes grew misty again as she remembered.

"I'm sorry," Michael said again. "Has this been painful for you?"

"In some ways, yes." Miss Ballard gave herself a little shake and smiled. "But I do have some wonderful memories of them both. And even after all these years, I still cherish them."

As they walked back through the library to her desk, she said suddenly, "Oh, there's someone you should meet. Inspector Handley, hello."

A tall, uniformed, and distinguished man with graying hair at his temples turned and smiled at her. At the same time giving Michael an appraising look.

"Miss Ballard." He gave her a wide smile. "I wondered why you weren't at your post."

"Paul, this is Michael Ballantyne. He is the new owner of Bedford Park."

"Are you now?" Inspector Paul Handley extended his hand. "About time that old place had some new life breathed into it."

"Pleased to meet you," Michael said, shaking the man's hand.

"American, eh?"

"From LA. You're with the Royston police department?"

"Abingdon, actually. It's a substation of Royston's main department and infinitely quieter." He smiled again. "Just the place to finish out my few years left before retirement." He handed Michael his card. "Call me if you have any problems over there at Bedford Park—though I sincerely doubt you will."

"Thanks." Michael pocketed the card.

"Well, very nice meeting you, Mr. Ballantyne. Welcome to England. Nice seeing you, Miss Ballard."

"Seems like a nice guy," Michael remarked as Miss Ballard tugged at his arm and they set off again towards her desk.

"His father was head of the Royston Police Department when your uncle died," she said quietly. "He and I had words over his handling of the situation, but his son Paul has always been fairly congenial. Well…" She smiled up at Michael. "It has been a delight talking with you, Michael. Please come in any time to see me."

§ § § §

Michael climbed out of the Rolls, leaving Matthew to wait for him at the cemetery gate. He walked slowly up the gravel path that lay between the rows of headstones. West Park Cemetery was well tended, the grass neatly mowed, the flower beds filled with a profusion and variety of blossoms. Miss Ballard had said his uncle's grave was easy to find, on the right hand side and sheltered by a Chestnut tree she herself had planted over sixty years ago.

"It was just a sapling then," she'd said wistfully. "Now you can't really miss it."

And he couldn't. The tree had grown to a majestic height, its branches thick with leaves and heavy with green chestnuts.

"He and Jonathan loved to play conkers when they were boys," she'd told Michael.

"Conkers?"

"When the green shells fall from the trees," Miss Ballard had explained, "they split open and the chestnut, brown and shiny, pops out. The boys bore a hole through them, string them, then try hitting them to see who can split the other boy's nuts first."

Michael had tried very hard to keep a straight face as he'd listened to her, but she saw his lips twist with the effort and laughed gaily, slapping his arm rather hard for an old lady.

Now he stood before his uncle's grave, and on reading the words carved into the stone, *Michael Thornton, 1922-1947, only beloved son of Richard and Martha Thornton*, he was filled with a deep sense of loss for the man he had never known. Under this earth lay a man whose life had been cruelly cut off, whose lover had possibly been murdered, and no one was brought to justice for the crime—or, perhaps, crimes.

Jonathan's words came back to haunt him: *Avenge us, my love, and set us free...* Michael shivered as the words echoed in his mind. He reached out to touch the stone, and as he grasped the cold marble, he could feel a presence near him. A shadow fell across the grave; he turned quickly and gasped with shock. Staring at the tall, dark-haired young man, casually dressed in a dark blue shirt and jeans, the blood drained from Michael's face, and for a moment he thought he was going to pass out.

"Dear God," he whispered, unable to believe his eyes. *"Jonathan..."*

The man stared back at Michael for a long moment, his finely chiseled face visibly paling. He struggled to speak. "You... you know me..." The words were torn from him on a whispered breath. He took a step nearer, his eyes searching the inscription on the headstone. "It's true then," he murmured. His gaze met and held Michael's again. "I can't believe who I'm looking at—you're Michael, aren't you?"

"Yes... but how...?" Michael couldn't find the words he needed.

"Dreams," Jonathan said. "I've been dreaming about you for weeks now." A faint smile crossed his handsome face. "You've been driving me quite mad."

"Oh..." Again Michael was at a loss for words. He felt the blood race back into his face as he digested the implication. "Yes, I've dreamed of you too... but this, this is incredible, and why did you come here, today of all days?"

"Perhaps we should find somewhere to talk," Jonathan suggested. "I have a car outside the gate."

"So do I... the Rolls... Matthew is waiting for me. I was taking him to lunch after..."

"Oh." Jonathan stared at him. "Matthew...?"

"He came with the house. I mean, I was left this house and Matthew's the chauffeur, butler, whatever..."

"You're American."

"Yes." Michael managed to smile. "What was your first clue?"

Jonathan chuckled and held out his hand. "This might seem a bit weird, but it's very nice to meet you, Michael."

Michael grasped Jonathan's warm hand in both of his. "I still don't believe this, but you are real, aren't you?"

"I think so." Jonathan's dark blue eyes twinkled, and he smiled at Michael. "At least I was, when I left the house this morning."

"I feel as though I already know you so well. Isn't that crazy?"

"Not so crazy," Jonathan replied, letting Michael hold on to his hand. "Not if your dreams have been anything like mine."

"Right... that..." Michael felt himself blush again. He released Jonathan's hand, his gaze shifting to Michael Thornton's headstone. "He was my uncle. An uncle I didn't even know I had until a few days ago."

Jonathan touched his arm. "We really need to find a place to talk."

"Yes, we do. I'll apologize to Matthew and promise him lunch another day. Maybe you could give me a ride home after we... uh, talk?"

"I can do that." They walked side by side through the cemetery to where Matthew sat patiently waiting in the car.

"Matthew, this is Jonathan... uh..."

"Robertson." Jonathan held out his hand to Matthew. "Pleased to meet you, Matthew."

"Yes, we met at my uncle's graveside," Michael said hurriedly. "Turns out he's a friend of the family on my, uh... mother's side. So we thought we'd go somewhere we can catch up, sort of... I'll take you to lunch tomorrow Matthew, if that's OK?"

"No problem." Matthew started the car. "You'll be getting a lift home then?"

"Yes. See you later, Matthew." He followed Jonathan to where his car was parked.

"Not a Rolls, I'm afraid," Jonathan said, opening the passenger door of his Ford Escort.

"That came with the house, too." Michael slid into the seat and pulled the belt around him. "Owning a Rolls Royce was never there, even in my wildest dreams." He turned to stare at Jonathan, admiring his strong profile and the way his dark curls tumbled over his forehead. "I still can't quite believe this is happening, you and me together in this car going... where are we going?"

"To Cambridge for lunch in a nice, quiet little pub I'm very fond of."

"Cambridge? Isn't that a long way off?"

"Not at all, not even a half hour away. You haven't been to the UK before?"

"No, this is my first time. I thought it was to be a flying visit, but it seems I'm going to be here for at least a year."

Jonathan glanced at him and smiled. "Good. Gives us lots of time to get to know one another."

Yes, it does, Michael thought happily. "Do you live in Cambridge?"

"Yes, I teach at one of the colleges."

"That's interesting."

"Not really."

"Yes it is. I mean the letter that Lionel wrote me explaining why he'd left me his estate mentioned the fact that my uncle Michael and his friend Jonathan were teachers after the war, at Cambridge."

"That part I did know," Jonathan said. "I'm interested to hear your side of the story." He touched Michael's hand lightly. "You said you'd had dreams about me?"

Michael looked down at Jonathan's long, slender fingers, barely resisting the temptation to curl his own fingers around Jonathan's hand. "Well, the man certainly looked like you," he began, "but I think it was the *original* Jonathan and my uncle in the dreams. I was really just the voyeur, so to speak—although it did seem like I was involved too," he added wistfully.

"You mean, like you could feel the smoothness of his skin under your hands, his warm breath on your lips, that kind of thing?"

"Y-yes... that kind of thing... Is that what your experience was?" Michael suddenly became aware of a pulsing heat in his groin.

"Exactly like that," Jonathan said. "I never felt like I was an onlooker; it truly seemed as though I was making love to you."

"To me?" Michael almost squeaked his surprise.

"Well, didn't it to you? Like you were there in my arms, returning my kisses? That's what it felt like to me, every time."

"Yes," Michael admitted. "I guess I was being a little, uh..."

"Coy?"

"*Coy*? Isn't that a word to describe nervous young girls?"

Jonathan laughed out loud. "Or nervous young men, it seems."

"Well, sorry, but we've just met, and I usually don't talk about this kind of thing on a first meeting."

"But we have met before, Michael, several times." He threw Michael a wicked smile. "There isn't a part of you I don't know."

"Oh, now..." Despite himself, Michael laughed. "You go too far, sir!"

"I'm sorry, I'm taking advantage of your good nature, I think." Jonathan squeezed his hand gently. "My friends will tell you I'm a bit of a tease and far too outspoken at times. I hope I haven't embarrassed you."

"I guess I *am* a bit coy about these things," Michael said ruefully. "Brad would be kicking me under the table if we were sitting at one."

"Brad? You keep throwing all these men's names at me: Matthew, Lionel, now Brad. Makes me think I may have to fight several duels to win your favor."

"Brad is my brother. Boy, you really are a tease, aren't you? Win my favor?" Michael decided he could afford to be just a little bolder. "Haven't you already done that?"

"Aha, so you admit to making love to me in your dreams."

Michael cleared his throat noisily. "You know, this is turning out to be one darned peculiar day."

Jonathan laughed out loud again. "Coy, the lad's most definitely coy. So this Lionel bloke who left you the house, was he also a relative of yours?"

"No, I'd never heard of him before. He left me a letter saying he wanted me to try to solve the mystery of Jonathan's disappearance."

"Why you?"

"He found out Michael was my uncle."

"And that was enough to leave you his house?"

"In the letter he said he had no family to leave it to," Michael explained. "But I was as surprised as you when the solicitor called to tell me I was the sole beneficiary."

"I can imagine. So what do you do in the States?

"I'm a graphic artist."

"Now *that* sounds interesting," Jonathan declared.

While they drove through the outskirts of Cambridge, their conversation became less personal, Michael taking on the role of the tourist, insisting that Jonathan point out the various points of interest. Jonathan stole furtive glances at the attractive young American who peered out through the car window at the fine buildings they passed. Amazing, he thought, that the man he had dreamed about for so many nights should now be sitting next to him in his car. They hadn't even begun to explore the reasons and the possibilities the dreams presented, and yet he could already feel a real bond between Michael and himself. Michael had asked him why he had gone to the cemetery on this particular day, and truth to tell, he really didn't know. He only knew that this morning in the shower he'd remembered the dream he'd had the night before, and was determined to visit the cemetery he'd walked through in his dream. Something had definitely urged him to make the trip today—but what it was he had no idea.

"This is such a great-looking place," Michael said with enthusiasm, breaking into Jonathan's thoughts.

Jonathan turned and smiled. "It has its charm."

"All I ever knew about Cambridge was from a couple of movies," Michael told him. "The famous university and the boat race, of course—how did Cambridge do in the boat race this year?"

"We won, of course."

"Of course? Doesn't Oxford usually win?"

"A pox on you," Jonathan laughed. "Say that out loud in this town and you'll be thrown into the stocks and pelted with rubbish."

"Oh, so it's a serious race then?"

Jonathan groaned. "You really are a Yank, aren't you?"

"Was that an insult? Jeez, we haven't known each other an hour yet, and you're calling me names."

"No, that's just what we Brits call you Americans—Yanks. Don't know why really. Anyway, here we are." He pulled up outside a small, whitewashed house with a thatched roof.

"Looks like somebody's home," Michael remarked.

"It was originally, about two hundred years ago. Now it's *The Hand in Hand*—a pub with good grub."

"Grub?"

"Food—sausage and mash, fish and chips, yum!"

"Lead the way, Limey."

"Now that *is* an insult."

"Sorry."

CHAPTER NINE

After they'd ordered their food and Jonathan had brought two pints of ale to their table, he smiled at Michael and said softly, "Cheers, Michael. Here's to a whole year of getting to know you better."

"I'll drink to that," Michael murmured, clinking his glass against Jonathan's. He still couldn't quite believe that he was sitting in an English pub staring at the man whose face he knew so well, whose lips looked just as soft and enticing as they had in his dreams, whose eyes of the darkest blue now gazed into his, making him warm all over. Tearing his gaze away from Jonathan's, he cleared his throat and said, "This is nice," making a determined effort to study the small, richly paneled interior of the pub.

Jonathan nodded, a trace of foam lingering on his upper lip. "My favorite spot," he said. "Gets a bit rowdy on a Saturday night, but the locals are a super lot."

Michael stared at the foam, wanting to lick it off Jonathan's lip. Well, he still wasn't *that* bold yet. "Uh, you have some foam." He pointed to his own upper lip, then watched, fascinated, as Jonathan's tongue snaked across his lip, his eyes, full of mischief, locked on Michael's.

"So..." Michael had to clear his throat again before speaking. "Do you know the story of Jonathan and Michael?"

Jonathan smiled. "It's waiting to be told, isn't it?"

"Be serious."

"I was being serious, but you meant the Jonathan and Michael in our dreams. A little, and only recently. I knew from research that Michael Thornton had committed suicide after Jonathan disappeared..."

"What made you research them?"

"The dreams. I happened to mention them to a girlfriend of mine, and she said she'd read an article some time ago about two men with those same names, Second World War Veterans who'd taught at Cambridge—one disappeared, presumed murdered, and the other committed suicide. I found the article in the library and did some more research and discovered that Michael Thornton was buried in Royston. You asked me why I showed up today of all days, but I really don't know why I chose today to go down to Royston... Except, I had a dream in which I was walking through a cemetery looking for you, or rather Michael—the other Michael. I vaguely remembered there being a West in the name, so I phoned the Town Council, and they gave me the location of the cemetery. I had no classes today, and although I could've spent the time doing a bunch of useful things, I decided to visit his grave."

"Almost like you had to?"

"Yes."

"That's how I felt after I'd talked with Miss Ballard at the library. She actually knew Jonathan and Michael. She'd been great friends of theirs, even admitted to being in love with both of them."

"Sounds kinky," Jonathan said, grinning.

"Grub's up for table six!" The call from the bartender had Jonathan jumping to his feet to collect their plates of food. Michael watched him joke with the bartender and a couple of customers seated on stools. Apart from the obvious physical resemblance to the Jonathan of his dreams, the real McCoy was nothing like Michael had imagined he'd be if they'd ever met. This man was fun, not the strong silent type Michael had expected. Well, not silent anyway...

Michael had ordered the sausage and mash Jonathan recommended. It smelled delicious.

"Tuck in before you go any further," Jonathan urged. "Don't let it get cold."

Michael took a large bite of sausage and winced. "Ouch, not much chance of it getting cold. It's blistering hot!"

"Just as it should be," Jonathan mumbled, shoveling mashed potatoes into his mouth. "Mmm, good. I was starving."

Michael smiled, watching Jonathan relish his food, then said, "So anyway, she told me something that Lionel, the man who willed me his estate, left out of his letter."

"Oh, yes?"

"Henry Bryant, the man who was suspected of murdering Jonathan Harcourt, apparently was jealous of their relationship. Michael told her that Bryant had tried to put the make on him."

"That wasn't in the article either."

"No, because in those days, according to Miss Ballard, people had to keep quiet about things like that—she called it 'the love that dared not speak its name.'"

Jonathan grinned at him. "Right, and now they call it 'the love that won't shut up.'"

"Be serious."

"You're *too* serious, Michael. Look, if we're going to try to solve the mystery of what happened to Jonathan and your uncle, that's serious enough. We'll need a little levity from time to time."

"Right, but here's the thing. Last night I had another dream, only this time it was more like a nightmare." Michael gave an involuntary shudder at the memory of it. "I, or rather my uncle, was looking for Jonathan. He was in this long passageway, only it came to a dead end. I... *he...* could hear Jonathan's voice on the other side of the wall yelling out, 'Get away, Michael.' Then his voice broke off, like he'd been silenced. It went dark, and I woke up, calling his name."

"My god, I'm sorry." Jonathan took Michael's hand. "I thought my dream of the cemetery was creepy enough, but yours—that really was a nightmare."

"Yeah." Michael looked down at the hand that held his, at the long, slender fingers that felt so warm and good. "I hate dreams that make you wake up sweating." With his free hand he reached inside his shirt pocket, remembering he was carrying the photograph Lionel had left him. "This was with the letter Lionel wrote—it's a bit disconcerting."

Jonathan took the photograph and studied it silently. Then he looked at Michael, a wry smile playing on his lips. "Disconcerting? It's bloody mind boggling. There was a photo of the two men in the article I read, but it was so old and grainy, I really couldn't see the connection at that time. But this is amazing... That could be you and me in those uniforms. It's an uncanny likeness, especially of you. You're your uncle's twin!"

"I know. That's what makes it all the more bizarre. And you... you must be related to Jonathan Harcourt. The likeness is unmistakable. Do you think you might be related to him?"

Jonathan looked at the photograph again, then back at Michael. "Well, here's the thing, Michael. I'm actually a bastard."

Michael chuckled. "Well, I wouldn't go that far."

"No, I mean, I really *am* a bastard. Born out of wedlock, that kind of thing." His full lips twisted wryly. "I have adoptive parents—well, had. My father died about five years ago."

"Oh wow, I'm sorry. I lost my parents in a car accident, so I know how that feels."

"Crikey, we are a pair, aren't we?" He put a comforting hand on Michael's arm.

Michael leaned closer. "You never asked who your real parents were?"

"No." Jonathan shook his head. "My adoptive parents were so wonderful to me, I didn't for a moment think they weren't my biological parents. Then, when I was told by a well-meaning but interfering relative, I really didn't care. I don't think any other two people could have been as loving to me as they were. My Mum's still alive, of course, but she's been ill for some time now and went to live with my sister in Manchester. I visit whenever I can."

He reached for his glass of ale and took a long swallow. After he put his glass down, he looked at Michael, an expression of affection mixed with a certain shyness that made

Michael's heart turn over. "Can I say now that I am very glad I went down to Royston today? I shudder to think how long it might have taken to meet you if I hadn't had that sudden urge to visit your uncle's grave."

"I'm very glad you did," Michael murmured, meeting Jonathan's blue-eyed gaze full on. "Very glad."

"I now have another urge…" Jonathan's voice was husky with desire. "I'd like to make another part of our dreams come true. By that, I mean I want to take you in my arms, and put my lips on your very kissable mouth."

"Right here?" Michael croaked. "But…"

His protests were muffled as Jonathan pulled him into his arms and delivered a hot, hotter than hot, kiss to his lips. God, this *was* just like in his dreams—only much, much better! He wound his arms around Jonathan's neck, deepening their kiss to the point of breathlessness. Then he became suddenly aware of a wolf whistle or two and a cheer from somewhere in the bar.

Oh my God! He pulled back from Jonathan's arms, his face glowing bright red. He was scared to death to look round the room.

Jonathan took his hand and kissed it, then looked up at him, a wicked smile dancing in his dark blue eyes. "I suppose I should've told you, before I did that, that this is a gay pub."

Michael laughed softly and rested his forehead against Jonathan's. "You really are a bastard," he murmured.

§ § § §

"So, where to now?' Michael asked as Jonathan pulled away from the pub that Michael would always remember with great affection.

"Home," Jonathan replied, then added, smiling, "*My* home. It's all part of the process of getting to know you better."

Michael shifted in his seat so he could stare at Jonathan. "I'm getting nervous."

"As long as you don't get coy again."

"I think I'm past the coy stage."

Jonathan flashed him his teasing smile. "Well, you did blush rather prettily when I kissed you back there in the pub."

"I think I'm past the blushing stage too—but I am nervous."

Jonathan gave him a surprised glance. "About what?"

"About what you have in mind. About what *I* have in mind. I don't want you to be disappointed."

"There's very little chance of that," Jonathan assured him. "It's not like we haven't, you know, done it before."

"But that was in a dream—this will be reality—and sometimes reality is a bit of a letdown."

"I won't let you down."

"I wasn't talking about you." Michael sighed. "I should tell you something."

Jonathan drew in a quick breath of mock apprehension. "You're not straight, are you?"

"No..." Michael laughed. "No, it's just that I've been kind of seeing someone."

"Kind of?"

"Yeah, kind of. He blows hot and cold, and lately I'd been telling myself that it was pointless, but..."

Jonathan glanced at him again, frowning slightly. "You love him?"

"Uh..."

"You're hesitating. You wouldn't hesitate if you loved him. So, that means I'm in with a chance, right?"

"A chance?"

"Yes, a chance to take you to my bed, rip off your clothes, and kiss every inch of that delectable body I've seen so many times in my dreams!"

"Wow," Michael gasped, once again feeling that pulse in his groin. "And I thought Englishmen were supposed to be slow."

"Only when we're enjoying ourselves," Jonathan said, chuckling. "But look, if you're unsure about this, I'll understand. We can still go back to my place, and just… talk. That's also part of the *getting to know you* process."

"You mean you won't try to get into my pants?"

"Of course I'll *try*—but I'll understand if you slap my groping hand away."

Michael chuckled. "You are something else, Jonathan man-of-my-dreams."

"And here we are." Jonathan pulled into a narrow side street and parked the car outside a garage door. Michael climbed out and looked around at the row of freshly painted two-story buildings that lined one side of the street. On the other side, a grassy slope led down to some tall trees, and beyond he could see what appeared to be a collection of spires.

"That's the university," Jonathan said, putting a hand on Michael's shoulder. "There's a better view from upstairs. Come on." He unlocked the front door and ushered Michael inside. A flight of stairs led from a tiny entryway. "These are called 'mews,'" Jonathan told him as they climbed. "Old stables really, converted to flats years ago. These have just been spruced up and modernized—central heating and showers in the bathroom, thank goodness."

"How long have you lived here?"

"In Cambridge, all my life. In this place, just over a year."

Michael walked into the living room at the top of the stairs and was immediately drawn to the large window overlooking the town. "Very nice," he said, "and you were right about the view, it's fantastic."

"It's rather nice from where I'm standing too," Jonathan murmured from behind Michael. He slipped his arms around Michael's waist and pressed his lips to the nape of Michael's neck. Shivering from the touch, Michael stepped away from Jonathan's embrace.

"Well, I did say I was going to try." Jonathan's smile was a shade rueful.

Michael stared at the handsome Englishman, the embodiment of the man he'd seen in his dreams for so many nights. "I'd be insulted if you hadn't," he said quietly. "But this is so sudden, don't you think?"

Jonathan reached out to stroke Michael's face gently with his fingertips. "I mentioned earlier there wasn't a part of you I didn't already know." He smiled softly. "I was teasing then, but I'm not being flippant now. Surely you must feel the same, Michael? It can't have been some sort of coincidence that we met today. All of this must appear slightly unreal to you—it does to me too, but being here with you now feels *right*. The kiss we shared back in the pub wasn't just a flirtatious move on my part; it was wonderful, heartfelt…"

Immensely touched by Jonathan's sentiment, Michael stepped forward and wrapped his arms around the slightly taller man's neck. For a long moment his green eyes were captured by Jonathan's dark blue gaze, and then, with soft sighs of longing, they kissed. Jonathan's lips on his made Michael's senses reel. Yes, this was sudden—or was it? Whatever it was, it felt wonderful, like nothing he had ever experienced before. He shivered again, this time with desire.

Jonathan's hands slipped inside the waistband of Michael's khakis, then under his briefs to caress the warm, round swell of his butt.

"Mmm…" Jonathan moaned his appreciation into Michael's mouth and pulled him in closer, grinding their crotches together, exulting in the sensation of Michael's rock-hard erection pushing against his own. Their kiss deepened, shirts were torn open and discarded, belt buckles were snapped open, zippers tugged at, and pants thrown to one side. When they were completely naked, Jonathan stepped back just a little and smiled.

"You are so beautiful, Michael Ballantyne," he murmured, admiring the slim, hard body in front of him. "But then, I always knew that."

His hand reached out to caress Michael's face, to slowly trail a line from his jaw down his throat to his chest, to gently tease both Michael's nipples and cause a shuddering breath to escape from Michael's parted lips. Jonathan leaned in and took those lips with his own, his tongue sweeping into Michael's mouth, caressing every part of his moist warmth. The men clung to one another, muscles straining in an effort to bond and mesh their bodies together. For them there was no closeness close enough. Jonathan's lips moved to Michael's neck, tracing a heated path across his shoulders, then down the centre of his torso. He knelt, nuzzling the head of Michael's erect cock with his lips, dipping the tip of his tongue into the slit to savor the salty sweetness of his precum.

Michael's fingers tangled in Jonathan's thick, curly hair. His head fell back as he gave in to the thrill of Jonathan's touch. He groaned, his eyes fluttered opened, and then he pulled back from Jonathan's embrace.

"Oh my God," he yelped.

"What's wrong?' Jonathan stared up at him, concern crinkling his forehead.

"I'm butt naked in front of this window," Michael gasped. "All of Cambridge can see my ass!"

Jonathan laughed and stood up. "Lucky Cambridge," he said, grabbing that part of Michael's anatomy with both hands and steering him away from the window. "Come with me to my boudoir, young man, and let me take care of that pretty arse of yours."

"You know just how to tempt a guy," Michael chuckled, letting himself be pushed through the bedroom door.

"Now, where were we?" Jonathan murmured, sliding his hands up the sides of Michael's torso, his thumbs circling Michael's nipples, bringing them once more to tiny, hard nubs. He bent to lick them. "Ah, yes, now I remember." Again he knelt in front of Michael, grasping the hard flesh that jutted from Michael's crotch, stroking its silky length before taking it into his mouth, all the way to the root. He buried his nose in the dark brown hair that curled around the base, inhaling Michael's musky scent. Cupping Michael's bottom with his big hands, he parted the cheeks, allowing his fingers to slip into the cleft and probe gently at his opening. Michael shuddered, pushing his pelvis forward, driving his cock into the hot depths of Jonathan's throat. Jonathan gulped at the salty nectar that leaked from Michael's cock, then pulled back slightly, his tongue swirling over the engorged head, laving the underside, then swallowing the hard shaft again. Michael's soft moans increased in volume, his fingers tangled once more in Jonathan's hair, his hips bucked as his orgasm coiled inside him.

"Uh… Jonathan… oh, God…"

Jonathan slipped his middle finger past Michael's resistance. It glided over Michael's prostate, sending his body into a paroxysm of ecstasy. He cried out as he climaxed, filling Jonathan's mouth with his hot, creamy semen. Jonathan held him in his mouth, sucking, milking him until every drop was wrung from him, then with a final lick and kiss, he stood and took a trembling Michael into his arms. For a long moment neither man could speak, but simply held one another in a tight embrace, their hands gently caressing and stroking each other's body.

Michael wound his fingers in Jonathan's hair. His lips moved over the smooth, warm skin of Jonathan's neck, across the faintly bristled jaw to his lips, claiming them with a kiss that was both sweet yet hungry. His hand slid to where Jonathan's cock, hard and erect, was pressing against his belly. He rubbed his thumb over the head, smearing it with the copious precum leaking from the slit. He slipped out of Jonathan's embrace and, still holding his lover's impressive erection, backed up to the edge of the bed where he sat and leaned forward to kiss the throbbing shaft. He paused for a moment, staring at the heated flesh he held in his hand. His entire life he'd only seen one or two uncut cocks, apart from those in porn photos, and he'd certainly never had one in his grasp.

"Has it passed your inspection?"

Michael looked up at Jonathan's amused smile. "It… it's beautiful," he said huskily. He eased back the foreskin and licked at the glistening head, the musky scent of male arousal intoxicating him. Hungrily he sucked the rock-hard cock into his mouth, his tongue moving with long, sure strokes over the pulsing flesh. Jonathan groaned out loud, and Michael, gripping his narrow hips, pulled him in deeper, his mouth taking all of Jonathan to the root.

"Oh… Michael… want to fuck you…" The words, wrung from Jonathan's lips and spoken on a long breathy sigh, caused Michael to look up at Jonathan, to see his face caught in an expression of pure pleasure. He released Jonathan's cock and scooted back on the bed. Jonathan covered Michael's body with his own.

"Now I can do what I promised earlier," he whispered. "Kiss every part of your delectable body…"

His lips traced a searing path over Michael's skin, lingering over each nipple, licking and teasing them into hard points. He knelt between Michael's thighs, kissed his softened cock, felt it stir beneath his lips. He inhaled the dizzying scent of spent semen and nuzzled Michael's balls, taking each one into his mouth, holding it gently, his tongue swirling around the soft, velvety skin. Michael writhed under him, shuddering with pleasure as Jonathan dragged his tongue along the sensitive path that led to Michael's opening. He bathed the puckered hole with his saliva, soaking it thoroughly before inserting his tongue, pushing the tip beyond the ring of muscle, causing whimpers of delight to escape Michael's lips. Jonathan, his erection now so hard it ached for release, raised his head, trailing his tongue back up over Michael's balls to his once-again rigid cock, where he paused to lick at the pearl-like drop of precum oozing from the slit. He leaned across Michael and grabbed a condom and lube from his nightstand drawer.

He smiled and dropped a kiss on Michael's lips as he pulled the condom on, smearing it with a generous amount of lube. Michael wound his legs round Jonathan's waist, giving him greater access, all the while gazing up at his lover through hooded eyes filled with an almost wanton longing. Jonathan coated his fingers with the lube, pushing one, then two, inside Michael's tight opening and gently easing out and replacing them with the swollen head of his cock. He pushed in slowly, and Michael grasped him by the shoulders, easing himself down, drawing Jonathan's thickness deep inside himself.

Jonathan began to pump rhythmically in and out of Michael's hot core with long, measured strokes, supporting himself with one hand while the other grasped Michael's erection, matching the rhythm he'd created.

Michael shuddered, waves of ecstasy flowing over and through him. He wrapped his arms around Jonathan's neck and brought him down for a long, loaded kiss. Their tongues intertwined, tussling inside each other's mouths, bringing Michael an erotic heat that set his blood on fire and his heart pounding so loudly inside his chest, he was sure Jonathan could hear it too. His hips moved in unison with Jonathan's rhythm. Gone was the initial pain of being impaled on Jonathan's hard-as-steel cock; now what he felt was a sensation of fulfillment he'd never known before. He gazed up into Jonathan's dark eyes, still finding it hard to believe that this man, the one he'd dreamed about for so many nights, was actually here, holding him, fucking him—and this he knew without a doubt, the fantasy had been eclipsed by the reality.

"Jonathan…" He ran his hands over Jonathan's back, loving the feel of the tightly bunched muscles under the smooth skin. Their bodies, now slick with sweat, were in perfect motion with one another. With each thrust Michael felt Jonathan go even deeper. He tightened his legs and arms around Jonathan's torso, clinging to the hard, muscular body as they rocked together. Jonathan quickened his rhythm; his breathing became deep and harsh, signaling his imminent climax. Michael bucked his hips upward, matching Jonathan's strokes, forcing his cock through Jonathan's fist, increasing the friction, determined that they would come together. He felt his orgasm build inside his balls, intense heat suffused his body, and he cried out as he came, unleashing a torrent of semen between their tightly pressed bodies.

Jonathan's body shuddered over Michael's. His lips took Michael's in a kiss that was hard and hungry, and Michael responded in kind, gasping with rapture as he felt Jonathan's pulsing cock fill the condom buried deep inside him.

They lay, arms and legs entwined, still and silent for a long time, no movement save for the occasional kiss or caress.

Michael found he couldn't speak, for what words could adequately describe his emotions at that moment? He couldn't remember ever feeling so good after sex, nor could he remember feeling so wanted, so cared for. Steve would pull out and roll off the bed to go wash himself immediately after he came, and never, not once had he allowed Michael to come in his mouth.

This man, this incredible Jonathan, the man who had filled his dreams night after night, now held him, stayed joined to him, making him feel complete. He smiled as Jonathan's forefinger traced the outline of his lips.

"Did I tell you that you have a very kissable mouth?"

Michael chuckled. "I believe you mentioned it in the pub, just before you embarrassed the hell out of me."

"And just look where it's got you."

"There's nowhere else I'd rather be. Even though I still can hardly believe this has really happened." Michael placed a gentle kiss on Jonathan's lips. "Mmm, did I feel something move inside me?"

"Just that smile of yours keeps me hard."

"The man's a marvel," Michael said with a happy sigh.

CHAPTER TEN

On the way back to Bedford Park, Michael sat as close to Jonathan as the handbrake between the seats would allow. His head rested on Jonathan's shoulder, while Jonathan's free hand was wedged firmly between Michael's thighs.

"This has been a most peculiar day," Michael murmured.

Jonathan squeezed Michael's thigh. "You said that before we made love. I was hoping you'd now think of a more flattering way to describe our time together. You know, like fabulous, fantastic, brilliant, mind-blowing…"

Michael chuckled and reached up to kiss Jonathan's neck. "It was all of those things too, and more. But you have to admit it was also peculiar. I mean, did you have any inkling that when you left home today, you'd meet a complete stranger in a graveyard, then take him home and have your way with him—three times?"

Jonathan laughed his robust laugh. "Only twice—you had your way with me the second time, remember?"

"How could I forget?"

"And it's not like we were complete strangers, Michael. What about all those times we made love in our mutual dreams?" He squeezed Michael's thigh again. "But I have to admit that although those dreams really got me going, the reality was a hundred times better."

"Only a hundred?" Michael quipped, slipping his hand inside Jonathan's shirt and teasing a nipple.

Jonathan groaned. "A million then. Careful or I'll have to pull over into those woods and have my way with you again."

"Sounds like a plan."

"It does, but at the risk of sounding sensible, it's late, and I do have classes tomorrow."

"Party-pooper," Michael muttered. "Does that mean you won't be spending the night with me?"

"'Fraid so."

"Tired of me already," Michael sighed dejectedly.

"Silly boy." Jonathan pulled his hand free from between Michael's thighs and put his arm around his shoulders, pulling him closer.

"I'll see you tomorrow, then?" Michael asked.

"Try and keep me away—oh, it's left at the junction, right?"

"Yeah... it's sign-posted with a funny name." Michael sat up straight, looking ahead at the darkened road. "There it is. Great and Little something..."

"Got it," Jonathan muttered.

"And left at the sign that says Bedford Park."

"Impressive," Jonathan said as he swung through the gates and stared at the big house ahead.

"Won't you come in for a few minutes at least?"

"Better not." He sat back in his seat and gazed at the front of the house, a strange, almost wistful expression on his handsome face.

"What's wrong?" Michael asked, taking his hand.

"Nothing, except that—this is going to sound corny, and I don't want it to—but, I seem to recognize this place."

"That's good, though, isn't it?" Michael squeezed Jonathan's hand. "The dreams I've had are more or less centered round the house and grounds. Aren't yours?"

Jonathan nodded slowly. "I hadn't really thought about where we were." He turned and gave Michael a sweet smile. "We were always sort of busy, you know."

Michael leaned in to kiss his lips. "I know. Why don't you come in?"

"Not tonight, but now that I know where you are, why don't I come a-calling tomorrow, after school, say around five? You can give me the grand tour." He leered at Michael. "And of the estate, too."

"Maybe the estate first," Michael chuckled as they pulled up in front of the house. "We might not have the strength after…"

Jonathan pulled him into his arms and kissed him with a fervency that took Michael's breath away. His tongue stroked and caressed Michael's, inflaming his senses once again with the desire to take the man and mark him as his own. Despite all the silly banter he'd engaged Michael in, Jonathan knew where his heart lay—securely in the hands of the man he'd known for less than a day, the man he now wished to never let out of his sight, not even for a moment, never mind until five tomorrow.

Michael moaned into Jonathan's mouth. He tried to climb over the handbrake and the gearshift in order to straddle Jonathan's lap. Instead, his knee came into hard contact with Jonathan's crotch, causing Jonathan to yelp out loud, and Michael to bang his head on the car roof.

"God, sorry." Michael fell back into his seat, rubbing his head and staring in horror at Jonathan's pained expression.

"It's all right," Jonathan croaked, holding his balls and trying to laugh through the pain. "Your eagerness is very flattering."

"I could kiss it better," Michael suggested.

"Let's wait until tomorrow, shall we?" Jonathan leaned over and kissed Michael's lips.

"I guess." Michael stroked Jonathan's cheek. "Sorry, again."

"I'll live. Goodnight, my sweet Michael."

Reluctantly, Michael got out of the car and watched as it pulled away from the house. He grinned as Jonathan's hand appeared from the side window, waving goodbye. Then he turned and walked up the steps to the massive front door, which swung open at his approach.

"Good evening, Mr. Michael." Matthew smiled as he opened the door.

"Hey, Matthew, were you watching for me?"

"It's a part of my job. Did you have a pleasant day?"

"Very…"

"You had two phone calls while you were out."

"Yeah, I forgot to take my cell with me."

"Your brother, Mr. Bradford Ballantyne, and a Mr. Steven Delaney."

"Steve?" Michael felt a twinge of guilt attack his stomach. "Did he leave a message?"

"They both left messages, Mr. Michael. I put them on the desk in the study."

"Thanks, Matthew."

Jack Trenton, watching from his window, narrowed his eyes as the blue car exited the grounds. He had been there when it had entered, and he knew who was driving. The voice that lived in his mind had told him that the *other one* would arrive soon. First, the one who knew too much would come, followed by the other. It was as the voice had said. He needed the two of them together—had to have them both side by side before he could move against them. The voice had been most explicit about that.

Trenton took a long swig from the rum bottle he'd been twisting in his hand all the while he'd waited for the car to leave. No doubt the new 'master' of the house was going to seek him out any day now, ask a lot of questions, and probably try to give him the sack. Well, he wasn't going anywhere, not until he'd done what he came here to do, not until he'd done what his father demanded he do. Not until then.

§ § § §

Michael found the messages on the study desk, and after he'd said goodnight to Matthew took them up to his room. He'd better call Brad first, he thought, looking at the message as he climbed the stairs. Matthew had marked it important. As he flipped on the light, he noticed that the room had been tidied, everything he'd left lying around had been put away, and the bed had been turned down.

"I could get used to this," he muttered, glancing about for his cell phone. "Ah, there it is." Before he punched in Brad's number, he noticed he'd had several messages. His brother picked up almost immediately.

"Hey, Michael, how's it goin'?"

"Great, really great," Michael told him. "I met the man of my dreams today."

"Already? Wow, I'm impressed. You work fast."

Michael chuckled. "I mean the guy I told you I was dreaming about."

"You *met* him? How the hell could you do that?"

"It's a long story, so I'll give you the *Readers Digest* version..." He went on to tell Brad about his meeting with Miss Ballard in the library, his visit to their uncle's grave, and how he'd met Jonathan there. "I couldn't believe it, Brad. I mean, what were the chances that he and I would be there at exactly the same time?"

"Remote, I'd say. So, what's he like?"

"Really nice, Brad. You'll like him. We got along so great."

"*How* great?"

"Brad, why do you ask me these things? You know it embarrasses me."

"That's why I ask, baby brother. Okay, I get the picture. Man, you *do* work fast. So I guess you don't care that Steve called me, looking for you?"

"He did?"

"Yeah, said he'd tried your cell a dozen times, then called me thinking maybe you were sick or something. I said, 'Oh no, not sick, he just flew to England.' You could've heard a pin drop, he went so quiet."

"Did he ask why?"

"Yeah, but I didn't tell him everything. I just told him it was a business trip, and you'd be back in a year's time."

"Brad!"

"Just kidding. I gave him your new house number, including that long, long code. He did seem a tad put out though, like he was looking to get some nookie, and you'd flown the coop."

Michael ground his teeth as he heard Brad trying to hold back his laughter. "You are really too much sometimes, Brad. I'm glad my sex life gives you so many laughs."

"Oh come on, bro, lighten up. You are far too serious for one so young and gay."

Despite himself, Michael chuckled. "I guess I can be too serious at times. Even Jonathan told me that today."

"So, what's his connection?" Brad asked. "Was he having dreams too? Was the missing Jonathan his uncle?"

"Yes, he was having the same kind of dreams as me, but no, we don't know his relation to Jonathan Harcourt yet. Jonathan *Robertson* was adopted. He doesn't know who his biological parents were, or are."

"Hmm, that complicates things a bit. But he must be related somehow to the dead Jonathan, otherwise why would he be having similar dreams to yours?"

"Right…" Michael paused, reflecting on what his brother had just said. "Brad, did you ever think that you and I would talk so easily about stuff like this? I mean, dreams and past lives and the like?"

His brother chuckled. "It does seem a bit far out, bro. But let's face it, none of what's happened to you in the last few days could be called, well, ordinary."

"True, and Jonathan and I hope it's a mystery we'll eventually solve. If we don't before you and Miranda come over, you can help out."

"Oh, Miranda would love that. She reads all those lady detective novels."

Michael yawned suddenly. "Wow, gotta get some shuteye, Brad. It's pretty late here, and I'm still a bit jet-lagged."

"And never mind what you got up to today," Brad teased. "You never told me how it was—was it *dreamy*?"

"There you go again, and I'm not telling you anymore than this—it was a whole lot better than the dreams."

"Oh, boy."

"Bye, Brad. Tell Miranda I said 'hi.'"

Michael smiled as he clicked off his cell and lay back on the bed. *I'll call Steve tomorrow morning,* he thought, ready to start remembering the fantastic time he'd spent with Jonathan. He jumped at the sound of his cell ringing. *Steve.* Once his name on the caller ID screen would have sent chills of anticipation racing through Michael's blood, not the sickening flip-flop he now felt in his stomach.

"Hi, Steve."

"Jeez, *finally*! I've been calling and calling since I got back; then Brad tells me you're in England. Why didn't you let me know?"

"Well, it all happened so fast. I meant to call you, but it's been kinda hectic here."

"So hectic you couldn't find five minutes to call me?"

Oh, oh, he sounds really mad.

"Well… uh, I'm really sorry, Steve…"

"So am I. The last time we talked, I told you I would be in LA and would call you so we could see each other. I thought that's what you wanted. You were always so whiny and needy when I couldn't come over, now, when I go out of my way to call and arrange a date, you're not there and don't even bother to call. Well, maybe we should call it a day."

Whiny and needy? Yeah, Steve, maybe we should.

"What was so all-fire important that you had to go flying off to freakin' England anyway?"

"Uh, well, I was left a country estate and five million pounds."

For a few moments the silence on the other end deafening. Then Michael heard an incredulous, "*What* did you say?"

"I said, I was left a country home, a really nice, big country home, Steve, and five million pounds in the bank. I think that translates to about eight million dollars in the bank, all taxes paid."

"But, but… *Mikey*, that's incredible." Steve didn't sound quite as mad any more. "I mean, you must be so… so…"

"Rich?" Michael suggested helpfully.

"Yes, no… I meant, so *happy* about this, Mikey. I mean, it's so great. So when are you coming back, or could I come see you, maybe?"

Man, could he be any more transparent?

"I thought you wanted to call it a day."

"No, no… that was before… I mean, I was a little pissed, but I understand, totally, that you'd be preoccupied with all that's been happening."

You don't know the half of it, Steve-o.

"Hey, Steve…" Michael yawned loudly into the mouthpiece. "I'm really bushed, y'know? Let me call you later, sometime."

"What? Wait, *Mikey*…"

But Michael closed his cell and lay back on the pillow, exhaling a long sigh of disappointment mixed with not just a little relief. So Brad had been right about Steve after all, and the obvious change in Steve's belligerent attitude when Michael had told him about the inheritance just about said it all. *Damn*… he wouldn't have guessed Steve would be the gold-digger kind, but then just how well did he know the man? Brad had been able to point out one or two of Steve's less than stellar attributes after only one dinner date. Michael sighed. When would he ever stop being so trusting and naïve?

CHAPTER ELEVEN

For a variety of reasons, Jonathan had trouble sleeping that night. The memory of what had passed between Michael and him earlier was the pleasant part, but he was vaguely uneasy about what he'd experienced when he'd driven into the estate at Bedford Park. There was some form of latent memory there, something he couldn't quite bring into focus. He didn't want to call it *déjà vu,* because to him that meant he'd been to the house before, and he knew he had not. Not in this life anyway.

Okay, stop that…

But then there was that photograph, that amazing photograph.

There had to be a rational explanation for all of this, although he was quick to admit that meeting Michael in the cemetery had been an extraordinary experience—but surely just a coincidence, nothing more.

But the photograph…

And Michael… Even now, several hours after they'd made love, he could still taste the sweetness of Michael's lips, feel the smooth firm muscle under his hands, hear the soft moans of ecstasy escape Michael's lips when he had brought him to climax. There was no doubt in his mind that Michael in the flesh definitely had a vast edge over the dream Michael—which led him to think about his own place in all of this.

Michael had asked him if he was related to the dead Jonathan, and he wondered if his mother—his adoptive mother—had some knowledge of it. But she was ill, and he really didn't want to bother her with this. There was always the Registrar's office, but now, when he thought about it, he wasn't even sure *where* he'd been born. He'd always presumed it had been in Cambridge; after all, that's what his birth certificate said, but what if that had been altered at the time of his adoption? What if there had been no original birth certificate?

Hmm… there were certainly questions now that he'd never thought to ask previously. *That's what happens when you're too complacent*, he thought, sitting up in bed and turning on the bedside lamp. He suspected that if his home life had been miserable, he'd have been much more interested in his biological parents' whereabouts, but there had never been an instant when he'd wished for another family. Now, of course, it had a certain fascination. What if he *was* related to Jonathan Harcourt? What would that actually mean now that he and Michael were going to try to solve the mystery of Jonathan Harcourt's disappearance? Would he feel more determined to find out what had happened if he discovered that Jonathan Harcourt was an uncle he'd never heard of?

Perhaps, but the reason he'd said he would help Michael was simply because he wanted to stay close to him. Michael had made a big impression on him, even though Jonathan wasn't usually very easily impressed. Michael was attractive, without a doubt, but it was more than that. Michael had touched him in more ways than just the physical appeal; he had made him feel good about himself again. After that disastrous affair with David, his self-esteem had taken a severe blow—but that was two years ago, and he'd festered for far too long. Now he found himself longing for the moment when he would see Michael again.

Perhaps, he thought ruefully, *I shouldn't have been in such a bloody rush to get home!* He reached across to switch off the light. Tomorrow, he'd try to solve at least parts of the mystery.

Just who were my parents, and what was Jonathan Harcourt to me?

§ § § §

"I think I need my own car," Michael said as Matthew drove him out through the gates the following day.

Matthew nodded. "I should think you would. The Rolls is your car, of course, and it's a beauty, but it's murder on the petrol. Mr. Burroughs thought it was prestigious."

"Well, it is, of course, and we'll keep it for his sake, but I'd like something sportier—a Jag maybe."

Matthew grinned. "They're not much better on the petrol, but more fitting for a young chap like yourself. There's a very good dealer up Cambridge way."

"Oh, yeah? Maybe I'll ask Jonathan to go with me this weekend. I hope Mrs. MacDonald didn't mind me inviting him for dinner tonight."

"Mr. Michael…" Matthew said with a sigh while slowing at the crossroads. "We are your staff. What you want is what we do."

"Uh, well, I'm just not used to that yet, I guess."

"Well, she didn't mind one bit. I think she misses the grand dinner parties Mr. Burroughs used to give—ten, twelve, fifteen people sometimes."

"She cooked for all of those people?"

"He employed caterers, but she liked to supervise, of course."

"My brother and his wife will be visiting soon," Michael said, looking out the car window at the houses and shops they were passing. "So, she'll have some more to look after. Oh, look…" He pointed at a men's clothing store. "Can we stop there, Matthew?"

"Of course." Matthew pulled over and stepped nimbly from the car, hurrying to the other side to open the passenger door.

"You don't have to do that, Matthew," Michael protested.

"It's my job. Are you trying to make me redundant before my time?"

Michael chuckled. "No, but you opening doors for me makes me feel guilty."

"No need, Mr. Michael. I'll wait in the car while you shop, make sure we don't get a parking ticket."

"Isn't there a lot somewhere around?"

"A lot of what, Mr. Michael?"

"A parking lot… for the car."

"Oh, a *car park*. No, we're a bit short of those in the center of town, I'm afraid."

"Right." Michael made a mental note. Car park, not parking lot; petrol, not gas; and what was it he'd said the other day that had made Matthew chuckle? Oh yeah— the trunk of the car, they call it the 'boot' over here... and the hood's the bonnet. A boot and a bonnet on a car—only in England!

He spent a pleasant hour in the store, buying underwear, shirts, jeans, and a couple of sweaters. He looked around for something to get for Jonathan. Could he use a new robe? Maybe if he could persuade him to stay over he'd need one in the morning. Michael smiled at the thought of waking up in Jonathan's arms, the two of them naked and ready for some lovin'... Oops, he was hard.

Man, just the thought of Jonathan's perfect, naked body has me going.

Holding the clothes he'd chosen in front of him to hide his obvious erection, he made his way over to where several robes hung on a rack, finally settling for one in terrycloth for himself and a silk one in rich burgundy for Jonathan. He asked that the silk one be gift-wrapped.

Matthew was snoozing in the front seat when he opened the car door and threw his shopping bags onto the back seat.

"Sorry, did I wake you?" he teased.

"Not at all, I was meditating."

"Ah, good for the soul, I hear."

"Extremely..."

As they approached the end of the street, Michael noticed a directional sign that read, *To the Cave.*

"There're caves near here, Matthew?"

"That's what they call it. Bit peculiar if you ask me, manmade and right under the centre of town. Somebody dug into the chalk hundreds of years ago and made what they think is some kind of temple."

"Really? You mean people worshipped there?"

"Well, a rum kind of worship it would have been. Rumor has it the Knights Templar met there."

"Knights Templar—the guys in the Crusades?"

"Correct. After the Crusades one of the Popes gave them a bad time, had them arrested, and confiscated their wealth. It's said they used the cave as a hideout during that time."

"Wow, I'm impressed, Matthew. You've done some research."

"Not really." Matthew laughed lightly. "It's open to tourists. Annie and I went there one afternoon, and I read the brochure. 'Course, it's all conjecture. Some say it might have been a prison, or somewhere for the monks to have a bit of a leg over."

"All right, you got me. What's a leg over?"

"Oh, you know, slap and tickle, a bit of the other—*sex*."

Michael roared with laughter. "God, you Brits! I'll have to get a translation book, Brit to American. Anyway, you have me suitably interested. Let's take a look at the caves, then I'll buy you lunch."

"Can't today, I'm afraid. They're only open Saturday and Sunday."

"Oh." Michael voiced his disappointment.

"So, it's lunch then?"

"I guess; your pick, Matthew."

"I know just the place."

§ § § §

The crowd that filled *The Dogcatcher's Arms* was big, loud, and friendly. Michael knew he'd never remember the names of all the people Matthew introduced him to on their way over to the bar.

"Is it always like this?" he asked, watching the bartender pull their pints of beer.

Matthew nodded. "Most days at lunchtime, when everyone comes in for a quick one before they go back to work."

"Wow…" Michael marveled at a custom he didn't think would sit too well with American employers—a liquid lunch, then back to work. "So what's good here?"

"Just about everything. I'm having the *Dogcatcher's Special.*"

"Which is?"

"Egg and bacon sandwich with chips."

"I see…" Michael stared at the menu on the wall behind the bar, looking for something light. He figured that if he kept eating this English fare he'd be a porker in no time. "Is there a gym in Royston?"

Matthew chuckled and patted Michael's shoulder. "Several, I think, not that I'd be interested. But you youngsters like to keep trim, I know."

"Well, in that case, I'll have the fish and chips."

Matthew placed their order, then raised his pint glass. "Cheers, Mr. Michael."

"Cheers. I wish you'd drop that Mister bit. Just Michael would be fine."

"Wouldn't feel right to me…" Matthew broke off, and his face darkened suddenly. "Look what the devil just dragged in."

Michael turned to look behind him. A tall, burly man with a ruddy complexion was striding through the bar towards them, his eyes fixed on Michael. For a moment, Michael thought the man's aggressive stare meant he wanted some kind of confrontation, but at the last second he veered away, a smirk etched on his face.

"Jack Trenton," Matthew muttered, his voice colored by his dislike for the man. "That's the bloke who's taken up residence in the lodge. You need to sort him out, Mr. Michael. He's not showing you any respect whatsoever. He should've stopped and introduced himself."

"I'm glad he didn't," Michael said dryly. "He'd have put me off my lunch. But you're right, Matthew. I'm going to have to have a talk with Mr. Trenton, sooner rather than later—and whether I like it or not." He took a long look at Trenton, who was busy talking with another man at the bar. Trenton looked to be in his mid-fifties, but tall and in good shape. Michael looked away quickly as Trenton's gaze met his. He glanced around the bar as he took a sip of his beer.

"That guy looks familiar," he said to Matthew. "Over there, in that group by the door."

"Abingdon police inspector," Matthew said. "Handley, I think his name is."

"Oh, right. I met him in the library the other day." He raised his hand in greeting as the man met his eyes across the bar. Handley smiled and walked over to where Michael and Matthew stood.

"I say, small world, isn't it? Twice in as many days." Handley shook Michael's hand and then Matthew's as he was introduced. "The butler at Bedford park, eh? Nice to have a new boss, is it?"

"Very nice," Matthew replied. "Mr. Michael makes a very fine lord of the manor."

"*Matthew*," Michael laughed. "Lord of the manor I am not!"

Handley chuckled. "Well, it's good to see you've settled in nicely."

"Oh, by the way…" Michael lowered his voice slightly. "What do you recommend I do about someone who's living on my property without my permission?"

Handley registered surprise. "Who might that be?"

"Guy standing at the end of the bar. Jack Trenton's his name, and he says he has a letter from Mr. Burroughs, the previous owner, giving him employment—but no one, not even the solicitor, knows anything about it."

Handley frowned. "Hmm, bit rum that is, without a doubt. Of course you can demand to see the letter he says he has, or simply tell him his employment is at an end. It's up to you, actually."

"And if he won't leave?"

"Then give me call, and I'll come talk to him."

"Why not talk to him now?" Matthew asked. "Sooner the better, I say."

"Not in a crowded pub," Handley said firmly "Phone me if you have any trouble, Mr. Ballantyne." He shook Michael's hand and abruptly went back to his friends on the other side of the bar.

"Fat lot of good he is," Matthew grumbled.

"Well, it could have become awkward, I suppose." Matthew cast a furtive glance over at Trenton, who looked as if he had been taking a keen interest in Inspector Handley's conversation with Michael. Nevertheless he couldn't help but think it would have been good if Handley had dealt with Trenton right then and there.

CHAPTER TWELVE

Later, getting himself ready for Jonathan's visit, Michael couldn't quite get the image of Jack Trenton out of his mind.

That's one angry dude, with a lot on his mind, and from the look he threw at me, none of it very pleasant.

After he'd showered, he pulled on the new pair of jeans and light crewneck sweater he'd bought earlier in the day. He wondered if he should mention Trenton to Jonathan, see what he thought the best course of action should be in dealing with him. But he wouldn't mention it tonight—tonight he wanted to be wonderful, a continuation of the time they'd spent together at Jonathan's house, kissing, caressing, and... Just the memory of Jonathan's soft lips on his was enough to... Ow, he was getting hard, and the jeans were just a shade tight around the crotch. Better cool the carnal thoughts for now. When Jonathan and he got going, the jeans would be history anyway.

The toot of a car horn had him rushing to the window, excitement surging in his blood as he saw Jonathan's blue car pulling up outside. He flew out of the bedroom, taking the stairs two and three at a time, then came to a screeching halt as he saw Matthew walk briskly to the front door.

Whoa, take it easy, he told himself. *Giving Jonathan a big sloppy kiss in front of Matthew is probably not the best of ideas!*

Matthew and his wife might seem quite liberal, but perhaps he'd better cool it 'til he and Jonathan were alone. He heard the murmur of voices, Jonathan's pleasant laugh, and then there he was, smiling up at him from the hallway and looking as gorgeous as Michael remembered.

"Hey..." Michael returned the smile as he descended the last few steps.

Jonathan winked at him. "Nice place you have here."

Michael chuckled. "It's not much, but I call it home."

"May I take your coat, sir?" Matthew, efficient as always, smiled benignly at the two men.

Jonathan slipped it off and handed it over. "Thanks, Matthew."

"Mrs. MacDonald has prepared some *hors d'ouvres*, and I've set them on the bar in the lounge."

"Great." Michael put his hand on Jonathan's shoulder and steered him across the hall. "I'll give you the Cook's tour, and you have to meet Mrs. MacDonald, Matthew's wife. The two of them look after me like I'm royalty."

"Which, of course, you are," Jonathan said, gently pinching Michael's arm. They laughed quietly together, and Michael pushed open the kitchen door.

"Mrs. MacDonald, I'd like you to meet my friend Jonathan Robertson."

She turned and beamed at them. "Robertson, is it? A good Scots name." She wiped her hands on her apron and took Jonathan's in a warm welcome.

"A pleasure," he murmured. "I think my grandfather hailed from over the border."

His adoptive grandfather, Michael thought. *I wonder what his real name is.*

"Dinner will be ready in an hour," Mrs. MacDonald told them, shooing them from her domain. "In the *dining room*," she added for Michael's benefit.

"Come on, let's have a drink, then I'll show you around." Michael grabbed Jonathan's arm, hustling him into the lounge. "What would you like?"

"You, on toast." Jonathan closed the door behind them and pulled Michael into his arms. "I've been waiting all day for this," he said, before taking Michael's lips in a hot kiss.

"Mmm..." Michael voiced his muffled approval as he melted into Jonathan's arms. He tilted his head back slightly. "I don't think there's been a moment in the day when I haven't thought of you."

"Ditto." Jonathan kissed him again. "But I did discover something you might find interesting." Their arms around each other's waists, they walked over to the bar.

"I'll pour you something while you tell me."

"Just some white wine."

"Coming up... Help yourself to some of those goodies Mrs. MacDonald made for us."

"I went to the Registrar's office this afternoon before I came down here." Jonathan picked up a small pastry and took a bite. "Gave them my name and driver's license, and they plunked it all into their computer and came up with some interesting stuff. Thanks." He took the glass of wine Michael handed him. "Bottoms up..."

Michael giggled as they clinked glasses. "Bottoms up? Isn't that for later?"

"You have a one-track mind, Michael my boy," Jonathan teased him. "I was referring to the bottom of the glass."

"Oh... Anyway, you were saying?"

"Apparently there are no records of me before my adoption. No mention at all of who my biological parents might be."

"Damn," Michael muttered, looking downcast.

"I know, you were hoping I'd be Mr. Harcourt's long lost nephew or second cousin or something."

"But there has to be a connection somewhere," Michael exclaimed. "Otherwise, why would you have been dreaming about me, or rather my uncle, and why did we know one another instantly? It doesn't make any sense."

"Well, my only other option is to ask my mother. I hadn't really wanted to do that because she hasn't been too well recently. But I know if I ask, she'll tell me."

"What about your sister; would she know?"

"She might." Jonathan considered that for a moment. "I'll phone her in the morning."

"Um…" Michael gave Jonathan a shy look. "I was wondering if you'd like to stay the night, spend the day with me tomorrow."

Jonathan leered at him. "What about the day after?"

"That too." Michael smiled happily.

"Well, at the risk of sounding presumptuous, and in the hope that you just might ask me to stay, I packed an overnight bag. It's in the car."

"Fantastic." Michael beamed at him. "I'm glad you can read my mind. Actually, I was hoping we could visit the Caves tomorrow at some point."

"Whatever for?"

"They sound interesting."

"It… there's only one cave, quite small really. Dug out of the chalk."

"Yes, that's what interests me, the chalk. The dream I told you about, or the nightmare, rather. I can't seem to forget the feel of the walls under my fingers—soft, porous, like chalk."

"Hmm…" Jonathan took a long sip of wine. "There's a lot of chalky soil around here. But you said you were in a passageway, not a cave."

"Right, but what if the passage was leading to a cave?"

"Michael, that was a dream."

"I know, but look what the other dreams have brought us. You and me, two total strangers until yesterday, and now we've met under really extraordinary circumstances. Why couldn't the nightmare have some relevance also?"

Jonathan nodded. "It could, I suppose. I just don't like to think of you wandering around looking for hidden passageways."

Michael grinned. "You can come too." He topped Jonathan's wine glass. "Matthew says Royston's an old town."

"Yes, it is, probably pre-Roman, or at least it flourished in Roman times. Then there was old King James the First from Scotland. He took over from good Queen Bess and had a hunting lodge built here, just for him and his courtiers, wouldn't you know. The peasants had to clear out of the way, of course."

"So it's possible there are tunnels and stuff everywhere around here," Michael said, enthused.

"It's possible. Are you thinking maybe Jonathan was buried in some out-of-the-way tunnel or cave?"

"It would make sense of my nightmare."

"Hmm… Well, like I said, I don't want you poking about on your own."

"Why don't we go for a stroll in the grounds?" Michael suggested. "It's still light outside, and there's a place I want to show you. We can take our wine with us."

"Lead on, MacDuff." Jonathan was glad Michael had got off the subject of tunnels and nightmares. He waited until Michael walked from behind the bar, then threw an arm over his shoulder, hugging him close. "When do I get to see the bedrooms?"

"How many do you need?"

"Just one at a time."

Michael chuckled and opened the French doors that led to the wide terrace outside. The evening sky still held a trace of blue behind small, puffy white clouds. They walked side by side across the lawn toward the orchard, enjoying the quiet serenity of the surroundings.

"So many of my dreams took place here," Michael said as they passed into the orchard, under the gently moving branches. "When we, I mean, *they* were boys, they played hide and seek here among the trees."

"Perfect place for it, but how do you know about that—them playing hide and seek here?"

"In one of my dreams."

"Of course." Jonathan slowed his steps, looking around and then upward through the leafy branches that rustled in the night breeze.

"Does it seem familiar to you?" Michael asked, taking his hand.

"Yes… yes, it does, strangely familiar. And I have to confess that last night when I drove you back here, the house also looked familiar. I've puzzled over that, telling myself it wasn't *déjà vu*, but now, being here with you, sensing somehow that I've been here before, I don't know what else to call it."

"I know what you mean," Michael said. "The first time I came into the orchard, it was almost as though I could feel their presence. That's the tree Jonathan hid behind in one of my dreams, and over there is where they made love before Jonathan was sent overseas."

Still holding hands they walked over to base of the tree Michael had indicated. Smiling, Jonathan sat down under the tree, pulling Michael down with him. They sat close together, Jonathan's arm around Michael's shoulders.

"How strange that all these years later, Michael and Jonathan should return to this place."

Michael felt a shiver run down his spine at Jonathan's words. He turned to look at him. "Do you think, is it at all possible that you and I are… are *them*?"

"You mean, reincarnated?" Jonathan let out a long sigh. "I've never believed in that kind of thing. It defies logic."

"Neither have I," Michael interrupted. "But the dreams aren't logical, and the fact that we both had the same kind of dreams, thousands of miles apart, and that we're now here together, sitting under this tree I dreamed about—what part of all that is logical?"

Jonathan was silent, not really knowing how to answer Michael's outburst. He was right of course, he mused; none of this was logical. Dreams rarely were, but then again, they didn't generally come true.

"And then there's the photograph," Michael continued. "The two of them, looking for all the world like the two of us, only in army uniforms. Miss Ballard at the library told me she took the photograph of them while they were home on leave."

Jonathan turned to look at Michael, then kissed him gently on the lips. "Well, if it is possible to have lived before, there is no one I would rather have lived with before than you. I don't pretend to know what it's all about, Michael, but I do know that what I already feel for you is quite amazing. Yesterday, I didn't know you actually existed, and now it's as though you've stepped out of my dreams, that you've become the man who now fills my thoughts every waking hour."

Michael stroked Jonathan's face with his fingertips. "That's how I feel too." He paused, then continued. "There's something I didn't tell you about what happened before the nightmare. I was in the master bedroom—Lionel said in his letter I should redecorate it to my taste before I moved in. Anyway, I was in there, and I felt this presence behind me, like it wrapped its... his... arms around me. I wasn't afraid, although I sorta freaked when it... *he*... kissed me..."

Jonathan gaped at him, his dark blue eyes wide with wonder. "*Kissed* you?"

"Well, it sure felt like a kiss, on the cheek, not the lips," he added for clarity's sake.

"A ghost kiss," Jonathan murmured. "I wouldn't have thought it possible."

"Nor me, it just kinda happened, out of the blue." He looked up at the darkening sky. "We should head back, I guess. Mrs. Mac will be wondering where we've got to." They stood and held each other for a moment, their faces pressed together. "After dinner, I'll show you the master."

Jonathan grinned. "You have a *master*?"

"I meant the master bedroom."

"You're being serious again."

"Sorry."

§ § § §

Mrs. MacDonald was waiting for them when they returned to the house. "Would you like to select a wine from the cellar, Mr., uh... Michael?" It had taken Michael almost a week to coax her into not calling him sir, or Mr. Ballantyne, and she still hesitated over what she considered the too familiar name.

"I'll let Jonathan choose," Michael told her. "What are we having?"

"Roast pork. I hope that's to both your liking."

"Lovely," Jonathan assured her, with a smile. "Michael tells me you're a wonderful cook."

Michael couldn't help but notice that his housekeeper fairly quivered with delight under Jonathan's charm—not that he could blame her for that. He'd felt himself quiver quite a few times.

"Let's go down to the cellar and you can pick what you want," he said, taking Jonathan's arm. "There's quite a selection down there." He flipped on the light as they descended the steep stairs. "Mind your step," he cautioned, leading the way.

Jonathan shivered as they reached the cellar floor. He wondered why this place made him feel so uncomfortable. It was just a wine cellar, yet there was something nagging at the back of his mind. Something he felt he should remember...

"See anything you fancy?"

Michael's voice echoing in the stone cellar made him jump slightly. "Um... just a sec..."

"You all right?" Michael looked at him with concern.

"Yes, yes... I'm fine..."

"No you're not. You're feeling something, aren't you?" Michael took his hand. "Something down here is troubling you."

Jonathan looked around, trying to figure out just why he was suddenly so ill at ease. "I'm not sure what it is," he muttered, squeezing Michael's hand. "I've never been here before, and yet..."

"Let's just grab a bottle and go back upstairs." Michael reached for the first one he could put his hand on and pulled it off the rack. "Come on," he said, tugging at Jonathan's arm. "Let's go."

"Wait…" Jonathan resisted Michael's pull and continued to gaze about him, staring at the wooden wine racks as if trying to see beyond them.

"Jonathan, you're worrying me." Michael gave his arm a gentle tug. "Let's go…"

"Right." He let Michael lead him back up the stairs, their hands tightly clasped. Once back in the kitchen, Michael handed Matthew the bottle of wine.

"Chianti with roast pork," the butler said, looking at the label. "Is that a favorite in America then?"

"What? Oh…" Michael forced out a chuckle. "Yeah, I mean no, it's a favorite of mine."

"Well, we'll have to order some more bottles," Matthew murmured. "Dinner will be served in about ten minutes."

"Thanks." Michael steered Jonathan out of the kitchen and back to the bar. "I think I need a stiff Scotch instead of wine," he muttered as they entered the lounge.

"Sorry, I didn't mean to go gaga on you down there." Jonathan pulled Michael close and kissed his forehead. "I think it must have been the confined space or something."

"It was more like you were having a bad memory," Michael said, hugging Jonathan to him. "The look on your face was… pained."

"Well, I refuse to have it spoil our time together." Jonathan kissed Michael soundly on the lips. "What were you saying about a Scotch?"

"Sounds like a good idea." He slipped behind the bar and poured them both a good shot of Glenfiddich. "Anything in it?"

"Good Lord, no. You don't add anything to good whisky, unless it's another shot."

"A man after my own heart," Michael chuckled. "Well, Skol…"

"Skol…" Jonathan tossed back his Scotch. "And here's to you, Michael, the man who has captured *my* heart in a very short space of time." Michael blushed, and Jonathan reached over the bar to kiss his cheek. "You are truly adorable, Michael Ballantyne."

"Keep that up and we'll be AWOL at dinner," Michael kidded.

Jonathan flashed him one of his wicked smiles. "I intend to keep that up—and anything else that comes to hand."

A discreet knock at the door had them looking ruefully at one another. Matthew popped his head in and announced, "Dinner is served, gentlemen."

"Thanks, Matthew." He grinned at Jonathan. "This is so much better than a frozen pizza on a TV tray."

Dinner was delicious, and the Chianti, slightly chilled, went well with the pork after all. The two men were left alone to enjoy the meal and each other's company by the always tactful Matthew and his wife, causing Jonathan to comment on it. "Do they know what's going on?" he asked. "With us, I mean."

"Well, they worked for Lionel for years—and his partner William—so they can't be blind to these things. I haven't actually discussed it with them, but they seem to have been fond of Lionel, and he must have thought highly of them to ensure they had a job, even after he passed."

Jonathan nodded. "They've never seen Jonathan Harcourt's ghost?"

"No, and according to Matthew, Lionel's partner William didn't either. He just went along with it so it wouldn't upset Lionel. But Emily, the housemaid, has seen him."

"Oh, yes?"

"Mmm, she told me the other day she has the 'sight.' She and her mother apparently see ghosts all the time."

Jonathan laughed. "Oh my God, Michael, can you imagine what tea at their house would be like? Would you like milk with your tea—or ectoplasm?"

"I know it sounds crazy…" Michael finished the last of his wine and twiddled the glass stem between his fingers. "…But, think about it, there's not much going on right now that isn't a little crazy. Weeks of dreaming about you, or the *original* you, making love to me, meeting you at my uncle's grave—an uncle I didn't even know I had until a few days ago—that strange encounter with *whatever* that kissed me, and then the nightmare I had about Jonathan Harcourt being in danger… All of it sounds like it belongs in a spooky movie, not in real life."

Jonathan smiled. "Even my making love to you?"

"No…" Michael felt himself blush again. "Not that… that was wonderful, and I can't wait for it to happen again."

"Then let's not wait." Jonathan stood up, and Michael's gaze zeroed in on the obvious tenting at his eye level.

"You're hard," he murmured, reaching out to stroke the enticing bulge.

"I told you, I just have to see you smile." He held out his hand. "Come on, I still have to see the bedrooms."

"You got it." Michael's smile got even bigger. "Let me just tell Matthew we're done, and thank Mrs. Mac for the dinner."

Once upstairs, the tour of the rooms took longer than Michael anticipated, with Jonathan insisting on some serious kissing in each bedroom. By the time they got to the master, their clothes were disheveled, and Michael's cheeks had taken on a rosy glow.

"This is where I had that strange experience." He indicated the corner of the room where he'd felt another's presence.

"Hmm…" Jonathan walked over and stood in the spot Michael had pointed to. "Don't feel anything…"

"I don't think ghosts come on demand," Michael said, chuckling. "Aren't they supposed to sneak up on you when you least expect them to?"

"That's how they do it in books and films," Jonathan remarked, looking around the room. "You know sliding panels and that sort of thing. Like that play, *The Cat and the Canary*, where dead bodies fall into the room from behind bookcases. Did you see it?"

"No, and right now I'd rather not think about dead bodies falling into this bedroom. I might be sleeping in here one of these days!"

Jonathan leered at him. "Just make sure you're not alone. It's a nice, big bedroom."

"Too big." Michael grimaced as he scanned the furnishings. "I'll have to do some major redecorating before I move in here. Brighten it up a bit. It's so dark, don't you think?"

"Mmm, brocade's never been my thing." Jonathan had that look in his eye again. "I know, let's go back to your room so I can make love to you without the possibility of a ghost peeking at us."

Michael laughed and took Jonathan's hand, leading him from the bedroom. "I'm all for that, without the peeking ghost—or the dead bodies." He pushed open the door to the guest room and ushered Jonathan inside.

"Ah, this is better." Jonathan looked around the comfortable guest room with appreciation. "Much more conducive to lovemaking…"

"Oh, here…" Michael handed Jonathan the gift-wrapped box. "I got you a little something when I went shopping earlier today."

"Michael, that is so sweet, but you don't have to buy me things."

"It's not much." Michael smiled mischievously. "But something you'll look great in, and I'll have fun taking off you."

Jonathan ripped off the paper and opened the box. Beaming at Michael, he unfolded the silk robe. "It's gorgeous." He slipped it on. "Almost as gorgeous as you…"

He pulled Michael into his arms and backed him up over to the bed. They fell on top of the quilt, Jonathan lying over Michael, his lips hovering a tantalizing inch or so from Michael's. "There's that most kissable mouth again," he murmured, brushing Michael's lips gently with his own. "And it's all mine tonight… and every night."

"Right," Michael whispered against Jonathan's lips. "So let's start with you losing that robe."

§ § § §

Jack Trenton paused in his prowling across the grounds outside the big house. He knew they were together inside, which meant it wouldn't be long before he could make his move. Just as had been predicted, the two had met and had cohabited—and just as predicted, they would meet the same fate as the two that had preceded them. It was inevitable, and he was the chosen instrument of their demise. His father had appointed him guardian of the secret—a secret that would have sent the old man to the gallows had it been discovered.

What his father had done all those years ago, he'd been forced to do. If the two hadn't meddled in his father's affairs, if Jonathan Harcourt hadn't threatened to expose him and bring the police into it, his father and the others would have had no reason to kill him. And then the other one… well, his father grieved over that one for a long time after. Some say he was never quite the same. But that was his father's weakness, and Jack thanked his lucky stars that he wasn't similarly afflicted. No, the two in the house wouldn't be able to use their charms on him—not on Jack Trenton. He scowled, his eyes catching some movement at one of the windows.

Matthew, he thought sourly. That old bugger was going to try to have him thrown off the property. Well, he was wasting his time. "I'm going nowhere 'til the job is done," he muttered to himself, turning away and walking slowly back to the lodge. "Not until the job is done…"

CHAPTER THIRTEEN

Michael and Jonathan lay on the bed, their arms and legs snugly intertwined, the warm mellow afterglow of their recent lovemaking rendering words unnecessary. Michael, his face resting on Jonathan's chest, his lips lightly touching a nipple, smiled with complete contentment. If he'd been a cat, he'd have been purring. *Boy, but this guy is a prize,* he thought, running his forefinger over the tiny nub of flesh that hardened at his touch. He tried to remember if sex with Steve had ever made him feel this way, and he could not think of one time when he'd been allowed to simply lie in the man's arms and enjoy the intimacy that being totally at ease with one another could bring.

"What are you thinking about?"

Well, he wasn't about to tell Jonathan he'd actually been thinking of another man. Even if it had been to compare said man unfavorably with the one in whose arms he now lay—no, that wouldn't be a very good idea.

"I was thinking I've never been happier," he replied, which, after all, was the truth.

Jonathan stretched, his lean muscles rippling against Michael's body. He kissed Michael's forehead. "I share that thought," he said, wrapping his arms around Michael again. "You have definitely lightened my life, young man."

"Even with all the spookiness involved?" Michael teased.

"Even with all of that." He pulled Michael up so his mouth was at a level with his own. He licked Michael's lower lip with the tip of his tongue, then slipped it between Michael's parted lips. As always, the effect on both men was electrifying, their bodies shuddering as, once more, desire swept through them.

Michael wriggled from Jonathan's arms and sat astride him, smiling down at him while his hands stroked and caressed Jonathan's hard chest muscles, lingering over the tiny nipples that hardened again under his touch. He leaned down to take each one in his mouth, nibbling on them gently, causing Jonathan to writhe under him and utter small gasps and moans that were music to Michael's ears. Michael scoured the warm flesh of his lover's torso with his lips and tongue. As he moved south, Jonathan's erection pressed into the cleft between his butt cheeks. He scooted down so he could take it into his mouth, his hand grasping it at the base, his tongue swirling around the swollen, silky head. The soft growling sound that came from Jonathan told Michael his lover was enjoying this as much as he was and encouraged him to explore further. His tongue skated over Jonathan's balls, licking and teasing each one, before exploring the smooth, sensitive path that led to his tight hole. Michael laved the ring of muscle with his saliva, then pushed his tongue deep inside. Jonathan shuddered and moaned as Michael fucked him with his tongue, his musk an aphrodisiac to Michael's senses, driving him wild with desire. He raised his head, licked his way back over Jonathan's balls, up his throbbing shaft, enclosing the head between his lips then taking it all with one long swallow.

"Ah... Michael..." Jonathan's cry was one of near-tortured ecstasy as he pumped his cock into Michael's mouth. Michael's hands stroked and caressed Jonathan's chest, the sides of his torso, the feel of the solid wall of warm flesh under him, filling him with an almost uncontrollable lust. He released Jonathan's cock only long enough to reach quickly for a condom and lube. Feverishly he stretched it over Jonathan's rock-hard erection, then coated it with the lube before easing himself down slowly onto the hard length of pulsing flesh. His breath escaped his lips in one long, ragged gasp as the initial pain was eclipsed by the incredible sensation of having Jonathan's cock fill him completely. Their eyes locked on one another; their bodies began to rock together, gently at first, then driven by passion and desire, with a fervor that had them both moaning out loud.

Michael bore down, his sphincter muscles pulsing around Jonathan's cock. He leaned back, supporting himself with his hands flat on the mattress while he moved rhythmically up and down on the hard length of his lover's cock. His eyes rolled back in his head, and he gave himself up to the rapture that being joined to Jonathan was bringing him. Jonathan grasped

Michael's hips, bucking under him hard and fast, driving his cock harder and deeper inside Michael, who bent forward to claim Jonathan's lips in a long, searing kiss that had them gasping into each other's mouths. His aching erection was gripped by Jonathan's warm hand, and the heat flooding his groin told him his orgasm was imminent.

He gritted his teeth, trying to prolong this moment of ecstasy, but his body shuddered as the pressure built inside his balls. With a guttural cry, he gave in to the overwhelming surge of his climax, splattering Jonathan's chest and chin with his semen. Jonathan gasped, his body tensing between Michael's thighs, then arching upward with the power of his orgasm, driving himself deeper inside Michael as he came in shuddering spasms. Michael collapsed on top of him, holding him, covering his mouth with a deep kiss until the throes of his climax stilled and his body relaxed. For a long time, they lay locked in each other's arms without moving, content to stay joined both physically and emotionally until sleep took them both away.

§ § § §

The following morning over breakfast, which Mrs. MacDonald had set up in the dining room, Michael brought up the subject of the cave again.

Jonathan stopped chewing on his toast long enough to ask, "You really want to see that place?"

"Well, yeah, it's just curiosity is all."

"And you know what that did, don't you?"

Michael ignored the cautionary remark. "Also, I'd like you to meet Miss Ballard at the library."

"The old girl who was in love with your uncle?"

"Yes. I think she'd be astounded to see the two of us together."

"It might be too much for the old bird's heart, you know," Jonathan warned. "Like a time warp or something."

"But it might help her remember what happened to Jonathan Harcourt's parents after they sold this place. They can't have just vanished off the face of the earth, and perhaps like my grandparents they had a son or daughter who then had you."

"And who put me up for adoption." Jonathan thought for a moment, then said, "It seems a bit odd that people like the Harcourts, who obviously were quite well heeled, wouldn't want a grandchild of their own. If they had a daughter, say, who had me out of wedlock, why would they insist she give me up?"

"The scandal, maybe?"

"People get over that stuff if they want to. Even if it was a son who got some girl in the family way, surely they'd want to keep the baby."

Michael smiled, and Jonathan raised an eyebrow. "What?"

"I was imagining you as a baby. I bet you were cute. Damn…" He broke off as his cell phone jangled in his pocket. He glanced at the ID screen and frowned. "It's my brother. I'd better take it. Hello, Brad."

"Michael, you okay?"

"Yeah, fine, what's up?"

"Your creepy boyfriend just called me."

"Steve?"

"Who else? How many creepy boyfriends do you have? Says you sounded upset with him last time you talked. Anyway, he wanted your address over there so he could send you a letter of apology."

"Steve—apologize?" Michael rolled his eyes. "That doesn't sound like him at all."

"Well, I gave it to him just to get him off my back, so look out for a letter full of baloney about how sorry he is that you're so far away, blah, blah, blah…"

"I can hardly wait. This is a first for Steve."

"So how's it goin' apart from that? You settling in OK?"

"Yes. When are you and Miranda coming over?"

"We should be there in about another week or so, if that's okay. You seen any more of that guy, Jonathan?"

Michael smiled. "Uh, yeah. As a matter of fact, we're having breakfast right now."

"Boy, that was fast." Brad chuckled. "He's not after your money, is he?"

Michael winked at Jonathan. "My brother wants to know if you're after my money."

"Michael!" His brother gasped his disbelief. "I can't believe you did that. Now, how am I going to look him in the eye when I meet him?"

Jonathan, grinning, held out his hand for Michael's phone. "Brad? This is Jonathan…"

"Oh my god, I was joking… joking, that's all…"

Jonathan laughed. "You sound like you're choking, not joking."

"You tell that bro of mine when I see him, I'll… I'll…"

"You'll give him a big hug? That's super, I'll let him know. I'm really looking forward to meeting you and your lovely wife when you visit Michael. He's told me lots about you."

"He has? Well, don't believe him. I'm a nice guy really." Brad laughed lightly. "Sorry for that bad joke earlier."

"No problem. And don't worry about his money. I won't spend it all before you get here." He handed the phone back to Michael.

"Brad, you still there?"

"He's a kidder, huh?" Brad sounded slightly unsure.

"Well, he's a match for you any day," Michael said dryly. "Thanks for letting me know about Steve's call. I won't hold my breath waiting for his letter."

"Right. Okay, brother mine, I'll call you in a few and let you know when we'll be arriving."

"Can't wait, and tell Miranda hello."

"Steve?" Jonathan gave Michael an inquiring look after he'd hung up.

"The guy I told you I was seeing before I came to England."

"Ah, yes... the one who blows hot and cold."

"That's him." Michael avoided Jonathan's intense gaze as he continued. "He called Brad asking for my address here so he could write me a letter of apology."

"For blowing hot and cold?"

"No." Michael looked up to meet Jonathan's eyes. "I didn't mention it, but he called the other night and was totally pissed at me for leaving without telling him. I kinda hung up on him."

Jonathan's mouth lifted at the corner in a half smile. "And he's apologizing to *you*?"

"Well," Michael said defensively, "he went from being pissed to really nice when I told him what Lionel had left me."

"Ah... so *he's* the one who's after your money."

Michael sighed. "I don't think so, not really. Besides, like I told you, we weren't really having a relationship."

Jonathan was silent for a moment, then asked, "Do you still have feelings for him?"

"I thought I did."

"What changed your mind?"

"Well... you did. I mean meeting you, having you in my life has made me realize what I've been missing."

Jonathan leaned forward and put his clasped hands on the table. "Do tell." He chuckled as Michael's face took on its habitual rosy glow. "You're blushing again," he teased.

"I have a hard time talking about really intimate things," Michael said quietly. "Not like my brother—he can be outrageous sometimes. He's given me a red face many a time."

"But you don't have any trouble expressing your feelings when we make love," Jonathan murmured, taking Michael's hand. "You're quite abandoned actually."

"Abandoned?" Michael laughed. "Never did I think I'd hear that word used to describe me."

"Well, you are. You're very passionate, a wonderful kisser—and I'm getting hard just talking about it."

"Now you're really making me blush." Michael smiled at his lover. "But this is what I mean. You are so different from Steve, and I don't mean just your accent."

"I have an accent?" Jonathan asked, wide eyed.

Michael chuckled. "No, I guess it's just we Yanks who have accents."

"That's what I've always believed." Jonathan's eyes twinkled. "But go on…"

"Well… gee, how do I say this without getting all red in the face again? When we, uh… make love… I really feel you're into it as much as I am. You know, like you care how I'm feeling all the time, not just wanting to get your rocks off, then either fall asleep right away or leap out of bed with a 'See you later!' kinda thing."

Jonathan shook his head. "Why on earth would you put up with that? If this is Steve you're talking about, then he's not worth a moment's consideration." He grinned. "I was thinking I might have to challenge him to a duel for your favor, but now if we ever met, I think I'd just kick him up the arse."

Michael grinned at the thought, then said, "You know, all this talk about me, I keep forgetting to ask about your past love life. I mean…" He broke off and did his famous blushing act. "…I mean, I'm presuming you are single. You're not hiding some English college hunk somewhere are you?"

Jonathan laughed. "You are so adorable when you get all flummoxed, Michael. No, I'm not hiding a lover under the bed. There was someone once, but we broke up over two years ago."

"Do you still miss him?"

"No, I can honestly say I don't." Jonathan sighed. "I did, for a time, but there was so much wrong with our relationship. David and I wanted different things from life, I suppose, and neither one of us was willing to compromise. He wanted to immigrate to Australia. I wanted to stay put. I happen to like living in England."

"And did he go to Australia?"

"Yes, he did. We corresponded for a time, but then I suspect he met someone, and that was that."

"David and Jonathan," Michael murmured. "The names of the biblical lovers…"

"Yes…" Jonathan laughed dryly. "And we know what happened to them, don't we?"

§ § § §

Lucy Ballard looked up from the pile of books she was sorting through and gasped as she caught sight of the two young men walking towards her desk. Her hand flew to her throat in a gesture of surprised shock.

"Jonathan," she murmured, staring at the man who stood in front of her next to Michael. She looked from one to the other, shaking her head. "It's just so unbelievable. You've found each other again after all these years." Tears sprang to her eyes, and she closed them for a moment as if to ensure that when she opened them again they would still be there and not just figments of her imagination.

"Miss Ballard," Michael smiled at the old lady. "This is Jonathan Robertson. We met the same day I talked with you, at my uncle's grave."

"Amazing," she whispered, tentatively taking the hand Jonathan proffered. "Both of you, so like the boys I knew so long ago…"

"We wondered if we might take a moment or two of your time," Jonathan said gently. "We have a few questions you might be able to answer."

"Oh, but of course." She turned to her assistant. "Miss Albright, I'll be gone for a few minutes." Again, without waiting for a reply from the woman, she slipped from behind the counter and led the way to the employees' break room.

"Tea?" she asked as she closed the door behind them.

"That would be very nice," Jonathan said, taking one of the seats at the table. "We won't keep you too long, but we're both a bit perplexed by the stories we've been hearing and reading concerning Jonathan Harcourt's disappearance."

"I'm sure you are." Miss Ballard set three cups on the table and poured a strong-looking brew from a large teapot. "Milk and sugar?"

"Please…" Jonathan nodded, while Michael shook his head and said, "Just like that is good."

The librarian sat at the table and gazed at the two men. "I could simply sit here and stare at you both all day. I feel like I've been taken back in time." She cleared her throat quietly. "But of course, you didn't come here just for my amazement. So, how can I help you?"

"Well," Michael began, "we know about my relation to Michael Thornton, but Jonathan here was adopted. He doesn't know who his biological parents were, and we wondered if you knew what happened to the Harcourts after they sold Bedford Park."

Miss Ballard took a dainty sip of her tea. "You mean after they *left* Bedford Park. The house wasn't sold until many years later. Emily, Mrs. Harcourt, died before the estate was sold. Roger, her husband, instructed his solicitors to put it up for sale shortly after she passed away."

"You were obviously in touch with them then," Jonathan said patiently.

"Oh yes, they didn't move too far away, only to Cambridge, so I was able to visit once in a while."

Michael met Jonathan's eyes across the table. *Cambridge…* where perhaps Jonathan was born.

"Did they have any other children?" Michael asked.

"No, Jonathan was their only child."

Jonathan sighed with disappointment. "What we were hoping for was some connection between the Harcourts and myself. I tried the Registrar's office but they have no record of me before I was adopted. I hadn't wanted to trouble my mother with this... she's been quite ill for some time."

Miss Ballard looked away from his earnest expression, a fleeting look of remorse clouding her eyes for just a moment. Michael had a sudden intuitive feeling she was about to tell them something she'd been holding secret for a long time.

"There is something you should know," she said slowly, looking at a spot above both men's heads. "I have kept this to myself for over sixty years, but seeing you two here together, it makes me wonder why on earth I should keep the secret any longer."

"Go on," Jonathan urged quietly.

Miss Ballard sat back in her seat and dabbed at her moist eyes with a lace handkerchief. "Jonathan and I had a child, a son..."

Michael stared at the old lady wide-eyed. "But Jonathan was gay... in love with my uncle."

"Yes, that is true, but as I told you we were, all three, very close." She paused to smile at Michael. "There was never any possibility of Jonathan leaving your uncle for me. Our relationship wasn't at all like that—I loved both of them equally. It was during the war. Jonathan came home on leave. Michael was stationed in Egypt at the time; they hadn't seen one another in over two years. They'd been in touch, of course, but getting leave together at the same time was almost an impossibility. I think it only happened twice in five years. Anyway, this particular time, Jonathan's despair was so intense, he turned to me for comfort, and before we actually knew what we were doing, we were... well, I'm sure I don't have to draw you a picture. Nine months later I gave birth to a baby boy and had him adopted. The scandal would have been too much I'm afraid. I would have had to move away and I had an ailing mother to care for..."

"But, Miss Ballard," Jonathan interrupted. "That child couldn't have been me. I'm only thirty!"

"No, of course not." She smiled wanly. "I'm not your mother, but I could very well be your grandmother."

"My God..." Michael gazed at her, astounded by the story he was still trying to digest. "Did you ever tell Jonathan he had a child?"

"Later..." Miss Ballard's eyes filled with tears. "After the child was adopted and the war was over. Jonathan noticed there was something different about me. I suppose he could tell I was keeping something from him. He asked several times what was wrong, even had Michael talk to me. At first, I just couldn't tell either of them what had happened, but I finally broke down and confessed. Jonathan was so angry, so *hurt*... and I... well, I hadn't quite forgiven myself for not telling him, and for giving the child away. It was a very stressful time for all of us. Jonathan avoided my company. Michael was sweetly sympathetic although I don't think even he quite understood my motives. It took Jonathan a long time to forgive me, and then he did so only shortly before his disappearance."

She paused to wipe her eyes, and Michael asked, "Your son... did you ever get in touch with him?"

"No, I did not. I did, however, find out many years later who had adopted him, and I'm afraid the end of this story is not very pleasant."

Jonathan and Michael sat silently waiting for her to continue, convinced that what she was about to say would reveal the mystery of Jonathan's parentage.

"Alistair, that was my son's name, was adopted by a couple who owned a farm in Cambridgeshire. A Mr. and Mrs. Hensley. He was a farmer's boy." She dabbed at her eyes again. "And he loved the land, they told me. He was engaged to be married, but a week before the wedding he was plowing part of a hillside attached to the farm. The tractor rolled over and crushed him to death."

"Jesus," Michael whispered.

"His fiancée, as you can imagine, was devastated, made even more so by the fact that she was pregnant with Alistair's child."

"Well..." Jonathan glanced at Michael. "I can see where the story's going now. She had the baby adopted, right?"

"Yes, but that's as much as I know, I'm afraid." Miss Ballard regarded Jonathan sadly. "The Hensleys were never told who adopted the child, but if I had to guess now by looking at you, Jonathan, I would have to say you are Alistair Hensley's son."

"And your grandson," Jonathan said, his eyes fixed on the old lady's.

She nodded. "It would appear so."

Sighing, Jonathan pushed himself against the back of his chair. "I'll call my mother and see if she can confirm any of this." He stood and walked over to Miss Ballard's side. He knelt in front of her and took her hand. "Thank you for being so honest about what happened. This must be very hard on you, having it all come back like this."

Her eyes brimmed again with tears, and she reached out to stroke Jonathan's dark hair. "If it means you are my grandson," she said gently, "then I'm very glad to be reminded of the past."

CHAPTER FOURTEEN

They were quiet as they left the library. Michael cast an anxious glance at Jonathan every now and then, trying to gauge his friend's mood after the surprising revelation from Miss Ballard.

"You all right?' he asked finally.

"Yes, though I think I could use a drink. There's a pub on the corner over there. Fancy a pint? We can leave the car here."

"Sounds like a plan," Michael replied.

"I'll phone my mother while we're there, if you don't mind."

"No, of course not. The sooner we find out the truth, the better."

There were only a few customers in the pub, a marked difference from the pub Matthew had taken Michael to the day before. Jonathan order two pints; then, with glasses in hand, they retreated to a booth in the corner. After a long swig of beer, Jonathan pulled out his mobile phone.

Michael said, "I'll just hit the john, give you some privacy while you talk to your mom."

"You don't have to do that, Michael."

"I know, but you can tell me all about it when I get back." He gripped Jonathan's hand, then left him alone.

Jonathan watched him go, feeling that now-familiar warmth the sight of Michael gave him. Then he punched in his mother's speed dial number. "Hello, Mum, how are you today?"

"Not so bad, dear."

He stifled his sigh on hearing her weak voice.

"It's nice to hear your voice, son."

"Mum, I have something to ask you."

"Oh, yes?"

He paused, not wanting to worry her too much. "I've had some strange things occur recently—made me start wondering about who I really am…"

"Who you are, Jonathan? Why, you're my son."

"Your adopted son."

"Yes, Jonathan, but you're as dear to me as though I had borne you myself."

"I know that, Mum, and I love you too. It's just that recently some things have happened that have made me curious as to who my biological parents are—or were."

"Oh, I see."

"If it's going to upset you, it'll keep for another day."

"No, no, that's all right. You have a right to be curious. I'm surprised you haven't asked before."

"I never saw the need until recently. I always considered you and Dad to be my only parents." He winced as he heard his mother's quiet sob. "Mum, don't get upset. You don't have to tell me today."

"No, that's all right, dear." There was a short silence, then his mother said, "The young lady, your mother, was engaged to a farmer. The poor man was killed a week before they were to be married."

Jonathan felt his heart thump in his chest as he asked, "Alistair Hensley?"

"Why yes, how did you know that?"

He let out the long breath he hadn't realized he'd been holding. "I was talking to someone earlier who knew them, or of them, rather. She works at the library in Royston."

"Royston? What on earth are you doing there?"

"It's a bit of a long story, and I think instead of telling you on the phone, I'll come and see you. How about next weekend?"

"That will be lovely, dear. I'll let Doreen know so she can make up the spare room."

"Um, I might be bringing a friend."

"That's fine, there's plenty of room for two. Who is it? Have I met him?"

Jonathan smiled at his mother's assumption it would be a man. There had never been any secrets between them. "No, you haven't met him." He looked up as Michael returned to their booth. "His name is Michael—he's a Yank, but don't let that put you off. He's very nice."

"I'm sure he is, dear. I'll tell Doreen to get some American beer, shall I?"

"Actually, he's quite taken to our British ale, so don't worry about that. I'll phone in a few days and let you know what time we'll be there. Give Doreen my love. Oh, I just have one more question, if you don't mind."

"What is it, dear?"

"Why did you choose to name me Jonathan?"

"That was the only request she made," his mother replied softly. "They had talked about names, your mother and father—Jonathan for a boy, Joanna for a girl."

"I see. Thanks, Mum. I was just curious. You take care now."

"I will. Bye, son."

"Bye, Mum."

His eyes glistened as he turned his gaze on Michael. "Well, that's that, then," he said. "She confirmed Alistair Hensley was my father."

"And he was Jonathan Harcourt's son." Michael moved closer to his lover to touch his hand discreetly. "So now we know how we're both connected to the past." He shivered slightly. "How do you feel about all this?"

"Okay. I mean, it's not like this is much of a shock," Jonathan said. "I've known for some time that I was adopted. I knew I had to have other parents out there somewhere. I only wish there hadn't been so much tragedy in their lives. Right from the beginning," he continued sadly. "When you think that Jonathan and Michael survived all those war years, and then when they were reunited and should've had their happy ever after, they were both dead within a year of each other. Not to mention my father, Jonathan's love child with Miss Ballard, killed a week before his wedding. It's almost like there was a curse put on them…"

"'Avenge us, and set us free…'" Michael stared at Jonathan wide eyed. "That's what Jonathan said to me in my dream one night. 'Avenge us…' D'you think maybe he meant there was a curse, and we have to free them of it?"

"But how?" Jonathan shook his head. "They're all dead, and whoever may have cursed them is most likely dead too."

"Henry Bryant," Michael said slowly. "Miss Ballard said he was without scruples and capable of murder."

"And he's gone too, Michael. There's no one still around who knew all of them except Miss Ballard, and I don't think she's the type to curse anyone."

"No, she loved them too much. But she did say that Henry Bryant was trying to put the make on my uncle Michael, and that he owed Jonathan a bunch of money. People have killed for less than that."

"That's true, but it doesn't change the fact that Bryant is dead, and if he did have something to do with my grandfather's death, it's rather too late to accuse him of it."

Michael sighed. "You're right, but it's going to bug me 'til I figure out what Jonathan meant when he said 'Avenge us.'"

As they drove through town, Jonathan asked, "Do you still want to visit the cave? It's only open Saturdays and Sundays."

"Oh yeah, let's do that. I'm kinda curious."

"All right, it's just round the corner here." Jonathan swung the car into the parking area provided for tourists. "I hope you're not disappointed," he said, leading Michael up to the entrance.

"I won't be. The fact that it's hundreds of years old is enough to interest me. We don't have Knights Templar stuff in the States."

Jonathan chuckled. "It's only a legend that they used the cave; no one really knows if they did or not."

Michael nudged his arm. "Don't spoil the romance of it all."

"Oh, right…" Jonathan rolled his eyes. "The romance of it all…"

Michael paid their entrance fees, and they descended into the cave via a long, sloping passageway that led into the high-domed round chamber. Michael gasped at the sight of so many wall carvings covering every part of the 'cave.' A handrail around the perimeter kept him from getting too close, but at one point he was able to touch the walls and run his hand over the surface. He closed his eyes, trying to remember the texture of the walls he had stumbled through in his dream.

"What are you doing?" Jonathan asked in a whisper.

Michael jumped with a guilty start. "Just wanted to know what these walls would feel like. I'll tell you later," he added, noticing Jonathan's skeptical stare. He listened to the guide's narration intently, the reference to the Knights Templar being overshadowed by more modern interpretations of what the cave was used for. He was interested, though, in the fact that several times the guide mentioned that, after the discovery of the cave, it was thought other small chambers and passageways may have been dug in the vicinity.

"So, did that satisfy your curiosity?' Jonathan asked as they walked back to his car.

"Yes, and no," Michael replied. "I told you about my dream when I was looking for Jonathan and going down long passageways. The walls were soft, porous, just like in that cave. If I have to believe, and I do, that the dreams we've shared have some kind of message, then somewhere, perhaps under the house, or the grounds of Bedford Park, there is a place just like that cave."

"Michael, if such a place existed," Jonathan protested, "surely it would have been discovered long ago."

"Not if it was meant to be a secret. Suppose it was there long before Bedford Park was built?"

"What an imagination you have," Jonathan said, unlocking the car doors.

"No more imaginative than those who discovered the cave and linked it to the Knights Templar. Our dreams must mean *something*, Jonathan. You suggested there might have been a curse placed on my uncle and your grandfather, and even on your father. If we follow that line of thought, what kind of person can put a curse on someone—and have it actually *work*?"

"Michael…"

"And who would be more knowledgeable about that kind of thing than a librarian?"

"Miss Ballard?" Jonathan gaped at him. "Surely you don't think…"

"No, no," Michael interrupted impatiently. "But she's surrounded by books, and… wait, come to think of it, there's a huge library at Bedford Park with *rare* books. They were mentioned specifically in the will—a collection of rare books. I haven't even had a chance to look at them yet. Maybe there's something there."

"Michael," Jonathan hung a left at the crossroads and headed back to Bedford Park. "You're letting your imagination run riot."

"No, I'm not. I'm just following the train of thought you put in my head about the possibility of a curse."

"You're becoming obsessed with it. There may not be any curse!"

"If there isn't, I'll shut up about it." Michael put his hand on Jonathan's thigh and squeezed gently. "It won't do any harm to do some research, now will it?"

Jonathan covered Michael's hand with his. "I suppose not. Just don't go around asking too many questions about curses and underground caves. People will think we're barmy. And if we do go to the library I'd rather not let Miss Ballard know what we're up to. It might upset her."

"Or she might know something about it," Michael countered. "Mrs. MacDonald told me there wasn't much Miss Ballard didn't know about the goings on around here. Besides, at some point, you need to tell her you really are her grandson."

"Yes, I must. I think that's probably the only bright spot in what we've discovered today. She's a sweet old lady."

"A sweet old lady with a lurid past," Michael said, chuckling.

"Not so lurid, really. She gave in to her love for my grandfather when he was lonely—pining for your uncle, don't forget—and just wanted to comfort him."

"Mmm, but it must have seemed like a dream come true for her at the time. One of the men she loved making love to her, regardless of the reasons." Michael smiled at the thought that had suddenly popped into his mind. "I wonder if he was thinking about my uncle when they were doing it."

Jonathan choked out a laugh of surprise. "Michael, for one who blushes like a virgin as easily as you do, you certainly do have a wicked mind."

Michael laughed. "I ain't no virgin, honey," he drawled. "You can attest to that!"

They were passing through the gates to the estate when Jonathan asked, "Who's that standing outside the lodge?"

Michael stared at the tall, burly man glowering at them and grimaced. "That's Jack Trenton," he said glumly. "I'll have to deal with him one of these days, I suppose."

"Deal with him?"

"Tell him to take a hike. He just showed up one day after Lionel passed, said Lionel employed him as a sort of security guard. Even the solicitor couldn't budge him, but now that I'm the owner, I guess I can fire him."

"He doesn't do a good job?"

"He doesn't do any job. He just hangs about giving everyone the creeps. I could swear he watches everything that goes on here. Mrs. MacDonald can't stand him. Anyway," he gave Jonathan a quick peck on the cheek, "that's my problem, and we've enough to think of at the moment without Jack Trenton."

They pulled up in front of the house and were greeted by Matthew, who swung the door open with a flourish.

"How do you do that, Matthew?" Michael asked.

"Do what, Mr. Michael?"

"You're always there to open the door no matter when I get here. You have built-in radar or something?"

Matthew chuckled politely. "It's part of my job, Mr. Michael. Now, would you care for a sherry before dinner?"

Michael grinned at Jonathan. "I think we'd rather have a stiff Scotch, Matthew. It's been another darned peculiar day."

"That's three in a row you've had since you've met me," Jonathan teased him as they went upstairs to freshen up.

"More than that, surely," Michael said, flashing him a mischievous smile.

Jonathan slapped him on the bottom. "I'm talking about your *darned peculiar days*, as well you know."

"Oh, more of that please!"

Laughing together, they raced up the last few steps and hurried into the bedroom where they threw themselves onto the bed in a tangle of arms and legs. Their laughter turned to quiet chuckles, then to soft moans and sighs, as they kissed and caressed, their desire for one another taking over.

"If you're going to do what I hope you're going to do, I need a shower first," Michael whispered in Jonathan's ear.

"Me too," Jonathan whispered back.

"Let's go, then."

In the bathroom, they stripped one another slowly, their hands caressing every part of their bodies as it was laid bare.

"Have I told you lately that you are a very beautiful man?" Jonathan murmured, tracing a pattern of kisses across Michael's shoulder.

"Yes, but tell me again so I can bask in your admiration."

Jonathan chuckled. "You are adorable, Michael Ballantyne, and so very beautiful." He turned on the shower spray and pulled Michael into the stall, holding him in his arms as the hot water cascaded over them. Jonathan slipped behind Michael and reached for the soap. He began soaping Michael's back, his strong fingers massaging first Michael's shoulders, then up and down the length of his spine.

"Mmm, that feels so wonderful," Michael murmured, giving himself up to Jonathan's ministrations. He let his head fall back onto Jonathan's shoulder and shuddered as Jonathan traced a trail of kisses over his throat. Jonathan's soapy fingers strayed over the cleft between Michael's buttocks, one finger probing and then finding its way inside his tight hole. Michael let out a long, breathy sigh as he bore down on Jonathan's finger, taking him all the way into his soft, moist heat. Jonathan encircled Michael's body with one arm, holding him close, covering his neck and shoulders with long, languorous kisses. Michael writhed against him, moaning softly as Jonathan's hand grasped his erection and pumped it with low, rhythmic strokes. Jonathan knelt behind Michael, replacing his finger with his tongue, burrowing deep inside him.

"Oh Jesus," Michael groaned, his body arching in ecstasy as he leaned back, moving his ass in slow circles around Jonathan's thrusting tongue. This blissful sensation almost proved to be too much. Michael felt his orgasm build inside him. Too soon. He wanted this, but he wanted all of Jonathan inside him— every inch of that beautiful, hard, uncut cock. As if he had intuited Michael's need, Jonathan stood slowly, his tongue sliding up the length of Michael's spine. He tightened his arms around his lover's slim torso.

"Ooh, baby." Michael wriggled inside Jonathan's arms. "What's that I feel knockin' at my door?"

Jonathan's deep chuckle vibrated on Michael's ear. "It wants in."

"Oh…"

"Don't worry." Jonathan slid the shower door open and reached for something on the vanity. He waved the foil wrapper in front of Michael. "Told you I was a Boy Scout once. I came prepared." After slipping on the latex sheath, he positioned his cock between Michael's butt cheeks and pushed slowly in. Michael bent over, supporting himself against the shower wall.

"Oh… yeah," he sighed as Jonathan filled him with one long, smooth stroke. "Oh, lover… you feel so good inside me." Once he felt Jonathan was all the way in, he stood, arching his back and leaning into Jonathan's body. He took Jonathan's hands in his and held them pressed tight against his chest. He exhaled a long sigh of happiness as he ground his hips into Jonathan's crotch. "If I could stop time right now, I would," he murmured, turning his head to kiss his lover's lips. "I want to hold you inside me forever. Feels so wonderful."

Jonathan caressed Michael's face, keeping their lips pressed together. "I love you, Michael," he said when they came up for air. He grasped Michael's cock and pumped slowly in rhythm with the movement of his hips.

Michael moaned long and low as the rush of his imminent release built inside him. "Jonathan," he gasped. "Oh, God… Jonathan." His body bucked and spasmed in the throes of ecstasy, his hands clutching at Jonathan's body even as he felt his lover's throbbing cock erupt inside him. Both men shuddered and arched in each other's arms as the intensity of their mutual orgasms rolled over them. Michael cried out while Jonathan muffled his groan of pleasure, his lips pressed to Michael's shoulder.

For a long time they stood there, locked together, Jonathan still deep inside Michael, while the shower spray enveloped them both in its steamy warmth.

CHAPTER FIFTEEN

Michael riffled through the pages of one of the books Lionel had kept under lock and key in a glass case. The book was bound in burgundy leather, and the pages were of the finest, almost fragile paper, edged with gold leaf.

"Don't think there's going to be anything about 'those who bring curses down on people' in here," he said to Jonathan, who was leafing through a tome he'd found on one of the study shelves. They had just finished dinner and decided to take their coffee into the study to make a quick sortie through some of the hundreds of books that lined the walls.

"Nothing in here either." Jonathan closed the book with a loud slap. "What we need is an inventory of the books you have here."

"Don't know where that might be," Michael muttered. "I haven't really had time to go through all this stuff." He added tartly, "A certain person I met shortly after I arrived in this fair country has been taking up most of my time in the most demanding ways."

"Oh?" Jonathan replaced the book on the shelf, then pulled Michael into his arms. "And who would that be?" He nuzzled Michael's nose. "Should I be jealous?"

"Mmm…" Michael gave in to the kiss Jonathan placed on his lips. "I could get so used to you," he murmured.

"I hope so." Jonathan's voice was husky. "I intend for you to get used to me."

A discreet knock on the study door had them standing back from one another and Jonathan picking another book from the shelf. Matthew poked his head in.

"Will there be anything else this evening, gentlemen?" he asked.

"No thanks, Matthew." Michael gave the butler a warm smile. "If we need anything, we'll just help ourselves. Tell Mrs. Mac the dinner was excellent as always. Oh... actually, there is something. Would you happen to know if there's an inventory for all the books in here?"

"Why yes, Mr. Burroughs was very particular about it," Matthew replied, walking towards the desk. "I believe he kept it in the top, right-hand drawer there. Some of the books he purchased along with the house. Dust collectors, my wife called them, but he wanted them all; wouldn't part with any of them."

Michael unlocked the top, right-hand drawer and pulled it open, drawing out a leather-bound file. "This must be it. Thanks again, Matthew."

"You're welcome, Mr. Michael. Now, if that's all, I shall retire for the evening. Goodnight, gentlemen."

"Goodnight," Michael and Jonathan chorused.

"Wow, look at this," Michael said, enthused. "Old Lionel was really particular about keeping records of what he had here—all alphabetized by author and title. Okay, let's see... Curses..."

"Look for witchcraft or warlocks," Jonathan suggested.

"Okay... yeah... two entries under warlocks: 'Warlocks, History of' and 'Warlocks in the Twentieth Century,' bay five, shelf six. Wow, he's making this really easy..."

"I'll say." Jonathan brandished the two books. "That's what I call organized."

"Okay, you take a look at those." Michael was turning back the pages of the inventory list. "There's something else I'm curious about... yeah, here it is, 'A History of Bedford Park,' bay three, shelf two." He got up from the desk and walked over to the designated bay. Pulling the book from the shelf, he said, "I'm hoping this will tell us what was here before it became the Bedford Park Estate."

"Good," Jonathan muttered, seated comfortably in a large, leather wing-back chair, and already lost in one of the warlock books. They were quiet for some time, reading while drinking their coffee, the only sound the occasional turn of a page and the ticking of the antique clock on the mantle. Then…

"Whoa, listen to this, Jonathan! Before the present estate was purchased and the grand house built in 1842, the land had been owned by the Crown, and subsequently requisitioned by Oliver Cromwell, who built a modest house for the use of himself and his officers while on furlough. After Cromwell's defeat and Charles the Second regained the throne, the land was returned to the Crown and the house destroyed." He brought the book for Jonathan to look at. "See, there's a drawing of the original house—doesn't look too modest to me."

"Their idea of modest and ours can be very different—quite plain looking though." Jonathan squinted at the artist's rendition. "I wonder where on the estate they built it."

"Matthew might know, or maybe Tom the gardener. We can ask him in the morning." Michael yawned loudly. "Anything in your books?"

"A couple of interesting things. The word 'warlock' means oath-breaker, and it's a hereditary title, generally passed from father to son. A warlock is a male witch."

"So he'd be able to throw curses about," Michael interrupted, easing himself into Jonathan's chair.

"Probably." Jonathan closed his book and slipped an arm around Michael's shoulders. "But how do you suppose we'll find a practicing warlock around here?"

"Not easily, that's for sure." Michael yawned again and laid his head on Jonathan's shoulder. "Mmm, Mrs. Mac's dinner was too filling, and that coffee's not working."

"Well, it's been a long and very full day, so seeing as how we're nice and cozy, why don't we have forty winks." Jonathan smiled as Michael's only reply was a soft snore. He closed his eyes and gave in to the feeling of drowsiness combined with well being. In a moment, he too was asleep.

In the darkness of night, the orchard had taken on a strange and sinister appearance. Overhead, the shadowy shapes of branches moved and creaked in protest, buffeted by a strong breeze that caused gooseflesh to ripple over Jonathan's bare arms.

"Where the devil is the man?" he said aloud, rubbing his cold arms impatiently. Michael would be waiting for him, wondering why he was late. Damn Bryant, the man was a menace. He should never have agreed to meet him out here even if it was to receive the money Bryant owed him.

"Just bring it to the house," he'd told him, but Bryant had begged for secrecy, not wanting anyone to know he'd been mismanaging his funds. Well, Michael knew, Lucy too, so Bryant's plea for anonymity had been pointless. Still he hadn't wanted to humiliate the man further, despite the fact that he couldn't stand the sight of him. The man was a coward, had used pitiful excuses to escape serving in the army during the war. Michael would be livid when he found out he'd met Bryant out here. Michael didn't trust Bryant either and had intimated that Bryant had made some unsavory suggestions to him.

Well, I'll take care of that little matter tonight also, he thought, shifting with impatience. A warning to keep his distance now that the debt was settled should suffice. He started as he heard a rustling and a snapping of twigs ahead of him.

"Bryant?"

"Yes, Harcourt, it's me."

"Well, let's get this over with quickly, shall we? I have other, more pressing things to do with my time."

"I'm sure you do."

Jonathan bristled at Bryant's sneering tone, then gasped with surprise as the man stepped out from the cover of the trees. He was wearing a long, dark robe—and he was not alone. He was flanked on either side by men similarly garbed in long robes. One of them produced a pistol and leveled it at Jonathan's chest.

"What the devil, Bryant? What's this all about?"

"What it's about, Harcourt, is your demise."

"Are you mad?" Jonathan took a step forward. "Murder is a hanging offence, Bryant."

"Only if the murderer is apprehended. Fortunately, I have two excellent witnesses who will swear I was in their company at the time of your…

disappearance." Bryant muttered something under his breath and the two men strode forward; one wrested Jonathan's arms behind his back, while the other delivered a vicious blow to Jonathan's forehead with the butt of his pistol. Jonathan dropped to his knees, stunned, blood dripping from the gash on his head onto the ground in front of him.

"Michael," he moaned. "Oh dear God, Michael…"

"Bring him," were the last words he heard before he blacked out.

"Michael, oh my God, Michael!"

"Jonathan, wake up." Michael gripped Jonathan's shoulder and shook him gently. "You've been dreaming, baby. It's okay, wake up."

Jonathan's eyes flew open, and he groaned as Michael's face swam in a blur in front of him. "Jesus, that was just a dream? It was so real, so *real!*" He leaned back into the chair. He was sweating; his eyes were hard, trying to focus, his mind still seething with images of dark trees and men in robes… "Christ," he muttered, running a hand through his hair. "Far too real…" He looked at Michael, his gaze softening. "Thank God, it was just a dream."

Michael kissed his cheek gently. "A bad dream. You want to tell me about it?"

Jonathan nodded. "I was outside in the orchard. Henry Bryant was there with two other men—they were wearing robes. One of them had a gun, hit me with it. After that, things went black."

"Henry Bryant," Michael murmured. "So it *was* him who killed your grandfather."

"It seems like it." Jonathan rubbed his head. "I could almost feel the blow… But there's more, Michael. I know this was a dream, but it felt like I was actually inside my grandfather's mind. I knew what he was thinking. How much he disliked Bryant, for a lot of reasons, one being he'd refused to serve during the war, and another that he was trying to get too close to you—I mean, your uncle. God, it's still so confusing at times…"

Michael gripped his arm. "You said Bryant and the other men were wearing robes. Do you think that's significant? That they might have been part of some secret cult or something?"

"It's possible."

"I wonder where they took you—I mean, your grandfather." Michael grimaced. "I know what you mean about it being confusing at times. It's hard to separate the Jonathan and Michael in the dreams from ourselves."

Jonathan gazed into Michael's eyes for a few moments before he spoke. Taking Michael's hand in his, he said softly, "I am actually beginning to believe in what you said the other day in the orchard, that we *are* them, living their lives again in the present. I know I said it wasn't logical, but then, none of this is."

Michael nodded his agreement. "I've often thought our dreams are like memories of what happened all those years ago. And then there's Jonathan's words, 'Avenge us, and set us free.' But how? Henry Bryant is dead, and most likely the other men involved are dead as well. How can we set them free? "

Jonathan shook his head. "I don't know, Michael. So much of this is still a mystery, and I doubt if the police would want to reopen the case based on our dreams of Bryant being the killer. The man is dead, they'll say, even if they believed us, which I'm sure they would not."

They were silent for a little time, finding comfort in sitting side by side in the big chair, holding one another. Jonathan was beginning to think that perhaps Michael's supposition that they were in fact the reincarnations of his grandfather and Michael's uncle was not so far-fetched after all. As hard as it was for him to accept this, it was starting to make sense. How else could they explain the dreams, or perhaps memories, that they had both experienced on opposite sides of the world? How else could they explain the almost instantaneous attraction that had flared between them and was now feeling very much like love to Jonathan? Yes, he was sure of that—he loved Michael—and if Michael loved him, then the circle had been made complete.

The lovers of the past were now the lovers of the present. Would that be enough to appease his grandfather's ghost?

His eyes were drawn to the window on the far side of the study. The curtains moved, stirred by a breeze through the open window. He blinked at the vague shape taking form. He gasped, unable to move, and beside him he felt Michael stiffen in his arms. It was as if his reflection stood by the window, but it was a sad Jonathan, lost and alone, looking out through the window across the moonlit streaked lawn towards the orchard. The apparition turned and gazed at Jonathan and Michael, a fleeting smile of sadness crossing his features—and then he was gone.

"Michael," Jonathan whispered. "Did you see him?"

"Yes… Jonathan, your grandfather. He looked so sad…"

"It's not over," Jonathan said. "And somehow I feel it won't be over until he's reunited with your uncle Michael."

"Emily, the housemaid, said something similar." Michael frowned as he remembered her words. "She said he wouldn't leave 'til things were sorted out. But how can we sort things out?"

Jonathan sighed, his face grim. "I don't know how, Michael. But somehow we have to find a way. Until then, until we can find a way to bring your uncle back to him, it won't be over."

CHAPTER SIXTEEN

Early the next morning, Michael was up, showered, and dressed before Jonathan even stirred. Michael let him sleep. He was aware of the restless night his lover had endured, most likely the aftermath of the traumatic dream and, followed by the eerie experience of seeing his grandfather's ghost in the study. Michael had hoped that their lovemaking would have calmed Jonathan's mind. It had been wonderful as always, and Jonathan had fallen asleep with his head on Michael's chest, the two securely wrapped in each other's arms. Before he left the room, Michael knelt by Jonathan's side and smoothed the tumble of hair from his forehead. He seemed less troubled, and so with a quick kiss to his lips, Michael left Jonathan to sleep a little longer.

He ran down the stairs to the kitchen and found Mrs. MacDonald and Tom Smithers at the table drinking tea.

"Good morning," he said brightly, heading for the coffee pot.

"Oh, Mr. Michael, sir, I'll make that," the housekeeper exclaimed, rising to her feet. "You're up ever so early for a Sunday morning."

"Sit, sit... I can do this," Michael told her. "I've lived on my own long enough to know how to make a pot of coffee."

"Hope you don't mind me 'avin' a cup of tea, sir," Tom mumbled.

"No, of course not. As a matter of fact, Tom, you're just the man I want to talk to this morning."

"Oh, aye?"

"Aye, I mean, yes... There used to be another house on the estate, built a long time ago and demolished by King Charles."

"Oh my," Mrs. MacDonald murmured. "Fancy that."

"I was wondering if you'd ever come across any sign of it, Tom, like the foundation buried under the soil, something like that."

Tom nodded. "Well, there were a pile of stones out there beyond the orchard, but Mr. Burroughs had 'em all removed and a rose garden put in. You haven't been out to see that yet, have you?"

Michael smiled at Tom's almost accusatory tone and shook his head. "No, I haven't, but I'd like you to show it to me this morning, if you have the time."

"Oh, 'course. Whenever you want, sir." He rose to go, tipping his cap at Michael.

"Terrific. I'll have my coffee, and then I'll come find you."

"Don't wait too long, sir. Looks like rain out there."

"Really?" Michael looked out the window. Sure enough, the sky had a dark, foreboding look. "Well, I haven't seen any of England's famous rain so far."

Mrs. MacDonald chuckled. "You'll see plenty of it before much longer. Mr. Jonathan still abed, is he?"

"Yeah, he'll be down shortly, I expect. Let him know I went exploring with Tom, will you? I think I'll take my coffee to go. Tom's right, looks like it might rain any minute."

"Take a brolly with you."

"A what?"

Mrs. MacDonald hurried to the broom closet and pulled out a large, black umbrella. "A brolly!" She poured him a mug of coffee. "Here you are."

"Oh, right, thanks, Mrs. Mac." Balancing his coffee mug in one hand, the umbrella in the other, he set off to find Tom.

The old gardener hadn't strayed too far from the house. He was staring up at the cloud-laden sky when Michael caught up with him.

"Shan't get too much done today, I fear," he said. "Looks like a right downpour and no mistake. I hope Dan gets back before it sets in."

"Your son, he's back today?"

"Aye, today. So if you hear him makin' a racket with that motorbike of his, you'll know he's back."

"Oh, okay…"

"Right then, let's hoof it over to the garden so you can maybe see what you're lookin' for."

"After you, Tom."

For an older man, Tom was fleet of foot, and Michael lost half of his coffee trying to keep up with him. They skirted the orchard, and Michael could see the lodge off to one side. He wondered if Jack Trenton was watching him and Tom. *Have to take care of that guy soon*, he thought.

"Here it be," Tom said proudly, pointing to a quite spectacular display of roses of every color and variety.

"Wow," Michael murmured. "That is beautiful, Tom. A pity it can't be seen from the house."

"The previous masters liked to sit out here on a sunny day. Said they liked the walk."

The previous masters…

Tom led him down one of the many brick pathways that crisscrossed the garden. There were arbors with benches, fountains and statuary scattered about, and at one end a stone wall set into an earthen bank covered with grass.

"It's just beautiful," Michael repeated. "I can see why they'd want to sit out here. What's that wall for at the far end?"

"That's what was left after the stones were taken away. Mr. Burroughs liked the look of it, rustic and all, he said, so we included it in the design as it were."

Part of the old house, Michael thought. *Interesting.*

A clap of thunder reverberated overhead, and several large drops of rain fell around them

"Here it comes," Tom said. "Well, I'll be off back to the cottage 'til it be over. Good morning to you, sir."

"Thanks, Tom. You've done a wonderful job here." Michael fiddled with the umbrella, just managing to get it over his head when the heavens opened, letting loose a veritable deluge of rain that battered the umbrella and sent cold rivulets down the back of Michael's neck.

"Ugh…" He took to his heels, galloping across the sodden grass as fast as he could. By the time he reached the back door to the kitchen, he was soaked through despite the brolly.

"Wow!" He laughed as he burst into the kitchen where Jonathan, wearing the robe Michael had bought for him, was sitting at the table with Matthew. "Hey, it's raining out there," he told them, while Mrs. MacDonald fussed over to him carrying a towel.

"Oh, you look like a drowned rat," she exclaimed, then added, "Oh, so sorry, Mr. Michael, not a drowned rat, I'm sure."

"I feel like a drowned rat," Michael said, taking the towel. "Look, my coffee mug's full of rainwater."

She took it from him. "I'll fetch you some more coffee, nice and hot."

"You should get out of those clothes," Jonathan said.

Matthew nodded. "You'll catch your death if you don't."

"Well, I better go upstairs first, I think." Michael winked at his housekeeper. "Unless you'd like a striptease, Mrs. Mac?"

"Ooh, you devil. Off with you." She pretended to cover her face as Michael laughed and ran from the kitchen. "Hurry back, I have your breakfast nearly ready," she called after him.

"Right-o!" Michael yelled as he dashed upstairs.

Jonathan chuckled as he sat back down at the table. "He's full of beans this morning."

"He's a good lad, is Mr. Michael," Matthew remarked. "Good for this house—it needed a spark like him after the gloom it's seen since Mr. Samuels passed. Mr. Burroughs just wasn't the same after… Could hardly raise a smile from him."

"The house has certainly seen its share of sorrow," Jonathan remarked. "First with my grandfather's disappearance…"

"Your *grandfather*?" Matthew gaped at him.

"Yes, Michael and I just found out from Miss Ballard at the library."

"She knows everything and everyone, that old lady," Mrs. MacDonald said. "I told Mr. Michael if there was anything he wanted to know, just ask her."

"But that's amazing," Matthew gasped. "First we find out that Mr. Michael's uncle was the one who committed suicide years ago, and now your grandfather's the one that disappeared." Matthew and his wife exchanged glances, then stared with startled expressions at Jonathan, who began to feel slightly uncomfortable under their scrutiny. The moment was compounded by Emily, who walked into the kitchen, took one look at Jonathan, turned pale, and gave out a sharp scream.

"Emily!" Mrs. MacDonald scolded her. "Stop that! You made me jump out of my skin."

"Oh, but I can't believe it," Emily mumbled still staring at Jonathan. "You… you look just like… just like the ghost I've seen here."

"Now stop that nonsense, Emily." Mrs. MacDonald shook her finger at the housemaid. "There's no such thing as a ghost here, is there, Matthew?"

Before Matthew could reply, Jonathan said, "I'm afraid there is. Michael and I both saw him last night in the study. It was my grandfather, Jonathan Harcourt."

"Well, I never," Matthew breathed. "So what Mr. Burroughs saw was there all along?"

"I told you so." Emily now looked defiant. "I know you didn't believe me, but I know what I saw."

"What did you see?" Michael asked, entering the kitchen. He was wearing clean sweats, his still damp hair slicked back, and looking, Jonathan thought despite the moment of tension, good enough to eat.

"The ghost, sir," Emily told him.

"Oh yes, the ghost..." Michael nodded. "Jonathan's grandfather."

"Well, you're all so very calm, I must say," Mrs. MacDonald huffed. "If I saw a bloomin' ghost, I'd faint dead away, and no mistake."

"He's a very nice ghost, Mrs. Mac," Michael said, smiling at his housekeeper. "He's just a bit sad and lost."

"I should think he is," Matthew exclaimed, "after all these years of wandering about. What do you suppose he's waiting for?"

Michael and Jonathan exchanged glances. "Uh, well, we're not quite sure about that," Jonathan said. "That's what we hope to find out."

Mrs. MacDonald looked agitated. "What? You're going to have a séance or something?"

"Ooh, I hope so," Emily squeaked. "Could my mum come, if you do? She loves a good séance, she does."

Michael laughed. "No, there's not going to be a séance. Now where's that breakfast you promised, Mrs. Mac?"

"Oh right, sorry..." The housekeeper bustled over to the stove and started banging pans about. "All this talk of ghosts has got me forgetting my duties. And you, Emily, off you go and start dusting!"

§ § § §

"I should get back home later today," Jonathan informed Michael as they strolled through the grounds, enjoying the smells of the wet grass and the clean cool air in the aftermath of the heavy rain.

"Do you have to?" Michael asked, not wanting the weekend to be over so soon.

"Well, I've run out of clean clothes to wear. I do have classes tomorrow, and I have some test papers I have to correct before then—so yes, I'm afraid I do have to go." He squeezed

Michael's hand. "But I can come back tomorrow night, if you like."

"I like." Michael smiled at him. "And somehow I'll get through the day 'til you're back."

"Yes, well, just don't go searching for tunnels or caves while I'm gone, will you?" He gave Michael a stern look. "That kind of thing we do together, agreed?"

"Agreed, oh Master," Michael kidded. "Which reminds me, Tom the gardener showed me the rose garden earlier today. There's a bit of the old house incorporated into the design. Like to see it?"

"Sounds interesting. Let's go."

The rose garden had taken a beating from the heavy rain, but the majority of the hardy blooms still stood tall and proud, and Tom was already there, pruning back the broken stems.

"Not too bad, sir," he said, thinking Michael had come to inspect the damage.

"Still looks terrific, Tom." Michael beckoned Jonathan over to the wall at the far end of the garden. "It just started to rain so I didn't get a good look at it earlier, but see, it seems original, doesn't it? Not built from stones just lying around."

"Well, I'm no expert on building." Jonathan knelt down to take a closer look. "But the mortar appears old and crumbly, so it could be an original part of the house."

Michael pushed against one of the stones. "Seems solid enough. I wonder how far under the earth the foundation goes."

"There should be some record of this in the library," Jonathan remarked. "Probably a tad more detailed than that sketch you showed me. If Oliver Cromwell had it built and it was used during the Civil War, some old records must exist somewhere."

"So, another trip to the library tomorrow. Miss Ballard's gonna be tired seeing me march in there." Michael turned a questioning gaze on his lover. "Should I tell her what we found out yesterday?"

"I think she already knows, don't you?" Jonathan took his arm and led him away from the rose garden. "If you do tell her, let her know that I'll call on her on my way over here tomorrow."

Once back in Michael's bedroom, they lost no time in getting out of their clothes and into bed. Michael knew he was going to miss Jonathan as soon as he left, and he wanted to enjoy every moment they had left of their time together. Of course, Jonathan would be back the following day, but Michael was going to miss his warm body next to him at night.

"Can you stay over tomorrow night?" he asked as he burrowed into Jonathan's arms.

"If you're a good boy," Jonathan teased him, kissing his chin. "But I'll have to be up and away at the crack of dawn. Classes start early, and the morning traffic in Cambridge around the colleges is miserable at best."

Michael stroked Jonathan's chest, running his fingertips over each nipple, smiling as he felt them harden at his touch. He kissed one, teasing it gently with his teeth, then the other, bringing small gasps of pleasure from Jonathan's lips. Jonathan's long, slender fingers tangled in Michael's hair, caressing his scalp, holding him pressed to his chest. Michael's hand strayed to the hard flesh rising from between Jonathan's thighs.

"Mmm," he sighed as he grasped the burgeoning erection, his touch bringing it to its impressive length and girth. He wove a trail of kisses from Jonathan's chest to the head of his pulsing cock. He pushed back the foreskin with his lips and ran his tongue around the swollen head, sucking up the juice that spilled from the slit. He heard Jonathan's now familiar growl of pleasure; felt warm, strong fingers caress his neck and shoulders. Jonathan's touch, his scent, his taste overwhelmed Michael's senses. He swirled his tongue over the sensitive flesh, taking it all into his mouth, licking and sucking with long, measured strokes then short, quick ones that had Jonathan's hips straining upwards. He slipped his other hand under

Jonathan's butt, his middle finger probing at his tight opening, pushing inside him, gliding through his silken heat, touching his sweet spot. Jonathan was moaning now, his hands gripping Michael's shoulders. His body tensed, then spasmed as his orgasm overtook him. Michael held him in his mouth, relishing the salty semen that flowed over his tongue, unwilling to release him until the last drop was wrung from him and his body had calmed once more. After a few moments, he eased himself up over Jonathan's body to lay his head again on Jonathan's chest and listen to the pounding of his heart.

Michael raised his head and smiled into Jonathan's eyes. "I love you," he said quietly. Jonathan's arms tightened around him, and he whispered, "I love you too. I always have." Michael found nothing strange in those added words. He understood them perfectly, for it now was clear to them both that they had loved one another through time, that their meeting was no accident, and that their lives were inexorably joined, and always would be.

CHAPTER SEVENTEEN

Michael didn't like waking up in the big bed alone. Although he had known Jonathan for only four days, it already seemed as if he had become the most important person in Michael's life. As he rolled out of bed and padded into the bathroom, his thoughts were firmly fixed on everything that had taken place over the past four days; some of it wonderful–more than wonderful, really—and some of it troubling; but all of it unforgettable. After he'd relieved himself and washed his hands and face, he pulled on his sweats and went in search of coffee.

Mrs. MacDonald must have heard him moving about upstairs, for she already had the coffee brewing when he ambled into the kitchen.

"'Morning si—I mean, Mr. Michael."

"'Morning, Mrs. Mac." He gave her a look of mock reproof at her near slip. "You can drop the Mister part any time you like. Mmm, that smells good."

"Would you like some fried bread with your coffee?"

Michael stared at her, unsure of what he'd just heard. "*Fried bread?*"

"Bread fried in bacon dripping. It goes down a treat—Matthew loves it."

Michael shuddered. "No thanks, Mrs. Mac, just the coffee." *Fried bread!* He really needed to find a gym—and a car. He couldn't be asking Matthew to drive him into town every day. "Matthew around?"

"He's outside polishing the Rolls. Looks after it like it's his own, he does."

"Hope it doesn't rain again today then."

"The forecast says no, but then, you can never be sure, can you?" She placed Michael's coffee in front of him. "Will you be going into town today?"

"Yes, I need to go to the library again, but Matthew can just drop me off and pick me up later. I'll call him when I'm ready to come home." *Home*—strange how he had so easily referred to this big house as home after just one week; and yet he did feel comfortable here, despite the ghosts and the mysteries. A lot of his feelings, of course, had to do with the fact that he had met Jonathan and they had become so close, so quickly. He wondered just how at home he would have felt if he and Jonathan hadn't met that day in the cemetery, if they had missed one another by just a few minutes. How different would all this have been? Fortunately, he didn't have to dwell on that for too long...

He looked up as Matthew came into the kitchen with his usual cheerful smile. "'Morning, Mr. Michael. Will you be going into town this morning?"

"Yes, to the library, thanks, Matthew. But you don't have to hang around. I'll call you when I'm ready to come back."

"No problem. Got a cuppa there, love?" he asked his wife.

"You enjoy your tea," Michael said, standing. "I'm going upstairs to shower. See you in a few."

Matthew frowned as he watched Michael leave. "I saw that blighter Jack Trenton this morning," he told his wife. "Out there prowling around as usual. I wish Mr. Michael would tell him to get gone. I don't like that scoundrel."

His wife sighed as she poured him his tea. "I'm sure the young sir will take care of it sooner or later. He's still feeling his way around, bless him. And all this strangeness with his uncle and Mr. Jonathan's grandfather must be a burden. I just hope they don't get in over their heads."

"Yes, well, I'm going to tell young Dan Smithers to keep an eye on that Trenton chap," Matthew said. "Dan got home late last night, so he'll be out on the grounds helping his old man. He can watch him without being too obvious like."

An hour later, when Michael strode into the library, he was disappointed to see that Miss Ballard had a line of young men and women at her counter all checking out books. Students who, no doubt, would keep her busy for some time. Instead of trying to attract her attention, he went in search of the local history section. Once he found it he hunted for any reference to Oliver Cromwell, the so-called Lord Protector of England who had Charles the First executed and who had ruled with Parliament for six years. He gave a little yelp of excitement when he found exactly what he was looking for: a reference to the house Cromwell had built as temporary headquarters for him and his officers during the Civil War. There were quite a few drawings of the house, but what gave Michael the most satisfaction was the description of an underground "escape passageway" that led from the house to the open countryside should Cromwell and his men have needed to make a quick getaway from Royalist forces.

According to the text, the passageway had been sealed after the house was destroyed—but there was no mention of the passageway being excavated or filled in. *Could it still be there?* he wondered; *and if it were, where would the entrance and exit be?* Under the part of the house that stood by the rose garden? As he stared at one of the artist's renditions of the house and the grounds surrounding it, he could figure out where the present house now stood, along with the lodge and Tom's cottage. It seemed likely to him that an underground passage would take the shortest possible route, which probably ruled out the old and present houses being linked—or did it?

Michael thought back to the time when he and Jonathan had been in the wine cellar and Jonathan had become distinctly uneasy. Something had bugged him down there, something he'd tried to brush off as of no importance. But Michael had seen the pained expression on his face and was sure a latent memory of some kind was involved. Now that they knew Henry Bryant was responsible for his grandfather's disappearance, Jonathan's dream, or vision, or *memory* of what had happened that night he'd met Bryant and his cohorts had become the most important clue as to what might have happened to Jonathan Harcourt.

What if Bryant knew of the underground passageway, had opened it up, and was using it for some kind of secret meeting? He and the men with him had been wearing robes. Robes meant something sinister in Michael's mind, and even if it was just in his highly overactive imagination, it should be checked out. There had to be a record of illegal or suspect covens or conclaves somewhere in the library, even if it was just rumors or unsuccessful investigations. Royston didn't seem the place for mysterious goings-on, but there *was* that cave with all those ancient carvings…

He looked over at the reception counter and jumped to his feet when he saw Miss Ballard finishing up with the last customer.

"Good morning, Miss Ballard."

The old lady looked up at him with a smile. "Why, Michael, you're becoming quite the regular here."

"Yes, I've been doing some research on Bedford Park— well, before it was Bedford Park."

"When it was requisitioned by Cromwell and then returned to the Crown, you mean?"

Well, of course I should have guessed she'd know all about that, he thought ruefully. *Should have asked her in the first place.*

"Right… Apparently there was an underground passageway used by Cromwell during the Civil War."

She nodded and signaled that he should follow her across the library floor. "There are more than one or two passages," she said as they walked. "The original plans for the house, the present house, took advantage of one of them, using part of it as the wine cellar. Have you been down there?"

"Yes, Jonathan and I were down there choosing some wine the other day."

"I used to hate it," she said with a shudder. "Of course it didn't help that your uncle would play all sorts of tricks on me while we'd be down there." She paused and smiled at the memory, while Michael had a vision of a young and vivacious

Lucy Ballard being teased unmercifully by his youthful uncle. He found he was smiling too.

"Ah, here we are." She pulled a book from a shelf and thumbed through it. "See, here is a very detailed map of what they unearthed during the time the house was being constructed in 1842. I expect quite a few of them were left untouched, probably considered worthless."

"Miss Ballard..." Michael took the book from her. "Have you ever heard of some kind of secret society in the area?"

"You mean like the Masons?"

"Well, perhaps more like a coven or something."

"Good Heavens, you mean like witches or warlocks?"

"Yes, exactly like that."

She shook her head. "No, I can't say I have, although I wouldn't put it past some people I've known over the years."

"Like Henry Bryant?"

"Henry?" She pursed her lips in thought. "He did mingle with some unsavory types, but I have to admit, I really don't know if he was mixed up in something like that."

"After Jonathan Harcourt disappeared, did you ever see Bryant again?"

She shuddered slightly. "Only in passing. We were never friends. Your uncle did tell me that Henry would phone him now and then."

"He did?" Michael stared at her in surprise. "Why would he do that?"

"Quite honestly, I don't think he ever gave up on the idea that one day Michael would come around and give in to his wishes." She shuddered again. "The thought of that makes me cringe."

"Bryant was a creep, huh?"

"Good looking, in a smarmy sort of way," she said. "Not at all in the same class as Jonathan and your uncle." She put a hand on Michael's arm. "Did your friend Jonathan talk to his mother the other day?"

"Yes. I think he'd rather tell you himself. He said he'd swing by the library on his way over to see me."

She smiled, her eyes glistening. "He seems like a nice young man."

"Yes," Michael agreed. "He is very nice."

"Well, I'll leave you to your research."

"Can I make a copy of the map?"

"Yes. Over there by the telephone, you'll find a copy machine." She turned to go, but Michael took her arm gently.

"I'd like you to join Jonathan and me for dinner one night soon."

"That would be lovely. I shall look forward to it."

CHAPTER EIGHTEEN

After he got back to the house, Michael had some time to spare before Jonathan arrived, so he thought he'd take a look down in the wine cellar. Miss Ballard had piqued his interest with her mention of it originally being part of one of the underground passages. After descending into its cool atmosphere, he stood looking around at the wooden shelves and racks that lined the walls, remembering how Jonathan had stared so hard at one particular wall, almost as though he had been trying to see what lay beyond.

So, what did lie beyond?

Michael took hold of the rack and tried shaking it. It was as solid as a house and didn't budge. He ducked down, pulling some bottles from their shelves, trying to see if the wall behind the rack afforded any clues.

Nothing.

He lay down on the ground, trying to see under the bottom of the rack. Still nothing. Well, he didn't think it was going to be easy, now did he? He stood up and prowled around the perimeter, looking for any gaps or fissures that might indicate *something*. He got down on his hands and knees, pushing his head as close as he could to the wall, hoping to hear something. He just wasn't sure what it was he wanted to hear or see.

"Mr. Michael, are you still down there?" At the sound of Matthew's voice coming so unexpectedly, Michael jumped up, knocking his head on one of the hard, wooden shelves.

"Ouch! God *dammit...* Yes, Matthew, I'm still here. What's up?"

"There's a gentleman here to see you. I told him to wait in the study."

"A gentleman?" Michael rubbed his head ruefully. *That hurt!* "Who is it? What's his name?"

"He wouldn't say, Mr. Michael. Said it was to be a surprise."

"Oh, it's Jonathan, right?' Michael chuckled as he climbed the steps. "He's early. Good, I want to show him something."

"No, it's not Mr. Jonathan. If it were Mr. Jonathan, I would have said 'Mr. Jonathan's here.'"

"Okay, Matthew," Michael growled. "I get the point." He gave the butler a light punch on the arm as he walked past him. "I banged my head down there when you yelled," he whined, rubbing the imaginary lump.

"Yelled? I don't recall *yelling*, Mr. Michael."

"Whatever." Michael grinned at him as he dusted off his jeans. "I'll *yell* if I need anything."

He ambled along the hall to the study, wondering who the heck could be calling on him out of the blue. *Hope it's not the tax man.* He pushed the study door open and froze. His mouth fell slightly open as he stared at the tall, blond man who stood in the centre of the study smiling at him.

"*Steve…*"

"Hey, Michael." Steve opened his arms expansively. "Surprised?"

"Dumbfounded is more like it," Michael said, not moving from the spot he seemed rooted to. "What… I mean how…?"

Steve strode forward, swept Michael into his arms, and delivered a smacking kiss to his lips that had Michael gasping for air.

"Whoa, Steve…" He pushed the taller man back. "What's that about?"

"What's that about?" Steve stared at him incredulously. "I've flown five thousand miles to see you, and that's all you can say—what's that about? Hell, I thought you'd be thrilled that I went to all this trouble to show how much I've missed you, Michael."

"Wow… yeah…" Michael cleared his throat, trying to pull himself together. *Jesus, Steve, here in the middle of all this—and Jonathan on his way.* He cast what he hoped was a surreptitious look at his watch. *Yep, definitely on his way.* "Gee, Steve, you're kinda the last person I expected to see here, after our last conversation."

"You hung up on me," Steve said in an accusatory tone. "And I couldn't let it go at that, not after all we've meant to each other."

Michael flinched. "You said I was needy and whiny, so you'll be glad to know I decided to do away with those annoying traits."

"Oh, come on, guy, you know I didn't mean that." Steve reached for him and pulled him hard against his body—the body that Michael had once considered perfect, and that now felt *bumpy.* Compared to Jonathan's sleekness, Steve seemed muscle bound and lunky. Whatever *that* meant.

Michael smothered a giggle and tugged himself free. "I think I need a drink," he muttered. "Let's have a drink and talk about this." He leaned out the study door and yelled, "Matthew!"

Almost as if he'd been waiting behind the door, Matthew appeared, wearing an urbane smile. "You yelled, sir?"

"Uh... yes... Sorry, Matthew. Would you bring us two Scotch on the rocks please?"

"At *once*, sir." They shared smirks at Matthew's show of obeisance.

"He's a bit fresh, isn't he?" Steve said, scowling at Matthew's back. "You *yelled*, sir?"

"Oh, that's just a little joke Matthew and I have, but you had to be there, and you weren't... uh, there. So, take a seat, Steve, and tell me what's been happening with you."

"Michael..." Steve ran a hand through his wavy blond hair as he sat on one of the leather wing-back chairs. "You're acting like you're not very pleased to see me. I've come a long way."

"Yes, I know it's a long way. When did you get here? Brad said you were going to write."

"I figured what I had to say would be better in person." Steve leaned forward in his seat, his expression earnest and concerned. "See, Michael, I've been doing a lot of thinking about you and me, and I admit I haven't really ever shown you just how much you mean to me. 'Course it's been difficult for me being out of town so much, but I'd like to change that if I can."

"You're planning on moving to England?"

"What? No... What I meant was, when you come back to LA we can spend more time together. Move in together even."

"Steve, I'm going to be living here for at least a year," Michael said, slightly stunned by Steve's solicitous attitude.

"Yes, that's what Brad said, but I intend to wait for you, then when you come back to LA, we can pick up where we left off."

"And where was that exactly?"

"Uh..." Steve broke off as Matthew entered the study carrying a tray with their drinks. Steve sat in stony, impatient silence as Matthew seemed to take his time, carefully laying down a napkin and swizzle stick beside each drink.

"I didn't add a twist, sir." This he said to Steve. "Would you care for one?"

"No, it's fine the way it is."

Matthew turned to Michael. "And what about you, sir?"

"No thanks, Matthew." Shielded from Steve's view by Matthew's body, Michael winked at him. Matthew slowly closed one eye, bowed, and left the room. Michael would have loved to be a fly on the kitchen wall when Matthew got back there.

Steve took a long swig of his drink, then looked around the study. "You've really done well here, Michael, haven't you?"

"Yes, I have." Michael smiled sweetly. "Impressed?"

"Very."

"But you were about to tell me about us picking up where we left off."

"Oh, well you know..." Steve took another long swig of the Scotch. "Us, the two of us making a go of it, together."

"Actually, Steve, where we left off was you on the phone telling me we should probably cool it."

And that I was needy and whiny.

Steve frowned. "I told you, I didn't mean that. I've done a lot of thinking."

"Yes, you said that."

"Michael, cut me a break here." Steve's face reddened. "I've flown five thousand miles to see you, and you're acting like you don't give a damn."

Michael's lips twisted. Oh, how he'd love to quote that famous line right now. *Frankly, my dear...* He took a deep breath. "Look, I'm sorry, Steve. I am acting like a spoiled brat. It was very nice of you to come all this way to see me. Where are you staying, by the way?"

"I was hoping I could stay here with you." He shifted uncomfortably in his chair. "But if that's *inconvenient*, I guess I can find somewhere in town."

"That would be a better idea," Michael said, nodding.

Steve gasped. "I can't believe you just said that. Michael, I have flown five thousand miles to see you, to tell you I'm sorry we had a misunderstanding on the phone, to ask you to share my life, and this is what I get—the brush-off?"

"Well, it's like this, Steve. I'm seeing someone else."

"*What?*" Steve gaped at him, his handsome face expressing petulance and disbelief. "You've only been here a week, and you're seeing someone else? What does that say about you, Michael?"

"I don't know," Michael replied coolly. "What *does* that say about me, Steve?"

"Well, for one thing, that you're not very damn loyal."

Michael sighed and began to show his annoyance. "Steve, I hate to sound like a broken record, but you are the one who last week was breaking up with me. In my book that made me single and fancy free. Now, I don't know what brought on this change of mind, although I can guess..."

Steve jumped to his feet, his fists clenched at his sides. "What the hell does that mean?"

"You must think I am so stupid, Steve." Michael stood to face him. "When we spoke on the phone last week, you were pissed at me and not very nice—until I told you about my inheritance. Suddenly, the mention of a country estate and a lot of money in the bank made you do a complete one-hundred-and-eighty degree turn back into being Mr. Nice Guy. If you think I couldn't see through that, then either you reckon I'm a total dumbass—or you are! Now, why don't you tell me the real reason you came *all this way* to see me."

Steve's mouth opened and closed several times without him saying anything. He looked thunderstruck, as if he had never considered Michael would act this way—it was patently obvious he had not. His shoulders sagged, he expelled a long, harsh breath, and for a moment Michael thought he was going to cry.

"Steve…" Despite the man's transparent attempt to con him, Michael was beginning to feel sorry for him. Something was wrong, something that Steve had thought Michael could fix. "What's wrong, Steve?"

"I'm broke," he rasped. "I borrowed on the business to buy the computer parts my clients were demanding, but now with the economy the way it is, nobody's buying anything. I can't sell the parts, and I can't pay back the loan. I spent my last eight hundred bucks coming here to see you. I thought… uh… I thought…"

"You thought that if you acted like you're still interested in me, I'd give you the money you need to get back on your feet."

Steve had the grace to look embarrassed. "Uh, well, when you put it like that, it sounds kinda worse than it is. I'm sorry. I still like you Michael, a lot."

Michael studied Steve's flushed face for so long that his ex-boyfriend shuffled his feet and looked away.

"Michael, *please…*"

Now Michael had to look away. To see Steve reduced to begging was not something he ever thought he'd witness. Not big and buff and oh-so-sure-of-himself Steve Miller. It didn't make Michael feel good, not one bit.

"How much d'you need?"

"Fifty thousand, but I'll pay it back, Michael. I swear, as soon as I can get a head start again, I'll pay you back—every penny."

The sound of a throat being quietly cleared had them both turning to stare at Jonathan, who stood framed in the doorway. "Am I interrupting?" he asked quietly.

"Oh, Jonathan, hi!" Michael exclaimed. "I didn't hear the doorbell."

"No, Matthew was his usual efficient self—saw me coming, he said."

"Jonathan, this is Steve."

The two men eyed each other with varying degrees of dislike and wariness, then Jonathan crossed the room and held out his hand. "How do you do?" Michael had never seen him so formal, stiff, and unfriendly.

Steve took the proffered hand for a cursory handshake. "Good," he said. "Yourself?"

"Fine." He gave Michael a tight smile. "I'll just go have a cuppa with Matthew and Mrs. Mac. Let me know when you're finished here." With that, he turned on his heel and left the room.

Oh boy, Michael groaned silently, *he is pissed... but at least he's not leaving.*

Steve looked grim. "*That's* the guy you're dating? Not very friendly."

"He obviously heard what we were talking about," Michael muttered.

"Well, it's not really any of his business, is it? I mean, you've only known him for a few days. How do you know he's not after your money?"

Michael sighed. "Unlike you, Steve, of course."

"Michael, I said I was sorry..."

"Yes, you did. And I'm sorry too, Steve. Sorry you're in such a bind."

"Then, you'll... you'll lend me the money?"

This really is too painful to draw out any longer, Michael thought. *Say yes, and get him out of here.* Any feelings he'd once harbored for Steve had evaporated in the half hour or so he'd been in his company. The man had a colossal nerve thinking that Michael was going to fall for all the baloney he'd spewed out when he first arrived. *Oh, Steve, what a shame.*

"Yes," he heard himself saying. "I'll lend you the money, Steve. I'll take care of it in the morning. Call me on my cell when you've found somewhere to stay tonight, and I'll meet you at my bank in Royston." He ignored the wince that crossed Steve's face. *Surely he didn't expect to be offered a bed for the night?*

"Thanks, Michael," Steve mumbled.

God, he did *expect me to offer!*

"Okay. Call me later, Steve."

Steve finally took the hint and headed for the door. Michael walked him down the steps to where a rental car was parked in front of Jonathan's blue Escort.

"Can I have a hug?" Steve asked.

Damn, he looks so beaten down. Who would have thought?

"Yes," Michael said, opening his arms. Steve hugged him to his body, pressing his face into the warmth of Michael's neck.

"Goodbye, Steve. Call me later." Michael broke the embrace and stepped back. Steve looked as if he wanted to say more—a lot more—but instead he gave Michael a watery smile and stepped into the car.

Michael walked slowly back into the house, feeling utterly drained. He went directly to the kitchen, sat at the table, and covered his face with his hands.

"Would you like another Scotch, Mr. Michael?" Matthew asked quietly.

Michael looked up at him. "No thanks, Matthew. Maybe later." He gazed across the table at Jonathan. "I'm so sorry about that. I had no idea he was coming here."

Jonathan shook his head. "You don't have to explain, Michael. What you were talking about in there is none of my business." He looked out through the window. "Would you like to go for a walk before it gets dark?"

Michael nodded. "That'd be good."

"And I'll have dinner ready for when you get back," Mrs. MacDonald said. "Matthew's already set the dining table."

"Thanks." Michael stood and followed Jonathan out the back kitchen door. The day was cooling as twilight approached, and a slight mist lingered over the lawn. They walked in silence for a few moments, and then Michael asked, "Did you stop in to see Miss Ballard?"

"Yes." Jonathan put a hand on Michael's shoulder and squeezed gently. Michael leaned in closer, happy that Jonathan didn't seem to be too upset after all about Steve's visit. "I told her what my mother had said, and that she was indeed my grandmother. She said it made her happy, and then she cried a little."

Michael slipped an arm around Jonathan's waist as they stepped inside the shelter of the orchard's trees. "I asked her to come here for dinner with us one night very soon."

"Yes, she mentioned it. That was very sweet of you, Michael."

They stopped walking and turned to face one another. Without a word, they stepped into one another's arms and kissed.

"I love you," Michael whispered, his lips trembling on Jonathan's. "I want you to know that now, more than ever."

"I love you too."

Jonathan led him to the base of the tree where Michael had dreamed of his uncle and Jonathan's grandfather making love. They sat on the ground together, arms around each other's shoulders, heads touching, the warmth of their bodies binding them together.

"So, another peculiar day for you," Jonathan said with a smile.

"*Darned* peculiar. When Matthew yelled down into the wine cellar that I had a visitor, Steve was the last person in the world I expected to find waiting for me in the study."

"He wanted money?"

"Yes."

"And? No wait, that's none of my business. What were you doing in the wine cellar?"

"It *is* your business, Jonathan." Michael kissed him on the corner of his mouth. "I don't want to have secrets from you. I'm lending him fifty thousand dollars to help him put his business back on its feet."

Jonathan whistled softly through his teeth. Then he chuckled. "I say, I'm in dire need of some help myself. How about a jolly loan of, oh, a hundred thousand?"

"Dollars or pounds?"

"No." He nuzzled Michael's nose. "Days spent with you."

"Done, with interest."

Their kiss was long and sweet. When they eventually came up for air, Jonathan asked, "So what were you doing in the wine cellar? Getting soused?"

"No, silly. Miss Ballard told me that it was part of one of the underground passageways Cromwell had dug. She showed me a map of what they found when they were building Bedford Park. I remembered you'd been uneasy when we were in the cellar the other night, so I thought I'd scope it out, see if there was a hidden door or something down there."

"And was there?"

"Well, that's when Steve showed and I had to give it up." He paused as a rustling sound in the trees behind them caught their attention. "Did you hear that?"

"Yes, probably a squirrel or something."

"A mighty big squirrel," Michael said, getting to his feet. "Somebody there?" he called out.

"I'll take a look." Jonathan jumped to his feet and strode over to where they thought the sound may have come from. Michael hurried after him, not wanting him to face some interloper on his own. "Nobody here." Jonathan studied the ground around the base of one of the taller trees. "But it looks like this spot has been disturbed recently."

"How do you know?"

"The damp leaves are lying on top of the dry ones. Weren't you a Boy Scout?"

"Uh, no. Never appealed to me," Michael admitted.

"Tsk, tsk. See what you might have learned along with the discipline?"

Michael stroked Jonathan's bottom. "Tell me later about the discipline," he said, grinning up at Jonathan.

"You are incorrigible, Michael Ballantyne." Jonathan studied the ground for a few more moments. "I suppose it could have been the gardeners coming through here earlier."

"Yeah, I guess so," Michael said, unconvinced.

Jonathan shivered slightly. "What's that saying about someone walking over your grave? I've just realized that this is where my grandfather met Henry Bryant the night he disappeared. Almost exactly on this spot. Of course, after they hit me—I mean, my grandfather—I couldn't tell where they took him."

"Do you suppose he's buried somewhere in this orchard?"

"I doubt it," Jonathan said quietly, his eyes scanning the trees ahead of them. "It's said they searched the grounds thoroughly. Surely they'd have come across a freshly dug grave."

Now it was Michael's turn to feel a shiver down his back. "God, it doesn't bear thinking about. Imagine what must have been going through his mind when he realized just what that bastard was going to do."

Jonathan put an arm around Michael, and the two men stood alone together under the suddenly still tree branches, both of them wondering just what the future held for them.

§ § § §

Jack Trenton breathed a sigh of relief when he reached the lodge. He was sweating and out of breath. That had been too close—so very nearly discovered. He'd been careless, trying to get near them to hear what they were talking about. He was sure he'd heard one of them mention the words *cellar* and *hidden door*. How would they know anything about any of that? Who could have told them about the wine cellar? Couldn't have been that old bugger Matthew or his hare-brained wife. They'd been working in the house for over thirty years and never suspected a thing. Even old Mr. Burroughs hadn't cottoned on, so there was no way these two interlopers could have found out—unless someone was helping them. Well, he'd have to be more vigilant in future. Follow the new master of the house around, see where he was going, who he was talking to...

Yes, that's what he had to do, without delay, for as each evening drew closer to the Time, he could feel the urgency build around him and inside him. He knew that if he failed to bring the two to their judgment, his punishment would be terrible—and if his father and he should come face to face in the aftermath of his failure... Well, he didn't want to think about that—ever.

CHAPTER NINETEEN

Michael couldn't quite free himself of the feeling that someone had been watching him and Jonathan in the orchard. It was an unsettling feeling, and one that grew more disquieting as night drew on and moonlit shadows lengthened across the grounds. For the first time since he had moved into Bedford Park, Michael felt unsafe. He stood by the French doors looking out, trying to see if that someone was still out there, prowling round the estate. His gut told him it was Jack Trenton, and he determined that the following day, after he'd dealt with Steve's loan, he would have words with Trenton and tell him his services were no longer required.

In other words, get the fuck off my property.

He hoped it wouldn't come to anything more than disgruntlement from Trenton, but he was quite prepared to hold his own if it got ugly.

Jonathan had been right, it had been another darned peculiar day, and he was beginning to wonder if there would ever be another non-peculiar day in his life. Brad had called earlier saying he and Miranda would be flying over to see him in ten days time, and Jonathan had invited him to his sister's home in Manchester the weekend before they arrived. Perhaps all of that would bring an air of normalcy back into his life. If only they could solve the mystery of Jonathan Harcourt's disappearance before much longer…

"You're very deep in thought." Michael smiled as Jonathan slipped his arms around him and kissed him on the neck. "Penny for them."

"Oh, just the usual thoughts I've been having ever since I got here. Plus I've been festering over who might have been out there watching us earlier."

"We don't actually know that there was someone watching us, Michael."

"I'm pretty sure there was," Michael said, hugging Jonathan's arms closer to him. He didn't say what was on his mind about Jack Trenton. He was going to handle that by himself in the morning. He turned in Jonathan's arms and kissed his lips gently. "Let's have a drink before dinner."

"Good idea, but just the one," Jonathan said, kissing him back. "I have to drive home tonight. We have an early morning call for a teacher's meeting."

"Oh, darn," Michael whined. "I thought you'd stay the night."

"Can't, I'm afraid, but tomorrow night's fine. I have Wednesday morning off, so if you like, you could come back with me and stay over at my place."

"I like that idea. It'll give Matthew and Mrs. Mac a break from us." Michael thought for a moment. "I could look for a car while you're teaching in the afternoon. I really want to get my own wheels, and I'm not crazy about driving the Rolls. A little sports car is more my style."

They moved over to the bar, and Michael poured them both a shot of Glenfiddich. "There's a car dealership quite near the University," Jonathan said, after taking an appreciative sip of his Scotch. "I could drop you off there if you like."

"Terrific." At that moment, Matthew announced that dinner was ready, so they trooped into the dining room and let him and Mrs. MacDonald fuss over them.

"I feel like I'm being spoiled every time I come here," Jonathan remarked once they were alone.

"Me too." Michael grinned at him. "But it's kinda nice, isn't it? And I think, so far, they get a kick out of having us to look after. It can't have been much fun for them when Lionel was so sick, and apparently distancing himself from all his friends."

"I wonder what this character Trenton's story is," Jonathan said suddenly.

Michael tensed, not wanting to talk about Trenton in case he slipped up about going over to the lodge in the morning. "What about him?"

"Well, you seem to be upset about the fact he's living here, yet he says Lionel hired him as security."

"I just don't like him. And he's not on the payroll, so why is he hanging around?"

"Maybe Lionel set up a trust account or something."

"Wouldn't Mr. Fortescue know about it?"

"Not necessarily," Jonathan said, helping himself to more potatoes. "It could have been a private agreement between Lionel and Trenton. But you could ask Trenton to show you the letter."

"I'll do that after I've taken care of Steve at the bank."

"No, I don't like the idea of you seeing Trenton on your own."

"Why?" Michael gave him a belligerent look. "I can take care of myself, Jonathan. Besides, the guy's not likely to get violent right here on the property, now is he?"

"You never know. If he's lying or hiding something, he could very well get angry about you questioning him."

"Okay then. I'll wait 'til you're here, and we can go over there together."

"Good." Jonathan gave him a peck on the cheek. "I'm glad you're being sensible about it."

Michael sighed. He guessed it was more *sensible* to wait and have Jonathan with him when he confronted Trenton, but he hadn't really wanted to involve Jonathan. There were some questions Michael wanted to ask the man that Jonathan might think too confrontational. But Michael was beginning to be very suspicious of Trenton and why he was there. He was sure Lionel hadn't hired him, and the letter, if it actually existed, had to be a forgery. He was even more certain that it was Trenton watching the house, and very possibly every move Michael made. But why? That was the question he wanted to ask the man, so maybe he wouldn't wait for Jonathan to go to the lodge with him.

He'd just have to suffer Jonathan's wrath when he found out.

§ § § §

The following morning, Steve was already waiting outside the bank when Michael's Rolls pulled up at the curb. Matthew hopped out and opened the door for Michael.

"Wow," Steve wasn't quite able to hide the envy in his voice. "That's some car."

"It came with the house," Michael told him. "I think I'm going to find me a smaller car."

"Well, you can certainly afford one," Steve said, trying hard not to sound snide. "What were you thinking about—a Ferrari?"

Michael laughed. "No, maybe a Jag or something sporty like that."

"Must be nice," Steve muttered under his breath.

Oh boy, Michael thought, *he's probably wishing he'd asked for more!* "Okay, let's go get you your money," he said, holding the door to the bank open for Steve.

Once again, Michael was fawned over by Bennett the bank manager. Michael found it funny. Steve's expression told him his ex was not only jealous of Michael's newfound wealth and social status, he was kicking himself for not being a part of it.

While Bennett arranged the transfer of funds to Steve's bank in LA, they sat in the waiting area in an uncomfortable silence. Finally Steve said, "I really appreciate you doing this for me, Michael."

Do you?

"No problem, Steve. Glad I could help get your business back on its feet. Let me know how it goes, won't you?"

"Mikey, I know you think badly of me right now…" Steve had a hard time getting the words out. "But I'm really sorry I wasn't more aware of how you felt about me. I'd like to make that up to you somehow."

God, where was this going? "Don't worry about that," Michael said quickly. "Just concentrate on getting your business going again. When I'm in LA I'll call you, and we can have lunch or dinner or something."

Steve looked at him morosely. "That's a year away."

"Yeah, but time flies, I'll be there before you know it."

"You'll be bringing the Englishman with you?"

"I hope so. Jonathan hasn't been to LA, just New York."

"So, it's serious with him?"

"Yes."

"But you've only known him for a few days. How can you be so sure he's the one? You and me, we'd been seeing each other for a couple of months, and we weren't ready to move in together."

"*You* weren't ready, Steve," Michael said. "Like you told me, you weren't aware of how I felt about you. But you don't have to worry about that now," he added hastily. "It's true Jonathan and I haven't known each other very long—at least not in the real world."

"What the heck does that mean?"

"If I told you you'd laugh," Michael said quietly. "So I'm not going to go there, but just let me say that Jonathan and I knew each other long before we met."

"Huh?"

Michael stood up, ending their conversation. "Here's Mr. Bennett now." He waited while Bennett handed Steve details of the transfer, then took the receipt for the funds. Hands were shaken all around, and Michael smiled politely as Bennett tried again to interest him in various investments.

"I'll be in touch, Mr. Bennett. Thanks."

Michael walked Steve to his car. "Are you going back to the States today?"

Steve's mouth did a downward dip. "Yeah, a short trip…"

"But a fruitful one," Michael said, smiling sweetly. "Have a good flight."

"Yeah, thanks again, Mikey. I'll be in touch."

With a surge of relief that Michael could feel all the way to his toes, he watched Steve drive away. Somehow he felt fairly sure that he would never see Steve, or the fifty thousand, again. With a sigh, he headed back to where Matthew was waiting.

"Where to now, Mr. Michael?"

"Home please, Matthew. I have something to take care of before lunch."

§ § § §

Steve wasn't aware that he was being followed. Even when he'd pulled into the car park outside the hotel where he'd spent the previous night, he failed to see the large man getting out of the black car behind him.

Up in his room, he hastily threw the few clothes he'd brought for his trip into his suitcase and zipped it closed. He looked round the room, making sure he'd not forgotten anything, then went into the bathroom to relieve himself. Staring at his reflection in the mirror, he wondered how he could have made his reunion with Mikey go better. He'd gotten the money he needed, but he'd hoped for more than that. Mikey had five million in the bank, plus a big estate. Steve now thought ruefully that if he'd just played his cards a little more carefully, he could have had a lot more than fifty grand. But little Mikey had found some English guy to fuck him, and he was all starry eyed with wonder—and just a bit too cocky about it.

A knock at the door interrupted his thoughts. Who the hell could that be? He marched over to the door and flung it open. He didn't even see the large fist that hit him hard in the centre of his forehead. He went down without a sound except for the thump as his body hit the floor.

With a grunt of satisfaction, Jack Trenton bent over and pulled Steve to his feet. Supporting him with one brawny arm he dragged Steve down the stairs and out the hotel door without anyone seeing them leave. Trenton opened the passenger door of his car, shoved Steve's inert body inside, and drove away, heading back to Bedford Park. Once there, he'd find out just who this man was, why he'd visited Michael Ballantyne the day before, and why they had gone to the bank today. In Trenton's mind it could mean only one thing— Michael Ballantyne was paying this man to investigate the deaths of Jonathan Harcourt and Michael Thornton.

Just like before, all those years ago when Thornton had hired a private investigator, now his nephew was pursuing the same path. Well, he, Jack Trenton, would put a stop to that. Once he found out what this man knew, he'd put the fear of death in him, send him off with so much terror in his heart that he'd never want to come near Bedford Park or contact Michael Ballantyne again. Trenton glanced at the unconscious man lolling in the seat next to him and smiled grimly. He wasn't much of a professional, wasn't carrying a gun, and he'd opened that door without any precaution whatsoever. What an idiot!

§ § § §

Michael let Matthew drive him all the way up to the house. There had been no sign of Trenton outside the lodge, but his car was there. He hadn't wanted Matthew to drop him off at the lodge, thinking it better that neither Matthew nor Mrs. MacDonald knew he was going to see the man. He knew Matthew would want to accompany him, and he really felt this would be done best by himself.

After he saw Matthew heading for the kitchen, he slipped out and walked down the long driveway toward the lodge. Taking a deep breath, he rapped on the door using the brass knocker, that sported a lion's head. For a long time there was no reply, but Michael had the strangest feeling there was someone directly on the other side of the door. Could he hear breathing? He knocked again, and this time the door swung open. Jack Trenton loomed in the doorway.

"Yes?" he all but snarled.

Michael steeled himself not to take a backward step from the man's intimidating presence. "Mr. Trenton, I'm Michael

Ballantyne, the new owner of Bedford Park. I think it's time we had a talk."

"What about?"

"About you being here on my property."

Trenton scowled. "Mr. Burroughs gave me leave to be here. Wanted security, he said."

"The solicitor who handled all Mr. Burroughs' affairs new nothing of it," Michael said evenly. "He also said you had been asked to leave but refused."

"Mr. Burroughs wrote a letter saying I was to be here."

"Can I see the letter, please?"

Trenton's scowl deepened. "Don't have it no more."

"That's convenient," Michael said with a half laugh. "Okay, Mr. Trenton, I have no further use for you on my property, so I'd appreciate it if you'd leave right away."

"Can't do that."

"Excuse me?" Michael looked up into Trenton's ruddy face. The man, though older than Michael, stood a good six inches taller and outweighed him by about fifty pounds; but Michael knew that if he backed down now, it would probably take a police order to get rid of Trenton—and that might take a long time.

"Mr. Trenton," he snapped. "You will be out of here by this afternoon. You are trespassing on my property. If you refuse to go, I will call the police. Do you understand?"

For an answer, Trenton's right hand shot out, grabbed Michael by his shirtfront and yanked him into the lodge, slamming the door behind him.

"What the fuck do you think you're doing?" Michael yelled, trying to tear himself free of the big man's grip.

Trenton backed him up against a wall. "You'll not be calling any police; you'll not be calling anyone."

Michael struggled in the man's grasp, but it was useless. Trenton was immensely strong. Michael tried to remember the best way to deal with a bigger man. He'd taken self defense classes some time back—oh yeah, get the nose. Swinging his hand upward, palm open, he caught the older man under his nose, hard. The big man grunted and stepped back. Michael then delivered what he knew rendered every man worthless—a kick to the balls. Trenton wheezed and doubled over. Michael pulled himself free and ran for the door. But Trenton wasn't so easily stopped. Snarling, he grabbed Michael and hit him hard on the jaw. Michael saw stars as he went down, only to be yanked to his feet again. There was another punch, this time to the side of his head, which laid him out cold.

Breathing heavily and holding his aching balls, Trenton stared at the man who lay at his feet. *Damn, this shouldn't have happened. Too soon, too soon—the time wasn't right. The interfering idiot had got in the way, and now he was going to have to keep him hidden 'til it was time. Another two days! But he couldn't let him go, that would ruin everything he had prepared.*

Swearing softly under his breath, Trenton fetched a rope and bound Michael's hands behind his back. He pushed back the soiled rug that covered part of the floor and pulled open the trap door he'd exposed. He hefted Michael over his shoulder, then slowly clambered down the steps, pulling the trapdoor closed behind him. His flashlight illuminated the long, narrow passageway ahead of him. Nothing for it, this is where he'd have to keep him 'til the time. Nuisance it might be, but an alternative didn't even exist. They'd come looking for him, no doubt of it, but he wouldn't be found—ever.

§ § § §

Matthew climbed the stairs and rapped softly on Michael's bedroom door. "Mr. Michael? Lunch is ready." When there was no customary cheerful reply from Michael, Matthew frowned and knocked again. "Mr. Michael, are you taking a nap?" He opened the door and peeked in. "Mr. Michael?" He stepped inside and looked around. The room was empty and the bathroom door open. "That's funny," he muttered. "He must have gone out, but I didn't see him go." He left the room, closed the door behind him, and trudged down the stairs.

His wife was setting the kitchen table when Matthew appeared in the doorway. "Young sir must have gone out," he said, scratching his head. "But I didn't see him go, did you?"

"No, but he might have just gone for a walk around the grounds before lunch."

"Now when I think about it, he did say he had to take care of something."

"Maybe see Tom about something?" his wife suggested.

"Maybe. I'll just go out and take a looksee."

"I won't serve 'til he gets back."

"Right; won't be long."

Matthew scanned the grounds as he stepped outside, but seeing no immediate sign of Michael, he walked towards the orchard where he could hear the sound of voices.

"That must be him," he muttered to himself. "Mr. Michael, you there?"

Tom and his son Dan appeared through the trees. "He's not here with us, Matthew," Tom said.

"He got lost then?" Dan asked, grinning.

"Not lost, I shouldn't think." Matthew frowned. "He said he had something to take care of before lunch, so I thought maybe he'd come out to see you."

"No, haven't seen him."

"Where the devil can he be then?"

"He likes that rose garden," Tom said. "Maybe he's wandered over there."

"I'll run over there," Dan offered. "Save your old legs, Matthew."

"Cheeky young devil—but off you go then. If he's there, just tell him lunch is ready."

"Will do." Dan set off at a brisk jog, but as he neared the rose garden, he could tell there was no one there. Just to be sure, he ran behind the stone wall at the far end where it marked the end of the property.

Matthew had a sudden feeling of unease as he saw Dan returning alone and shaking his head. "No sign of him over there."

Matthew looked towards the lodge. *Would he have gone to see Trenton by himself?* "Dan," he said grimly, "let's you and me take a walk over to the lodge. See if he went to see Trenton."

"That rum character?" Dan stared at Matthew. "What would he want with him?"

"To tell him to get gone, I suspect. He knows Trenton's not supposed to be here."

"That Jack Trenton's a bad egg," Tom said. "I'll be glad when the young master gives him the sack."

"Let's go then." Dan started off towards the lodge, Matthew at his heels. They hesitated outside the lodge door. Neither man was looking forward to speaking to Trenton. The big, burly man made no bones about the fact he had no time for the staff at Bedford Park.

"Go on then, Dan, knock."

Dan knocked, then stepped back from the door. It was immediately swung open to reveal Trenton's scowling face. "What d'you want, you two?"

"We're looking for Mr. Ballantyne." Matthew tried to peer into the darkness behind Trenton, but the man's big frame seemed to fill the whole doorway. "Is he here with you?"

Trenton's scowl deepened. "No one's here with me," he rasped. "Why would he be here?"

"We're just looking for him," Dan said mildly. "Thought he might have stopped by to have a word with you."

"Well, he didn't, and I haven't seen him all day, so bugger off and leave me be."

"With pleasure," Matthew muttered, turning away. "Miserable git," he hissed at Dan, who nodded his agreement.

"Maybe he's back at the house by now," the young gardener suggested as they walked away from the lodge.

"Wouldn't that just be my luck, traipsing all over for nothing."

But Michael wasn't at the house, and Matthew and Mrs. MacDonald exchanged worried looks as an hour passed and there was still so sign of him.

"Maybe you should call the police, Matthew."

"They won't come out looking for him when he's only been missing for an hour, Annie." He paced the kitchen, stopping to look out of the window every two seconds. "He must still be on the grounds somewhere. I'm going out again for another look."

CHAPTER TWENTY

Jonathan pulled through the gates of Bedford Park and was surprised to see Matthew, Tom, and his son, Dan, all in heated conversation in the middle of the driveway. He pulled over and rolled down his window.

"What's the powwow about?" he asked breezily.

"Oh, Mr. Jonathan, Mr. Michael's gone missing," Matthew explained, his forehead creased with worry. "We've been searching high and low for hours, and there's no sign of him."

"Have you called the police?"

"Yes, and they said they couldn't do anything 'til he's missing twenty-four hours."

"All right, let's talk about this inside. Jump in, Matthew. Have you tried calling his mobile?" he asked as Matthew climbed into the car.

"Yes, but it just goes to his answering service. We even went to ask that scoundrel Jack Trenton if he'd seen Mr. Michael, and he told us no, he hadn't seen him, and for us to bugger off."

"Nice chap." Jonathan pulled his car up in front of the house. As they got out of the car and walked into the house, he pulled out his mobile phone and punched in Michael's number. Michael's cheerful voice told him he couldn't take his call but please leave a message. "Michael, it's Jonathan. We're all worried sick. Please call me as soon as you get this message." A bit pointless he realized, but just in case...

"Michael... wake up..."

From somewhere far off it seemed, he could hear Jonathan's voice. He tried to move, but then realized he was tied to a table by thick ropes. He looked around him at the strange stone walls and ceiling of a place he did not recognize. The face of his dead lover, sadness filling his eyes, stared down at him.

"Jonathan... How... where am I?"

"They have you in the same place they took me. They found out you suspected Henry Bryant. The police officer you spoke to is a friend of Bryant's—he was with Bryant on the night they took me here."

"So, I've fallen into the same trap."

"I'm afraid so, and I am powerless to help you, Michael. Bryant and his followers have imbued themselves with an ancient power. They intend to separate us forever, in death, just as they did in life."

"No, Jonathan..." Michael struggled to free himself. *"I won't let them. Somehow I'll find a way to stop them."*

Jonathan's image began to fade from Michael's vision. *"I'm sorry, Michael. Sorry I couldn't save you. Just remember, I will always love you... always..."*

"Jonathan!"

"Mikey... Mikey... for God's sake wake up, Mikey!"

Michael groaned as he regained consciousness, his mind in turmoil from the trauma of his encounter with Jack Trenton and the dream he'd just had. His throbbing head felt as though it were being held in a vice. He was lying on his side on a stone floor, his hands tied securely behind him.

Jack Trenton... he must have carried him here after knocking him out. He pushed himself up so that he was sitting with his back against the wall. He peered into the gloom that surrounded him.

"Mikey!"

Michael gasped with shock. Sitting on the ground, his hands tied to what looked like an iron ring embedded in the wall, was—

"Steve... how on earth...?"

His ex-boyfriend's face was contorted with rage. An ugly bruise covered his forehead. "That fucking madman you've got living up there did this," he rasped. *"Kidnapped* me, asked me all kinds of fucking stupid questions. I had no idea what he was talking about, and when I told him that, he threw me down here."

Michael winced at the pain in his head. "What kind of questions?"

"Who I was working for, how much had you told me about him. All crap I hadn't a clue about. What the hell *is* this all about?"

Michael shook his head and winced again. "I don't know, Steve. I came here to tell him to leave. He dragged me inside the lodge and started to beat the crap outta me." A faint light some distance away helped him make out the shape of a long passageway to his right. Realizing his feet were not tied, he struggled into a standing position.

"What is this place anyways?" Steve whined.

"I'm guessing we're in one of the passages that had been dug under the estate hundreds of years ago during Cromwell's war against the Royalists."

"Well, thanks for the history lesson," Steve sneered. "Now how do we get out of here?"

Michael remembered that Miss Ballard had mentioned that part of a passageway had been used as the house's wine cellar. Could it be that if he walked far enough, he would find himself under the house and on the other side of the wine cellar? If he yelled loud enough, would Matthew or Mrs. MacDonald hear him? It seemed unlikely, yet it was worth a shot. What other option did they have? At some point Trenton was going to come down to check them out, and God alone knew what the cretin was capable of. That thought spurred him into action, and he set off down the dimly lit passage.

"Where are you goin'?" Steve yelled. "Mikey, don't leave me."

"I'm just going to check something out. Hopefully get someone to hear me."

"Hear you? Are you nuts? No one's going to hear you down here 'cept that madman!"

Michael ignored Steve. He stumbled down the passageway, all the while wriggling his wrists inside his bonds, trying to loosen them just enough to enable him to slip his hands free. From the length of the passage, Michael figured it had to go all the way to the house. Despite his and Steve's predicament, he found himself wondering why Cromwell would have needed such a long escape route—or had this just been some form of ruse to lead any pursuers in the wrong direction? There might be other passageways leading in all sorts of directions. Ahead Michael could see a blank wall, and he was suddenly reminded of the dream he'd had recently where he'd stumbled down a dimly lit passage looking for Jonathan. Only, if he didn't find a way out, it would be Jonathan looking for him! Hopefully.

He jumped as he heard a door slam somewhere behind him and Steve scream out a warning. *Damn*, Trenton was back. He'd be coming after him. His eyes could just about make out a recess in the wall—a door! He leaned on it with his shoulder and it creaked open. Slipping through, he closed it behind him and stood in the darkness, trying not to breathe too loudly. His heart pounded like mad as he heard footsteps approaching.

Shit, Trenton's bound to know I'm in here. He'll open the door, shine a light in my face, and it'll be all over. He braced himself for the inevitable. *If I could just get my hands free...* He backed up as the door was pushed open, and as he'd feared he was instantly blinded by a beam of light from Trenton's flashlight.

"You little fool!" Trenton barged into the room and grabbed Michael by the arm, hustling him out to the passageway. "There's no way out down here."

Michael twisted out of the man's grip and ran for the wall blocking the passageway. "Help," he yelled at the top of his voice. "Help! Anybody... help me! I'm under the house...!"

Trenton snarled something unintelligible and swung his fist at Michael's head. Michael screamed with pain but kept yelling until Trenton slapped a big hand over his mouth, then head-butted him. Michael's legs buckled under him, and he went down like a rag doll. He lay staring up at the man, unable to move, his vision blurring, his voice now no more than a whisper.

"Help me…"

From far away he heard Steve's plaintive cry, "*Mikey…*"

Jonathan jumped to his feet, startled. "Did you hear that? It sounded like someone shouting for help."

"I heard it," Matthew said, frowning. "But from where?"

Jonathan looked at the cellar door. "Am I barmy or what? It sounded like it was coming from the cellar."

"But I looked down there earlier, Mr. Jonathan. There was no sign of him, and it's not big enough to get lost in."

"Let's take another look, shall we?" Jonathan pulled the door open, switched on the light, and ran down the steps with Matthew at his heels.

"See? Nobody here, and there's nowhere to hide if he was just trying to pull our legs."

"This has been going on too long for it to be a joke, Matthew. Michael would have tired of it by now." He felt the hair on the back of his neck prickle with apprehension. *What was it about this cellar?* "Miss Ballard told Michael there were passageways under the grounds here," he said tersely. "Part of one was sealed off to build the wine cellar—which means that behind one of these walls is an old passageway."

"But how could he have got down there?"

"You said he might have been out for a walk in the grounds. What if there's a weak spot over one of the tunnels and he fell in?"

Matthew looked skeptical. "Surely Tom or Dan would have spotted that at some time or another—and if he did fall through a hole, they'd have seen it while we were searching for him."

"Yes…" Jonathan's shoulders slumped. "You're right, of course. Then how?" He frowned, thinking. "Michael said he'd brought a map of the tunnels home with him. We were going to look at it together, but his friend showed up, which put the kybosh on it. It's probably up in his room or the study. Let's find it. There might just be a clue there. You check the study, Matthew, while I run upstairs."

"Right-o!"

Jonathan took the stairs two at a time. He had a sick feeling in the pit of his stomach. This was beginning to feel like history repeating itself, except this time it was Michael who had disappeared. *God, please don't let anything bad have happened to him.* What if, just as in his grandfather's disappearance, Michael was never found? Jonathan couldn't bear to think of that just yet. Entering Michael's room, he spotted the map rolled up on one of the nightstands next to Michael's cell phone. No wonder he wasn't answering his calls.

Jonathan whistled through his teeth as he studied the photocopy. "There's a veritable warren under these grounds," he muttered. Running downstairs, he yelled for Matthew. "I found it! Let's take a look at it in the kitchen."

He spread the map out on the kitchen table with an anxious Mrs. MacDonald hovering at his side. He had to turn it round a couple of times to get his bearings on the present layout.

"This is where the present house sits," he said, pointing to the northwest corner of the map. "That would be the gates, down here." He took in a sharp breath.

"The lodge," Matthew said. "Look where that tunnel starts and finishes!"

"The lodge!" Jonathan felt a cold anger sweep through him. "That bastard said he hadn't seen Michael."

"But why on earth would he put Mr. Michael down in one of those tunnels?" Mrs. MacDonald's voice held a querulous tone. "The poor boy, down there in the dark all by himself."

"Now, now, Annie, we don't know for certain that he is down there," Matthew said, trying to placate her.

"Well, I'm bloody well going to find out," Jonathan rasped, heading for the back door. Matthew ran after him, shouting for Tom and Dan.

"What's up?" Dan asked.

"That bugger in the lodge most likely lied to us," Matthew explained as he tried to keep pace with Jonathan. "We think we heard Mr. Michael yelling for help from somewhere near the wine cellar. There are tunnels under here."

"Oh, yes that's right," Tom said. "All sealed up though."

"Not all of them, seems like…"

They caught up with Jonathan as he banged on the lodge door. "Open up, Trenton," he yelled. "Now!" But the door remained closed. "You have a key?" Jonathan asked Matthew.

"Should be one on this ring," Matthew replied, handing over the bunch of keys he always had fastened to his belt.

Jonathan tried one or two likely looking keys, and on the third he was rewarded by the sound of the latch unlocking. He pushed the door open and entered quickly, the other men behind him. He gasped as he saw the open trapdoor in front of him. Just then Trenton's head and shoulders appeared through the trap, the look on his face one of astounded disbelief.

With a roar of rage, he grabbed Jonathan's leg, trying to pull him into the trap, but Dan, moving fast, brought the trapdoor down on the man's head, knocking him back down the steps. Jonathan leaped down after him, Dan at his heels. The big man was lying sprawled out on the ground, moaning.

"Michael!" Jonathan shouted.

"Over here!"

The men peered into the gloom and could just make out Michael's form huddled in a corner.

"Jesus…" Jonathan handed Dan his mobile. "Call the police…" He hurried over to where Michael was lying, hands still tied behind his back. Jonathan seethed with rage at the sight of his lover's bruised and swollen face. "That bastard!" He hugged Michael to him as he untied his hands.

"I'm okay, I'm okay," Michael whispered. "Thank God you found me. That Trenton guy is nuts! He's got Steve too, over there."

Jonathan helped him to his feet, then threw Dan the rope that had bound Michael's wrists. "Tie the bugger up 'til the police get here. Then they can deal with him." He looked down at the dazed Trenton as Dan ran the rope round the man's wrists good and tight. "What the hell are you up to, anyway? Do you know the kind of trouble you're in?"

Trenton said nothing, not even when Dan chortled, "It's the clink for you, Jackie boy, and no mistake. We won't be seeing you for a long time."

"Fuck him," Steve whined. "Somebody untie me and get me outta this hellhole!"

Jonathan loosened the rope that had Steve tied to the wall and helped him to his feet. Without a word of thanks, Steve pushed past Jonathan and strode over to where Trenton lay, securely tied. He kicked Trenton in the ribs.

"Fucking bastard," he raged at the big man and delivered another kick to his side.

"Steve, stop that!" Michael pulled Steve away before he could kick Trenton again. "There's no need to kick him when he's down. The police are on their way. They'll deal with him."

"Look what he did to my head!" Steve fingered the bruised lump on his forehead. "What kind of craziness do you have goin' on here?"

"That we don't know," Michael told him. "I'm sorry you got mixed up in this, Steve, but I have no idea why Trenton wanted to kidnap you."

Before Michael could stop him, Steve kicked Trenton again. "Why did you come after me, you bastard?" he yelled.

Jonathan stepped between Steve and Trenton. "I suggest we leave the questioning to the police. Don't you have a plane to catch?"

Steve stared at Jonathan, his hands trembling with rage and balling into fists. For a moment Michael thought his former lover was going to punch Jonathan, and he instinctively stepped forward. But then his ex-boyfriend must have thought better of it, because he simply sputtered, "Yes... Yes, I have a plane to catch, and thank God, so I can get away from this fucking country and all of you *crazies*."

"*Steve.*" Michael glared at him. "These people saved you and me from god-knows-what, and instead of being grateful, you're acting like it's their fault. Cut it out!"

"Just get me out of here," Steve mumbled, turning away from Michael's angry look.

"Dan, why don't you drive the gentleman back to his hotel?" Jonathan handed the gardener his keys. "You can use my car." He looked at Steve, his expression one of cool dismissal. "Unless you want to stay until the police get here and make a complaint against Trenton. You will, of course, miss your plane."

"No, I don't want to do that." Steve made an effort to pull himself together. "Sorry Mikey," he muttered. Without another word, he climbed the steps back up to the lodge. Dan rolled his eyes, then reluctantly followed. Now, more than ever, Michael was convinced he'd never hear from Steve again.

§ § § §

"I know this isn't the best time to chew you out for going to see that madman alone," Jonathan said, sitting on the side of Michael's bed. He was trying for a stern expression but couldn't quite pull it off. Michael was propped against several pillows and holding a bag of ice to his bruised face. He looked extremely vulnerable at that moment.

"I hear a *but* coming," Michael said through swollen lips.

"Well, you did say you'd wait for me so we could go over there together—safety in numbers and all that."

Michael sighed and pressed the bag of ice to his left eye. "I just didn't want to get you involved. Jack Trenton was my problem, and quite honestly I never dreamed he'd go berserk the way he did. The man's a total nutcase."

"Did he say anything to you? Like why he was behaving in such a crazy manner?"

"No… he just kept muttering about it not being the right time."

"The right time for what, I wonder." Jonathan took Michael's free hand in his own. "Well, the police will probably get something out of him. The good thing is, he won't be coming back here. You won't have to worry about having to evict him from the lodge. He took care of that himself."

"But why go after Steve?" Michael still couldn't forget the tirade Steve had let loose at Trenton once the big man was safely tied up. Not that he could blame his ex for wanting to kick Trenton into the middle of next week. "Imagine him thinking Steve was a private investigator I had hired to watch him. Where the hell did he get that idea?"

Jonathan shrugged his wide shoulders. "Trenton's paranoid. I wonder what it is he's hiding from—or from whom, perhaps."

"Jonathan…" Michael gazed intently at his lover. "Somewhere in those underground passageways is the answer to your grandfather's disappearance. I had this dream while I was down there, about him—and my uncle too. I don't know quite how to explain this to you, but it was like they were trying to help me solve the mystery of their deaths. I know everyone thinks I have an overactive imagination, but I wasn't imagining what just happened, and if you and the others hadn't found me, well, I'm sure Trenton was planning something really nasty. Why else would he have gone nuts and thrown me down there?"

Jonathan squeezed Michael's hand and leaned in to gently kiss his swollen lips. "Try not to think about what might have happened. You're safe now."

"I want to go back down there," Michael said with determination.

"No, Michael." Jonathan shook his head for emphasis. "You've had enough trauma to last a long time. Dan and I will go down there and check it out in the morning."

"Fine, Dan can come too, but I'm not going to be left out."

"Michael, you've been through enough—now just relax, please, and get some sleep."

"I'll never sleep tonight. I'm too wired up."

Jonathan smiled and slipped his hands under Michael's tee-shirt. "I have the perfect remedy for that. It's guaranteed to reduce stress, and promote a feeling of well being."

"Guaranteed?"

"An unlimited guarantee." Jonathan pulled Michael's tee off, then bent to feast on both his nipples. Michael squirmed under him, the pain in his head forgotten as he gave himself up to the pleasure Jonathan's mouth was bringing him.

§ § § §

Despite the ecstatic release Jonathan had brought him, Michael could not sleep. His mind was still in turmoil from the events of the day, and from his eagerness to find out just what had taken place all those years ago, and what was hidden in the underground passageways. Quietly he slipped from the bed and pulled on the jeans he'd discarded on a nearby chair. Without turning on a light, he found a sweatshirt and pair of trainers, then tip-toed from the room. He knew Jonathan would be pissed, but he didn't want to wait until the morning to go exploring the passageways.

In the kitchen closet, he found the key marked *Lodge* and a large flashlight. After checking to make sure it was in working order, he slipped out the back door and made his way in the darkness over to the lodge. He paused outside the door, wondering if this was such a smart idea after all. The sound of the key grating in the lock sounded overly loud to his ears, and his skin grew cold with apprehension as he pushed the door open all the way and stepped inside. He shone his flashlight around the room, and his heart leaped into his mouth when he saw that the rug had been pushed back and the trapdoor raised.

His mind screamed, *Okay, time to go back and wake Jonathan,* yet he just couldn't resist inching his way over to the open trapdoor to peer down the flight of steps that led to one of the passages. He could hear the low murmur of voices, and one of them sounded familiar—*Jack Trenton*.

They'd let the bastard out already?

"Shit..." His muttered oath sounded loud in the deathly stillness of the room, and he clapped his hand over his mouth, then winced as he hit his still swollen lips. The voices suddenly ceased. Had they heard him? *Oh, shit...* But no, the low murmur started again, and Trenton didn't come bounding up the steps to beat the crap out of him. In fact, the voices seemed to be getting fainter, like the men were walking away from the steps.

Okay, time to go for broke. He put one foot on the first step, then froze as it creaked under his weight. *No way could they have heard that.* He climbed slowly down the rest of the steps. He reached the bottom step just in time to see Trenton disappear round a corner at the far end of the passage. Keeping his flashlight aimed at the ground he followed, but stopped just short of the corner in order to peek round without being seen. There was no one in sight.

Must be a door down there, he thought, sidling round the corner. But there was no sign of a door, or even a trapdoor in the stone floor. *Where the hell...?* It was as though they had vanished into thin air. He stood staring at the chalky walls, trying to see if there was any telltale crack or indentation that might mean there was an opening of some kind somewhere in the walls. He could see nothing.

Okay, time to go. He was at a dead end, and if the men should suddenly reappear, he didn't want to be quite as visible as he was now. When Jonathan woke up, Michael would confess where he'd been, and then he would call the police to ask why they had released Trenton. Jonathan would be angry, but he'd take care of that.

After Michael had climbed back up through the trapdoor, he dropped the door back into place and pulled a heavy dresser over the top, effectively trapping Trenton and whoever was down there with him. *Hah! Let's see you get out of there, Jack, old boy.*

As he locked the front door to the lodge, a hand gripped his shoulder. He jumped almost three feet into the air. "*Fuck...*"

He whirled round, ready to defend himself. "*Jonathan!* Jesus, you scared the shit outta me!"

"What the hell are you doing out here at this time of the night?" Jonathan's expression was grim and angry. "I told you we'd do this in the morning."

"I... I couldn't sleep," Michael stammered.

"Michael, after what you've been through today, this was not a good idea. Why the devil couldn't you have waited?"

Michael bristled at Jonathan's domineering attitude. "Hey, just wait a minute, Mister," he growled. "You're not the boss of me!"

"No, I'm not the boss of you, Michael," Jonathan said quietly. "What I am is someone who cares for your well being. You were beaten and traumatized earlier today, and traipsing into the night on some midnight exploration is hardly a clever thing to be doing."

Michael looked away from Jonathan's searching gaze, shuffling his feet uncomfortably. "I... I'm sorry," he mumbled. "I just had to come back here—and Jonathan, *Trenton's* down there—with someone else."

"What? That's impossible! The police said they'd hold him 'til he sees a judge."

"I *heard* him, Jonathan. I couldn't mistake that voice for anyone else's."

Jonathan pulled his mobile phone from his back pocket. "I'll call the police, have them pick him up, and whoever is in there with him."

"They can't get out," Michael told him. "I pulled a heavy piece of furniture over the trapdoor.

"Good thinking." Jonathan listened to a recorded message telling him no one could take his call at the moment. "That's strange. I thought they'd have had someone on night duty." He snapped shut his mobile. "Well, they're not going anywhere," he said, nodding at the lodge. "They'll keep until morning. Let's get you back to bed where you belong, young man." He took Michael by the arm and marched him towards the house.

"You're still mad at me, aren't you?" Michael said needlessly.

"Yes, very mad indeed."

"I'm sorry for what I said back there. It was uncalled for."

"Yes, it was."

"I should've known you were only thinking of me."

"Yes, you should."

"I'll make it up to you, I promise."

Jonathan chuckled. "That's one promise you'll not be allowed to break."

CHAPTER TWENTY-ONE

Michael looked at his watch for the tenth time since he and Jonathan had got out of bed and come downstairs for morning coffee. "Almost eight," he announced to everyone in the kitchen. "I'm calling the Abingdon police station." He punched in the number from the card one of the officers had given Jonathan when they had arrested Trenton. "Oh, yes, hi, this is Michael Ballantyne at Bedford Park. I'm calling 'cause you need to come over here and re-arrest Jack Trenton."

"I beg your pardon, sir?" the officer who'd answered said politely. "But why would we do that?"

"Because you let him go yesterday, and the first thing he did was break into the lodge on my property."

"That's impossible, sir. Jack Trenton is in custody, at least until he sees the judge later today."

"Well, I think you'd better go check and see if he's actually there," Michael said sarcastically, "because last night I heard him and someone else in those passageways under the estate. *And* I blocked their escape route by pulling a heavy piece of furniture over the trapdoor—so they're still in there!"

"Sir, I truly hate to disagree with you, but I personally took a cup of tea to Jack Trenton about a half hour ago. He's here all right, locked up good and tight."

"But... but that's impossible. I was there—I heard him talking to another man."

The police officer let out a heavy sigh. "You may have heard *someone,* sir, but it wasn't Trenton. However, I'll dispatch a car over to Bedford Park so they can take a looksee. Should be there in a few minutes, sir."

Michael looked at Jonathan and Matthew in stunned disbelief. "Trenton's at the police station, locked up good and tight, the officer said. He brought him a cup of tea a half hour ago. How the hell is that possible?"

Matthew and Jonathan exchanged glances. "You're sure it was Trenton you heard last night?" Jonathan asked quietly.

"Yes, I'm sure," Michael rasped. "I couldn't forget that damned voice—ever!"

"Maybe we should get over there," Matthew suggested. "See who it is the coppers drag out. They'll need us to let them in, anyway."

"Right." Michael pushed himself away from the table, tense and frustrated by the police officer's words. *How could it be possible that Trenton was there at the station? It just didn't make any sense.*

Jonathan put his arm around Michael's shoulders. "Chin up," he murmured. "We'll get all this straightened out once the police get here."

They didn't have long to wait. As they approached the lodge, a car pulled in through the gates, and a tall, uniformed policeman climbed out.

"'Morning officer," Matthew greeted them. "I've got the key here to let you in."

The young policeman nodded acknowledgement, then zeroed in on Michael's face. "Nasty bruises there, sir,' he said. "You've been in a fight?"

"You could say that," Michael replied tersely, looking at the officer's nametag. *P.C. Bradley.* "Jack Trenton, the man arrested yesterday did this."

"How could you not know that?" Jonathan asked. "Abingdon Police Department is hardly Waterloo Station. I would have thought an arrest for assault and holding someone against his will would have been the main topic of conversation among you chaps."

Bradley's face stiffened. "Wasn't on duty yesterday, sir." Abruptly, he turned to Matthew. "Better open up then, and let's see what's going on."

Matthew unlocked the door, and Bradley brushed past him, with Michael and Jonathan following quickly. Michael gasped in surprise. The heavy dresser he'd pulled over the trapdoor was now back in its position against the wall.

"Wait a minute," he said, his heart sinking. "I moved that dresser over the trapdoor so they couldn't get out."

"What trapdoor, sir?"

"The one under the rug," Michael fumed, pulling the rug back. "This trapdoor!" He pulled it open and stared into the darkness below. "They were down there last night. I followed them for a bit; then they disappeared."

"Who was down there, sir?"

"Jack Trenton and someone else. I don't know who the other guy was, but I know I blocked the trapdoor with that dresser."

Bradley cleared his throat noisily, and Michael had the distinct impression he was trying not to laugh. "You said they disappeared. Did you get a good look at them before they, uh... disappeared?"

"No. I didn't *see* them at all. I told you I heard them." Michael's expression reflected his frustration. "Then when I got to the end of the first passageway, they had disappeared."

"Into thin air, was it, sir?"

Michael resisted the temptation to smack the smirk off Bradley's handsome face, but Jonathan had listened to enough. "Listen, chum, you're not here to make fun of the situation. You are here to investigate a complaint made by the owner of this estate. Now, do your job or we'll make sure your superintendent knows about your lack of concern for Mr. Ballantyne's safety. If he says he heard Trenton down there, then that's what happened."

"Well, I'm sorry, sir, I'm sure." Bradley didn't sound the least bit sorry, and Michael began to wonder about the validity of the Abingdon Police Department. Bradley was way too arrogant, and he obviously didn't believe a word of Michael's story.

"Okay," Michael said, turning away from Bradley. "Thanks for coming by. Sorry we wasted your time. Have a nice day."

Bradley seemed confused by Michael's dismissal. "Well, I think I should check down there, don't you?"

"No, there's no need," Michael told him. "The police were here yesterday when I was being held by Trenton. I'm sure they took a good look around. Whoever was here last night is long gone; the fact that they moved the dresser away from the trapdoor is evidence of that. But thanks again." And with that he walked out of the lodge and headed back to the house.

Bradley stared at Matthew and Jonathan as if for help in deciding what to do next. "I didn't mean to upset the gentleman," he said lamely.

"Really?" Jonathan gave him a hard look. "You certainly gave us a different impression."

"Mr. Michael had a terrible experience yesterday," Matthew said, rattling his keys to indicate he was ready to lock up the lodge. "I think he expected you to be a little more helpful."

Bradley took the hint and walked outside. "Well, there's no evidence of what he said—the dresser wasn't on top of the trapdoor."

"You're very observant," Jonathan remarked dryly. "Thank goodness for that at least."

Bradley bristled. "Now look here, sir…"

"No, you look here, officer. I suggest you go back to the station and read the report on what happened here yesterday. Then, when you are sufficiently ashamed of the way you have acted, you might call Mr. Ballantyne and apologize for your incredibly unprofessional behavior."

Red faced, but unable to come up with a reply, Bradley turned on his heel and walked quickly to his car. Matthew and Jonathan watched as he sped out through the gates with a squeal of rubber. Matthew shook his head in disbelief, then followed Jonathan as he made for the house.

Jonathan found Michael up in his room looking despondent. "That cop had me doubting my own sanity." Michael looked helplessly at Jonathan. "If you hadn't been there with me, I might start thinking I'd dreamed the whole thing."

"But you didn't dream it, Michael. It happened just the way you said."

"Then how did they get out?"

"That I don't know." Jonathan gently rubbed the back of Michael's neck. "There must be another way out of the tunnels, most likely into the grounds somewhere." He paused, thinking. "This might explain why we couldn't find anyone that day we were in the orchard and thought someone was watching us."

"And I just bet it was Trenton," Michael said with a deal of vehemence. "I want to go to his hearing this afternoon and make sure the bastard's locked up for a while."

"You sure you want to put yourself through that?"

"You bet I'm sure—and I want to go back and check out those tunnels again. Those guys just disappeared when I was following them. There has to be some kind of hidden door or *something* down there. I just wish I knew what it was they were doing—what Trenton's up to."

"We could check out the tunnels now if you like," Jonathan said. "I'd rather we do that together. I'm going to call the college office and tell them I won't be in today, or possibly tomorrow. I also want to go with you to the courtroom when Trenton goes before the judge."

"Thanks." He leaned in to kiss Jonathan on the lips. "And thanks for backing me up when that cop tried to make me look stupid."

"He's the stupid one, but I sent him off with a flea in his ear and told him to read the report of what happened to you yesterday."

Michael hooted. "With a flea in his ear? God, you Brits have the craziest way of talking."

"Well," Jonathan chuckled, "at least I can make you laugh."

"You can do a lot more than that, baby." Michael kissed him again. "A *lot* more."

§ § § §

"Looks like rain again," Jonathan observed as they made their way back to the lodge.

"I like the rain," Michael said. "We don't get a lot of it in California. Perpetual sunshine is was we get."

"And that's bad because?"

"It's not bad, just kinda boring." He unlocked the lodge door and stepped inside. "I'm going to have this place fumigated and repainted now that Trenton's out of here," he said, looking round at the messy room. "He was a slob." A peal of thunder overhead made him jump. "Jesus, now I'm getting all jittery."

"It's no wonder," Jonathan said, prying the trapdoor open, "after what you've been through recently."

"Yeah, well," Michael chuckled to himself. "I used to have nerves of steel."

They climbed down the steps, the beams from their flashlights picking out the chalky gray walls ahead of them.

"Along there on the right is the room I tried to hide in when I heard Trenton coming back." Michael shone his flashlight onto the wooden door, then pushed it open. "I didn't have time to see what was in here."

Jonathan peered inside, raking the walls with a beam of light. "Nothing much here. Could have been used as some kind of cell, I suppose."

Michael shivered. "Probably where he was going to keep me if you hadn't shown up in the nick o' time." He pointed his flashlight at the far end of the passageway. "That's as far as I got when I started yelling."

"So the wine cellar must be behind this wall." Jonathan rapped it with his flashlight. "Feels solid enough. We're under the house now."

Michael said, "That long passage to your left is where they disappeared. I followed them to this corner, but when I looked round here, they'd gone."

"Let's take a look." As they walked the length of the tunnel, they could hear a thrumming noise overhead.

"What's that?"

They stood still, listening. "My guess is it's the rain," Jonathan said. "We must be outside the perimeter of the house again."

"Somewhere here," Michael muttered, "there must be a hidden door. I didn't have time to look properly last night, but now…" He knocked on the wall at intervals as he slowly moved toward the end of the passageway.

"I'll check this side," Jonathan said. He was about to start when he heard Michael yelp.

"Over here! It sounds hollow, right here." Michael pushed at the wall, but nothing gave, nothing opened. "Damn, it's gotta be here somewhere."

"Look! What's that?" Jonathan pointed at a small stone lying by itself at the base of the wall.

"Just a stone," Michael said, kicking at it. It didn't budge.

Jonathan stood on it, and Michael yelped again as the wall he was leaning on slid open. "Jesus—Jonathan, look at this, will you?"

They shone their flashlights into a small chamber, the walls of which were painted and carved much like the walls in the Royston cave. However, rather than being religious, they had a decidedly sinister appearance. Pentagrams and other symbols neither Michael nor Jonathan had ever seen before covered nearly every part of every wall, including the ceiling.

"What the hell…?" Michael stared at the walls around him open mouthed.

"This is amazing," Jonathan muttered. "But what on earth could it have been used for?"

"You think Oliver Cromwell was into black magic or something?"

"I wouldn't have thought so." Jonathan stepped nearer the wall to take a closer look. "He was a Puritan, and as such would have stayed away from witchcraft of any kind."

"This circle on the floor…" Michael traced the patterns with the beam from his flashlight. "What do you suppose this is?"

"Looks like a marker of some kind."

"Like something's buried under here?"

"Something—or *someone.*"

Michael gasped at the implication and locked eyes with Jonathan. "You don't think…?"

"It could account for his body never being found." Jonathan knelt by the circle, tracing the carved patterns with his fingers. "This indentation in the middle of the circle looks like something's been taken out—or something's supposed to fit into it. That map you got of these tunnels from the library, the one I used to find you. It doesn't include this chamber."

"Which means that this was dug out after Bedford Park House was built."

"Exactly, but by whom, and for what purpose?" Jonathan stood and stared around at the walls again. "I would bet that this hasn't been used for a long time, but the fact that you heard Trenton and some other man down here makes me think they intend, or intended, to use it in the near future."

"The dream I had when Trenton held me prisoner down here…" Michael shivered as he remembered. "My uncle was tied down, and he said something about falling into the same trap as your grandfather. If Henry Bryant was responsible for your grandfather's death, then it sounds like he killed my uncle too."

"In some kind of ritual, and made it look like suicide?"

"And that fits with the idea that Bryant may have been a warlock, perhaps even head of a cult, meeting here in secret."

Jonathan nodded his agreement. "A warlock's power is handed down to his son. Maybe the man Trenton was with last night is Henry Bryant's son, or grandson even."

"But what business can they have here?"

"I hate to say this Michael, but the recent dreams we've been having all point to some kind of danger." He hesitated for a moment, then said, "I have a feeling that whatever Trenton and his friend were planning, it includes us."

"So what do we do? Let the police know of our suspicions?" Michael smiled ruefully. "It's all going to sound like so much hocus-pocus to them. They won't believe us."

"They will when we show them this chamber and these weird symbols. When we go to court this afternoon, we can get the officers who'll be presenting their evidence to come back here with us." Jonathan looked down at the circular marker by his feet. "Then we can maybe find out what, or who, lies under here."

CHAPTER TWENTY-TWO

The courtroom in Abingdon was a small affair and not very busy. Michael guessed there wasn't a whole lot of crime, or at least *reported* crime in the town. Then too, the nasty change in the weather may have deterred people from turning out to watch the few larcenous residents face the music. When Michael and Jonathan entered the courtroom, Trenton was already before the judge with one of the police officers who had arrested him giving evidence. Trenton looked suitably hangdog, standing with his shoulders slumped, staring at the floor.

Michael had to admit to a feeling of surprise at seeing the man there. He had been almost sure that when they arrived they'd have found the proceedings postponed until Trenton had been found. But there he was, as large as life—so who had it been he'd heard in those passageways the night before? He watched as a young man in a business suit stood and told the judge that Trenton had never been in any trouble before; that he had mistaken Michael Ballantyne for a burglar and had only been trying to defend himself.

"That's a crock!" Every eye in the room turned to stare at Michael as he stood red-faced mad and pointed at Trenton. "That son-of-a-bitch knew exactly who I was."

The judge's hammer hit the bench so hard it echoed through the room. "Order! Who are you, sir?"

Michael strode forward, glaring at Trenton, who now did not look quite as subdued. "I am Michael Ballantyne, the owner of Bedford Park. This man was trespassing on my property, living in the lodge when he had no right to be."

"I had a letter, I told you," Trenton snarled.

"A letter you couldn't produce when I asked to see it. Instead you dragged me inside and beat the shit out of me!"

"Mr. Ballantyne, control yourself," the judge exclaimed. "Do you have witnesses to corroborate your allegations?"

"Of course I do." He turned to Jonathan who had joined him at the bench. "My friend here, Jonathan Robertson, my butler Matthew MacDonald, and the gardeners all saw me and my friend Steve Miller, who was visiting from America, tied up and held prisoner in the passageways under the lodge."

"Well…" The judge looked at Trenton and his solicitor. "This altogether changes things. I'm remanding you for trial, Mr. Trenton. Date will be set for as soon as possible. Bail is set at five hundred pounds."

"*Five hundred?*" Michael stared at the judge in dismay. "That's all? You'd be as well letting him go right now!"

"Mr. Ballantyne, you will refrain from further comment, or I will find you in contempt." The judge rose to go. "My decision stands." He slammed his hammer down again and swept out in a flurry of black robes.

Michael seethed as he watched Trenton being led away. "Look at the smirking bastard," he said from between clenched teeth. "Just don't come anywhere near my property, Trenton," he yelled at the man's back.

Jonathan took his arm and led him out of the courtroom. "Relax, Michael. At least he's going to trial."

"Yes, but he'll be out and about in no time flat." Michael was still fuming. "We'll have to be on our guard twenty-four seven."

"Let me go talk to the officers who made the arrest," Jonathan said. "Wait here, I'll be right back."

Sighing, Michael took a seat outside the courtroom. He looked up as he heard footsteps and saw Handley and another man approaching.

"Inspector Handley," he said without warmth.

Handley smiled briefly and gestured to the man by his side. "This is Police Detective Harold Anderson, Mr. Ballantyne." Anderson nodded but didn't offer to shake hands. That suited Michael just fine as he was in no mood for niceties.

"Does the law always let felons off so easily around here?" Michael asked bluntly.

Anderson frowned. "He's going to trial, isn't he?"

"If he's still around," Michael countered. "That bail amount was a joke."

"I spoke to the judge about it," Handley said stiffly. "Apparently your attitude ticked him off."

"My *attitude*? How was I supposed to react to that lying sack o' shit who attacked me and would have probably done me in if my friends hadn't found out where I was?" Michael looked angrily at the two policemen. "That guy shouldn't have been allowed bail at all. He should be behind bars until his trial."

"Well, perhaps that's how they do things in *America*," Anderson sneered. "But here, even someone like Trenton is innocent until proven guilty."

Michael stared at him with hard eyes. "Let me tell you something. I am going to hire the best attorney money can buy. I'm going to find out just who Trenton is, where he came from, and why he ever came to Bedford Park. And if I find out that he or anyone else has some kind of devious plan directed against me, I will see to it that they are put away for a long, long time. That's how we do it in *America*."

The two men looked at each other. Handley glared down at Michael, who met his stare calmly. Without a word they turned away and walked toward the courtroom entrance. Michael watched them go with a sinking feeling that he had just alienated the only men who could have helped him. *But man, they pissed me off.* Sighing, he peered at his cell phone's ID screen as it jangled in his hand.

"Hi, Brad."

"Well, don't sound so pleased to hear from your big brother."

"Sorry, it's been a rough couple of days."

"What's going on?"

"Oh, too much to go into over the phone. When are you and Miranda coming over?"

"That's what I'm calling about. I booked us a flight for next week... uh, Wednesday. Get's into Gatwick in the morning, uh... ten-thirty. How's that?"

"Great—I just wish you were here now, is all."

"Michael..." Brad's voice was filled with concern. "What's wrong? Did something happen with you and Jonathan?"

"Oh no, that couldn't be better. It's just every other fucking thing. But I'm really glad you'll be here soon. Steve was here."

"What? Is that why you're upset?"

"Not really. It was a bit of a shock, him arriving out of the blue—but he's gone now, and somehow I don't think I'll ever be hearing from him again."

"Let me guess," Brad said, sighing. "He tapped you for some money."

"You should be a detective, brother mine."

"That s.o.b. is way too easy to read. What a loser."

"Yeah, I should've listened to you sooner. A detective and a psychic." Michael chuckled ruefully. "I could use your expertise right now."

"Will you please tell me what's wrong?" Brad pleaded.

Michael looked up and saw Jonathan and a familiar looking police officer walking towards him. "There's just too much to go into right now. I'll call you later and fill you in when I have some more information. Gotta go..."

"Okay, but you take care, little brother. I love you."

"Love you too. Tell Miranda hello."

Michael stood as Jonathan and P.C. Bradley approached him. Much to Michael's surprise, Bradley extended his hand.

"I believe I owe you an apology, sir," he said as Michael shook his hand. "I took Mr. Robertson's advice and read the report on what happened to you yesterday. That, and with what your friend has just told me you discovered earlier today made me realize I was being... er, a bit *bumptious*, to say the least."

Michael smiled at the good looking police officer. "Your apology is accepted. I'm glad someone official finally believes me."

"I'd like to take a look at what you found," he said. "I'm off duty 'til later in the afternoon, but if you can give me a lift…?"

"Absolutely. Let's go; and by the way, it's Michael, and this is Jonathan. I don't think we need to stand on formality, do you?"

Bradley smiled. "The name's Arthur."

§ § § §

Trenton's visitor looked at him grimly. "You have made a muck of things, Jack. There is no way we can go ahead with what we planned until things quiet down. What the hell persuaded you to kidnap that American?"

"I was sure Ballantyne had hired him to investigate me," Trenton fumed. "I didn't know he was just a friend of his."

"You should have been more careful about Ballantyne."

"I couldn't help it," Trenton hissed. "He came barging over and telling me to get gone or he'd call the police, the interfering little squirt. I couldn't rely on you being the one he'd call. When I get out of here, I'll take care of him once and for all."

"You'll keep a low profile until I say different. Don't go near Bedford Park, d'you hear? Stay away from Ballantyne and the other one. We have to lull them into a false sense of security, then, when they least expect it, we'll get them."

"Shouldn't be too difficult. They've become inseparable, it seems."

"I've got someone keeping an eye on them. He'll report back to me regularly. Now for God's sake, Jack, stay away from them until I say different!"

"There's one thing wrong with that request." Trenton looked away from his visitor's sharp eyes. "The medallion's still at the lodge."

"*What?*"

"It's hidden away, but I didn't have time to put it back where it belongs. Once you pay my bail, I'll go over there and get it."

"I don't like the idea of you going back there. Just tell me where it is, and I'll go get it."

§ § § §

P.C. Arthur Bradley looked around at the chamber walls, an expression of mystified disbelief on his face. "What the hell can this have been used for?" he muttered as he shone his flashlight over the carved symbols.

"Has there ever been any mention of a secret cult in the area, Arthur?" Michael asked. "You know, black magic, warlocks, that kind of thing?"

Bradley shook his head. "Not that I've heard of, but I've only been on the force here three years. I came up from London. I could ask around."

"No, don't do that," Jonathan said quickly. "We'd rather you kept this quiet for the time being. Perhaps you could check out some old, archival records."

Bradley nodded. "I can do some snooping when I'm on the early shift tomorrow morning. Can't think though that there was anything like that going on around here."

"It's a little hard to imagine, I know," Jonathan agreed. "Doesn't quite fit with the air of respectability that permeates Abingdon." He looked at Michael for a moment, then back at Bradley. "Would you like to hear a rather bizarre story?"

Bradley raised an eyebrow. "As bizarre as this place?"

Michael grimaced. "Maybe even more so. Let's go back upstairs. This place gives me the creeps." He walked out of the chamber ahead of Jonathan and Bradley. The steady thrum of the rain overhead sounded louder in the passageway, and as he looked further down into the gloom beyond he could hear what sounded like water dripping. He directed his flashlight in the direction of the sound.

"Look, down there!" he exclaimed. "We've got a leak." Shining their flashlights at the source, they could see water seeping through and dripping onto the passage floor. "Why do you suppose it's happening only in this one spot?"

"That looks like wood up there," Jonathan said, jumping up to give it a push. It moved under the pressure of his hand and more water poured in. "Another trapdoor by the looks of things. Give me a boost, Arthur." The policeman cupped his hands together, and Jonathan placed one foot in them, giving himself just enough height to push the trapdoor open and peer out. "Trees," he muttered, jumping back down. "It's the orchard we're under." His eyes widened with sudden realization. "That day we thought we were being watched, Michael—whoever it was, most likely Trenton, must have used this to disappear so quickly."

"Why would Trenton be watching you?" Bradley asked as they made their way back along the passageway to the steps beneath the trapdoor.

"We're not completely sure," Jonathan told him, "but we think he might be tied in to what happened here some years ago." Once back in the lodge, they found chairs in the small kitchen and sat around the table. "Michael and I have only recently discovered that I'm related to the son of the previous owners of Bedford Park," Jonathan continued. "He was actually my grandfather, and his, uh… his best friend was Michael's uncle."

"They were gay?"

"Yes."

"Like us," Michael said, determined to get that out of the way from the start.

Arthur smiled and leaned back in his chair. "I'm in good company then."

"You too? Wow…" Michael shook his head. *Boy,* he thought, *my gaydar didn't pick that up. Never would I have thought Arthur was gay.* "Why did you leave London for this little town?"

"It's a long story, and I want to hear yours first."

For the next hour or so Arthur Bradley sat, apparently transfixed by the story Jonathan had termed bizarre.

"Just wait 'til I tell Erick about all this," he said finally.

"Erick?"

"My boyfriend. He'll never believe it."

"But you do?" Jonathan asked.

Arthur shrugged. "No reason not to. Why would you bother spinning a tale like this just to impress me? I'm a police officer. I can check out just about every aspect of your story. Your grandfather's disappearance and your uncle's suicide, Michael, are public record. Also, Henry Bryant's statement must be on record somewhere."

He paused for a moment, before adding, "But I still don't get Trenton's involvement in this."

"Okay," Michael said. "You have to take a leap of faith to believe that Jonathan and I are reincarnations of his grandfather and my uncle. If we in fact are, then why couldn't Jack Trenton be a reincarnation of, say, Henry Bryant or one of the other men who killed Jonathan Harcourt sixty years ago?"

"All right, let's say he is." Arthur drummed his fingers on the table. "Are you saying he's going to attempt to repeat what happened all those years ago?"

Michael gave an emphatic nod. "I think so. While he had me tied up down there, I heard him say it wasn't time. He said it over and over, like a mantra almost, like he was *willing* it to be 'time.' Whatever was on his mind definitely involved me—and I'm sure Jonathan also. The dreams we've told you about have become darker recently, almost like predictions."

"But why do you think you would be reincarnated only to die again in a similar fashion?" Arthur asked, perplexed. "I thought reincarnation was supposed to help humans achieve a higher station in life, a sort of journey to the betterment of the soul."

"You believe in it?" Jonathan couldn't keep the surprise out of his voice.

"Erick and I have talked about it now and then." Arthur smiled. "He's read some of the Buddhist teachings and says he likes the idea of meeting me on a higher plain of existence."

"Really? Funny, but I've never seen the logical side of it."

"And I've never given it a second thought," Michael said. "Yet here we are, the two of us, now convinced we lived before. It's crazy."

"Not so crazy, really." Arthur looked at them both intently. "What if you're here to make right the wrong that was done to the original Jonathan and Michael?" He dropped his gaze for a moment. "Um, I'm presuming that you two are lovers..."

"Yes, we are," Michael said immediately, making Jonathan smile.

"So, that makes it even better," Arthur exclaimed, as if warming to his theory. "I bet that you're here to solve the mystery of what happened all those years ago—but not only that, to find out what is keeping Jonathan and Michael apart in the afterlife!"

Jonathan groaned and shook his head. "Lord," he muttered, "all the elements I've never really believed in."

"But you can't deny that it is bloomin' amazing that you two have met," Arthur persisted. "I mean, from so far away from one another—no idea that either of you existed even." He grinned. "I can't wait to tell Erick all this. He'll be gobsmacked!"

"Is that good?" Michael asked.

Jonathan and Arthur chuckled at Michael's question. "Good, in an astounded way," Jonathan told him. "So, we have to find out what Trenton's little game is. Any ideas on that, Arthur?"

"Well, he's going to make bail, for certain. Probably already out and about." He looked at Michael as he continued. "You said Trenton seemed concerned with time."

"Yes, he said it over and over—'not the time.'"

"And having him thrown out of here has most likely put the kybosh on his plans. After seeing that room down there, it would seem the most likely place for whatever he's planning." Arthur started drumming on the table again. "I can find out where he's gone and keep an eye on him for the next few days."

"Might be good to find out who paid his bail, if he didn't himself," Jonathan suggested. "Surely he can't be the only one involved in this."

"Right, I'll check up on that too." He pushed his chair back and stood up. "I should be going. I'm on duty in a half hour, but I'll keep in touch, let you know what I find out, if anything."

"Why don't you drive Arthur back to the police station?" Michael said. "It's stopped raining, so I'll just walk back to the house and wait for you there."

"Okay." Jonathan gave Michael a quick kiss on the cheek. "I should be back in about twenty minutes. *Don't* go back down there," he added, pointing toward the trapdoor.

"I won't," Michael kissed him back. "'Bye then, Arthur. Thanks for believing our bizarre story."

"No problem. Like I said, this is all amazing, and I want to find out just what it's all about."

Michael grinned at him. "That makes three of us."

After they had gone, instead of leaving for the house, Michael snooped around the lodge, taking stock of what needed to be repaired or replaced. *Best bring Matthew down here so we can make a list...* The bedroom Trenton had used was a mess. *Typical straight guy, can't clean up after himself* was his uncharitable thought as he surveyed the dirty sheets and clothes flung on the floor. He pulled open a dresser drawer, more out of curiosity than anything else. He really didn't want to *touch* anything in there. Before he knew it, he'd opened every drawer, peering inside at the jumble of shirts, socks, and underwear.

He was just about to close the last drawer when something caught his eye—a metal chain. He pulled on it, and a large circular piece of stone slid out from under Trenton's clothes. Michael gazed at the strange, carved symbols cut into the stone, similar to the ones on the chamber walls. He suddenly remembered the circle in the middle of the chamber and what Jonathan had said.

This indentation in the middle of the circle looks like something's been taken out—or something's supposed to fit into it.

Could this be what he'd meant, this round piece of stone? Could it be the key to what was under the chamber? He shuddered as he imagined what they might find—Jonathan Harcourt's remains. Then, excited, he headed for the trapdoor.

Boy, wait 'til I show Jonathan what I found... Wait, he said don't go back down there.

Michael dithered at the edge of the rug that covered the trapdoor. He so wanted to run down those steps and find out just what this stone would do, but on the other hand he didn't want to piss Jonathan off *again*. Still, he hadn't stayed mad too long the last time. Kisses are an amazing way of mellowing him out...

Ack, what's a guy to do?

CHAPTER TWENTY-THREE

"We didn't get around to the story of why you left London for the glitter and excitement of Abingdon," Jonathan remarked as he drove Arthur back to the station.

The policeman chuckled. "It is a bit surprising, isn't it? Actually, my mum and dad live here, but I moved to London when I met Erick one wild weekend about five years ago."

"And you came back. Why?"

"Erick and I broke up, and I came home to lick my wounds, so to speak."

"Oh, I thought you and Erick were boyfriends."

"We are." Arthur laughed ruefully. "We made up about a year ago. I applied for a transfer back to London, but I'm afraid the wheels of London Metro grind exceedingly slow. So for now it's the occasional weekend when either he or I can get away. He's a freelance computer programmer, so he takes the jobs when he can, regardless of the days of the week."

"Do you really believe in reincarnation?" Jonathan asked. "Or were you just trying to humour us?"

"Oh, I'm a believer all right. 'Course, I wouldn't say it out loud among the fellows at work. I get enough funny looks as it is!"

Jonathan said, "I have to admit you'd have got one from me too before all this. It's just so hard to rationalize it, to try and have it make sense. I mean, yes, the dreams now seem to have meaning. Before I met Michael, I thought it was just a product of me feeling randy."

They laughed together, then Arthur asked, "But you said they'd turned darker."

"Yes, like they're warnings or predictions of a kind. Michael had what was almost a vision while he was being held by

Trenton. It was like he was watching something being played out."

"Like what?"

"He saw his uncle tied to some sort of table." Jonathan sighed before continuing. "My grandfather was there too, but not in corporeal form—as a ghost."

"Jesus," Arthur murmured.

"Quite." Jonathan gave him a sideways glance. "It's all still so hard for me to comprehend at times, but I can't argue with what Michael and I have both experienced, before and since we've been together."

"So when he saw his uncle and your grandfather in that vision, what does he think was actually happening?"

"His uncle realized he had fallen into some kind of trap, and Jonathan, my grandfather, said he was sorry that he couldn't save him."

"Sounds like Michael's uncle didn't hang himself after all," Arthur said. "Tied to a table—an altar maybe—ready for sacrifice?"

Jonathan shuddered. "Michael did say my grandfather mentioned an ancient power. Could it really be this bizarre? Warlocks, ancient curses, reincarnation?" He shook his head in wonder. "It's so hard for me to get my mind around this. It defies all logic." He paused as he pulled up in front of the police station. "Anyway, Arthur, thanks for your help in this."

"No problem." He pulled a card from his inside pocket. "Here's my mobile number. Let me have yours. I'll phone soon as I have anything." Jonathan recited the number, then shook Arthur's hand. "Don't worry," the young policeman said, getting out of the car. "I'll be in touch."

§ § § §

Michael swept the rug back and stared at the trapdoor imbedded in the floor. All right, Jonathan was going to be pissed when he told him he'd gone back down there, but he just had to know if this stone fit that indentation in the circle—he just had to! He stooped and pulled the trapdoor open. The sudden slam of a car door outside had him dropping the trapdoor handle like it was scalding hot.

Oops... Jonathan's back—but that's okay, 'cause now we can both go find out if this stone works.

He tried hard not to look too guilty as Jonathan appeared in the doorway. "Hi. Look what I found." He held up the round stone by its chain.

Jonathan's eyes went from the stone swinging on its chain to the pulled-back rug. His lips twitched. "What is it?" he asked, walking towards Michael.

"Some kind of stone medallion, I think. It's got some funny markings on it." Michael held it out for Jonathan to see. "I thought it might have something to do with that circular stone in the chamber floor."

"And you were just about to go down there and find out, weren't you?" He took Michael into his arms and held him for a long moment without speaking. Finally he said, "Come on then, let's see if what you've found is a part of that marker down there."

"You're not mad at me?"

"Michael, I have no right to be mad at you. You're your own man, used to making your own decisions." He kissed him gently on the cheek. "Now, let's go."

"You're mad at me," Michael said dejectedly. "I've done it again, haven't I?"

"Look…" Jonathan smiled sadly at him. "I know you're anxious to find out what all this is about, but you taking that stone medallion, or whatever it is down there, not knowing what it might do, fills me with dread. The more into this we get, the closer I feel we are to discovering something very unsavory. I told Arthur about your vision while you were being held here by Trenton, and like you, he immediately jumped to the conclusion that your uncle didn't commit suicide. If what you 'saw' was real, then it means your uncle Michael was murdered, presumably by the same people who murdered my grandfather.

The reference to an *ancient power* might even mean they were sacrificed for some reason we can't even guess at. That's why I don't want you investigating on your own." He touched Michael's face gently. "I'm not saying I would be the conquering hero in an emergency, but I'd just feel better if I was with you when things like this stone show up."

Michael leaned his head on Jonathan's shoulder. "Sorry," he mumbled. "I was being my usual foolhardy self."

"You're not foolhardy, Michael. You're adorable, and brave, and I love you—even if your can be a trifle stubborn at times." He cupped Michael's bruised face gently between his hands and kissed his lips. "Now come on, let's get cracking." He pulled open the trapdoor and started down the steps, Michael close behind, clutching the round stone in both hands.

Michael's heart pounded with excitement and not a little trepidation as they made their way along the passage leading to the chamber. What he held in his hands might just unlock a clue to the mystery surrounding Jonathan Harcourt's disappearance, and he wasn't quite sure if he really wanted to know the gory details. What Jonathan had just hinted at, that they might discover something unsavory, had him more than a little apprehensive. They entered the chamber, and he handed Jonathan the stone. He watched with bated breath as his lover knelt by the circle, carefully inserting the stone into the indentation in the centre. The stone sank all the way in and both men stared at it, waiting.

Nothing happened.

Michael let out the breath he'd been holding. "Maybe if you turned it?" he whispered, kneeling beside Jonathan.

"Right." Jonathan turned the stone to the left, then to the right, then in a full rotation. Still nothing. "Hmm…" He sat back on his haunches. "I'm not sure what I was expecting, but this wasn't it." He pulled the stone out and examined the symbols carved round the edges. "Maybe they have to line up with the carvings on the big stone. Do you see anything on both that looks similar?"

Michael leaned over the circular stone to get a better look. "This one that looks like a pyramid is repeated several times round the edge here, see? Here, here, and here." He pointed to each one.

"There's only one like that on the small stone," Jonathan said. "Let's try pointing it at each one slowly." He replaced the stone, then turned it slowly to face each pyramid shaped symbol in turn.

Nothing.

"Damn," Michael muttered, feeling a surge of disappointment. "I really thought we had something here. Oh well." He broke off as a loud bang sounded somewhere above them. He gripped Jonathan's arm. "Someone's upstairs!" Together, they bolted from the chamber and along the passageway to the steps. "Son of a bitch!" Michael stared up the trapdoor, now closed firmly in place.

Jonathan ran up the first few steps and pushed up at the trap. "It won't budge." He pounded on the door. "Hey, who's ever up there, open this door!"

"I bet it's that bastard Trenton," Michael seethed. "He probably came back, looking for the medallion."

"And he's most likely gone for reinforcements, whoever they are," Jonathan said. "We have to get out of here. He thinks he's got us trapped—he won't know we found that other exit when it was raining. Come on!" They ran along the passage, stopping for a moment to collect the stone, then continued to the far end where they had found the second trapdoor that would take them outside.

"I'll go first," Jonathan said. "Just give me a boost so I can open the door, then I'll pull you up."

"Okay." Michael cupped his hands so Jonathan could stand on them and reach the door. He pushed it open, then clung to the edge, heaving himself up and out onto the damp, leafy ground. Michael slipped the stone's chain around his neck, then reached up to grab Jonathan's hand, using his feet against the tunnel wall for leverage. When Michael was able to grab the edge, Jonathan slipped both arms under his lover's' armpits and dragged him up through the trap. They lay on the damp ground for a moment or two getting their breath back.

"Damn," Michael muttered, standing and brushing himself free of wet leaves. "Well, now we know this stone has some importance if Trenton risked coming back for it."

Jonathan pulled his mobile phone from his pocket and, after glancing at the card Arthur had given him, punched in the number. "Arthur? Listen, we just had a rather narrow escape." He explained what Michael had found and what had happened subsequently.

"We think Trenton went to alert whoever's in this with him—*what?*" He looked over at Michael. "Trenton's still in custody," he said. "So, we were right," he told Arthur. "Trenton's got help in whatever he's planning to do. We have to find out who it is, and quickly. Maybe whoever pays his bail? Okay, Arthur, keep us informed. Thanks."

He hung up and stared grimly at Michael. "So, it can't have been Trenton who was in the lodge."

"But who then?" Michael looked down at the stone still hanging from its chain round his neck. "Who else knew where this was? Someone Trenton had to have told since he's been in custody, someone who visited him in jail. Arthur should be able to find out who that was easily enough."

"Yes, he's going to check into that." He looked up at the darkening sky as several large drops of rain fell around them. "You go on up to the house. I'll just go get my car."

"Okay, I'll see you in a few."

As Michael ran up the steps to the house, the door swung open and Matthew appeared in the doorway. *He must have a built-in radar device*, Michael thought, managing to smile at the older man. "Hi, Matthew."

Matthew raised an eyebrow as he took in Michael's appearance. "Mr. Michael, you look like you've been rolling around in wet leaves."

Michael grimaced. "I was, but I wasn't having any fun." He swiped a few more leaves off himself. "I'll just run upstairs and get out of these wet clothes. Jonathan's right behind me with the car. Send him up, would you?"

"Of course. Would you care for an aperitif before dinner?"

"You bet. Soon as we come back down." He ran upstairs, discarding the stone medallion on the bed, and stripping off his damp clothes. He towel-dried his hair, then slipped on a tee shirt and a pair of lounge pants. As he combed his hair, he examined the discoloration on the side of his face and smiled ruefully at his reflection in the bathroom mirror.

Could this get any weirder? Every day seems to bring something else that's close to being unbelievable. Thank God Jonathan is here with me, or I'd think I was going out of my mind. Man, I do need that drink! He walked back into the bedroom and sat on the bed. Picking up the stone medallion, he examined it closely. "You were supposed to solve this whole mess," he told it, then tossed it back onto the comforter.

"Who were you talking to?" Jonathan asked as he entered the bedroom.

"The medallion. I think I am finally going out of my mind."

"Not allowed." Jonathan pulled his wet shirt over his head and bent to kiss Michael's cheek. "Most definitely not allowed," he murmured, his lips capturing Michael's. Michael wrapped his arms around Jonathan's damp body and pulled him down on top of himself.

"You make everything seem okay," he said, nibbling Jonathan's ear.

"Just okay?"

"I mean, the shit that's going on around us. I was just thinking that if I didn't have you here, I'd be going nuts by now."

Jonathan kissed him tenderly. "Despite all the *shit*, as you call it, I wouldn't want to change the fact I have you in my life, for anything in the world."

Michael ran his fingertips up Jonathan's spine. "Oh God, that makes two of us. I just wish we could put all this behind us and get on with our lives—our real lives."

"We will." Jonathan rolled onto his side then stood up. "I need to get out of these jeans. Do you have another pair of those sweet pajama pants I could borrow?"

"They're called *lounge* pants, and yes, I bought a bunch when I was shopping the other day." Michael sighed. "Apart from the time I've spent with you, shopping is the only sane thing I've done since I've been here. Everything else seems so... so fucking *weird*." He got up and rummaged in his dresser drawer, pulling out a pair of dark blue lounge pants. "Here, these might be a tad short, but maybe if you wore them low on your hips..."

He gasped, mesmerized once again by the sight of Jonathan's sleek, smooth body as he stripped off his damp jeans and briefs and stood there naked. Michael's lustful gaze took in every nuance of Jonathan's toned musculature, his defined torso, his hard abs...

"On second thought," Michael murmured, moving into Jonathans' arms, "never wear clothes again."

CHAPTER TWENTY-FOUR

The following day Arthur called with the news that Trenton had been released on bail, but he'd been unable to find out who'd paid it.

"Paid by a delivery boy with cash," he told Jonathan. "Didn't want a receipt, and the boy didn't have any information to give me. But I did find out that your friend Trenton was, or perhaps still is, a private investigator."

"Really? Wonder what the heck he was doing snooping around Bedford Park. What do you suppose he thought he was investigating?"

"Dunno, unless someone hired him."

"But that wouldn't give him the right to take residence in the lodge," Jonathan said. "He claimed he had a letter from Lionel Burroughs, the deceased owner, but couldn't produce it when Michael asked to see it."

"Mmm... Well, anyway, he did a bunk soon as he was let out. Shouldn't think you'll see him again."

"I hope not." Jonathan put the phone down, frowning. So, an anonymous person had bailed out Trenton, which was a reason to worry right there, even if Arthur didn't seem to think it was a problem.

"What's up?" Michael asked as he came out of the bathroom.

"That was Arthur on the phone. Trenton's been released— and apparently he's a private investigator."

Michael gaped. "What? Jeez, you just can't tell anymore, can you? Trenton a private investigator; that's the second time I've been surprised about people."

"Who was the first?"

"Arthur... Didn't get the gay vibe at all from him."

Jonathan chuckled. "There are such things as gay bobbies, you know."

"Oh, I'm sure there are; I just didn't see it in him, but he seems hot enough for his boyfriend Erick."

"Your face looks a little better today," Jonathan remarked, kissing Michael's cheek. "I propose that we forget all this mayhem we've been caught up in the last few days and drive up to Cambridge for lunch, just get away for the day. How does that grab you, sir?"

"Sounds like heaven. Can we go to your place after lunch?"

"Why on earth would you want to go there?" Jonathan asked, a teasing light in his eyes.

"You know very well why—for the view, of course."

They chuckled together, their foreheads touching, their lips tracing each other's jaw lines. "Come on then," Jonathan whispered. "Let's hit the road."

"Can we stop at the library on the way?" Michael asked as they climbed into Jonathan's car. "I'd like to thank Miss Ballard for her help, and tell her what we found in those passageways."

"Good idea. I should ask her out for lunch, get to know her better."

"I bet she'd like that."

Miss Ballard was again busy with another long line of students checking out textbooks, but she smiled and waved, indicating she'd be free in a few minutes. While Jonathan thumbed through a sports magazine, Michael browsed in the 'supernatural' section, hoping for some more information on warlocks. He looked round as he heard Jonathan call his name, and hurried over to where his lover was standing with Miss Ballard.

She looked at him with dismay. "Michael, my dear boy, what happened to your face?"

"You should see the other guy," Michael quipped.

"A fight?" she gasped.

Jonathan explained. "Jack Trenton, who's being living in the lodge uninvited, got nasty when Michael asked him to leave."

"And threw me into one of those underground tunnels I asked you about," Michael added. "You were right, there's a veritable warren down there, and we found some kind of secret chamber when we went snooping."

Miss Ballard looked at him aghast. "But this is terrible. Was he arrested?"

"Yes, and released this morning. Anyway, I'm okay really." Michael smiled reassuringly. "Jonathan's taking me up to Cambridge to get away from it all for a day or so."

"A very nice idea." Miss Ballard gestured to a small table where they could sit and talk. "I'm glad you came by today," she said when they were settled. "You asked me when last we spoke if I had heard of any secret societies or covens, and I had to admit I had not. But I was gossiping with a friend of mine the other day over a cup of tea, and mentioned it to her. Much to my surprise, she remembered some sort of rumor that went about many years ago involving Henry Bryant and some others. While she was talking, I had a vague recollection of it." She smiled an apology. "It *did* happen a long time ago."

"Henry Bryant, eh?" Jonathan looked thoughtful, and Michael knew he was thinking of the dream he'd had of his grandfather meeting Bryant in the orchard at Bedford Park. "I suppose nothing came of the rumor?"

Miss Ballard gave her head a little shake. "Amy, that's my friend, said he denied it, of course, but then he denied having anything to do with Jonathan's disappearance. He really was a wretched man. I know one shouldn't speak ill of the dead, but Henry Bryant endeared himself to no one."

"Did he ever marry?" Michael asked.

"Yes. Poor girl. It didn't last, not surprisingly."

"Did he have any children?"

"A son, but I have no idea what happened to him. His mother took him with her after the divorce. He'd be in his late fifties by now."

Jonathan and Michael exchanged glances—a *son*. Michael's skin prickled at the implication. "If Bryant actually was a warlock, it just might mean that his son, wherever he is, has some knowledge of what his father was up to."

"You don't know where Mrs. Bryant went after she left?" Jonathan asked.

"I'm afraid not." Miss Ballard looked at him apologetically. "It all happened so many years ago, and I was caught up in my grief over losing my two best friends. I didn't know Mrs. Bryant at all well, and I only heard about her leaving through the gossip mill."

"You think anyone might know?" Michael persisted. "Your friend Amy, for instance?"

"I can certainly ask her. Is this of some importance to you?"

"Well, with what's been happening recently," Jonathan said, "we're beginning to think that Lionel Burroughs was correct when he said Jonathan Harcourt haunted the house at Bedford Park." He hesitated for a moment, then said, "Actually, more than think—we've both seen it, or rather, *him.*"

"Oh, good gracious."

"Something we haven't told you, Miss Ballard," Michael said quietly, "is that Jonathan and I, for weeks now, have both had amazing dreams. Even before we met, we dreamed of one another. Now that we *have* met, the dreams have become more like visions. Jonathan had one the other night where he saw his grandfather being attacked by two men under Bryant's orders, and while I was being held in the tunnels by Trenton, I saw my uncle tied to some kind of table. The incredible part was that Jonathan Harcourt was there with him, but unable to help because he was, uh… well, a ghost."

"Oh…" Miss Ballard had turned quite pale. "But this is unbelievable. Are you saying you know for sure that Michael and Jonathan were murdered by Henry Bryant?"

"Unless we're both going loony-toons, then yes."

"And these other men," she asked Jonathan. "Could you tell who they were?"

"No, they wore cloaks and hoods, but it's unlikely I would have known them even had I seen their faces."

"That's why we asked you about covens and stuff," Michael said. "The cloaks, the chamber, the symbols we found in there all point to some kind of ritual being carried out."

Miss Ballard gasped. "You mean sacrifice?"

"In Michael's vision, my grandfather mentioned that Bryant had some kind of ancient power," Jonathan said. "We've been talking to a P.C. Bradley in Abingdon. He thinks perhaps Michael's uncle might have been tied to an altar of some kind."

"Oh, dear God."

"There's no sign of an altar in the chamber we found," Michael told her. "But then again, it didn't look like the chamber had been used recently."

Jonathan nodded. "Something occurred to me the night we saw my grandfather's ghost, and I've been thinking about it quite a bit since, especially after Michael's vision. My grandfather said something about Bryant keeping them apart— in death as well as in life. I'm thinking that somehow Bryant was able to stop Jonathan and Michael being reunited in the afterlife." He shook his head ruefully. "Something that, up until all this happened, I didn't even believe in."

Miss Ballard stared hard at Jonathan for a moment. Then she rose from the table. "I'll be right back." Michael watched her go. Then he turned to Jonathan.

"You think maybe that's what it's all about? That we've been brought together to reunite my uncle and your grandfather? You think Bryant had enough power to keep them apart?"

"I'm not sure. I'm not sure of anything anymore, Michael." Jonathan looked at him and smiled. "Well, I'm sure of how I feel about you, but all this supernatural stuff has my head in a spin. Half of me still doesn't buy it, and yet what we're learning as each day goes by tends to make my cynicism seem foolish."

"I know what you mean." Michael reached under the table to give Jonathan's thigh a surreptitious squeeze. "I never believed in witchies and goblins either. I've always maintained an open mind about ghosts—just maybe they could exist—and I'm glad I did, 'cause they do, and we have our own very special ghost." He looked up as Miss Ballard returned. He hastily withdrew his hand from Jonathan's thigh. She placed a book on the table in front of them.

"This might be of interest," she said, sitting down.

Jonathan picked it up and glanced at the title. "*Captive Souls*," he read aloud.

"I read it years ago," Miss Ballard said. "I found it quite interesting, although somewhat bizarre. Never did I think it might apply to what happened to Michael and Jonathan." She shuddered. "But it might give you some insight into what you'd be dealing with should you go further with what you obviously have in mind. I just pray that you will both be very careful."

On the way to Cambridge, Michael opened the book Miss Ballard had given them. "*Captive Souls*," he murmured. "Sounds like a romance novel instead of something supernatural." He scanned the list of chapters. "Hmm, this sounds like what we want… 'Origins of Soul Catching'" He flipped to the indicated page. "Want me to read you this?"

"Go ahead."

"'*It is thought that the first people to successfully capture and hold a departing soul in this earthly realm were Mayan priests. This mystical practice so fascinated a Spanish general by the name of Carlos Fuentes that he promised to spare the lives of the priests if they divulged their secrets to him. This they did, after which the redoubtable General Fuentes had them slaughtered. He then attempted to capture their souls.*'"

"Nice chap," Jonathan remarked.

"Tell me… '*It is not known whether the General succeeded in his first attempts, but according to his recently discovered diaries, he continued the practice on the poor residents of his estate in Alicante, Spain. He instructed his eldest son, with whom he had shared the Mayan knowledge, to secure his soul at the moment of his death. Again it is not known whether the son was successful, but somehow the secret found its way into the hands of worshippers of a demon named Aristonas, a pagan cult that*" *thrived for many years in the British Isles alongside Christianity. The cult was eventually outlawed, but it is believed that small, isolated gatherings are still quite prevalent to this day.* "

"To this day," Michael muttered, flipping to the copyright page. "First edition printed 1944. Wow, this is an old book."

"What's the date on that particular edition?" Jonathan asked.

"Uh… 1998…"

"And they didn't edit out that last part, so either the author or his heirs knew for sure that the cult still existed. Interesting!"

"Are you thinking Bryant might have been a worshipper of this Aristonas?"

"Very possibly, but the success of soul catching seems sketchy at best. According to what you just read, no one appears to have actually captured a soul—or at least they didn't own up to it if they did."

"Mmm… But here's another chapter headed 'Accounts of Successful Soul Capture.'"

"Aha! That's what we want to hear about. Read on, MacDuff."

Michael chuckled. "That's the second time you've called me that. Please tell me that's not going to be your nickname for me."

"No, of course not—actually I was considering 'Plumduff.'"

"*What*? What the heck is a plumduff?"

"It's a rather delicious English dessert, very sweet, very fruity…"

"That's enough of that," Michael growled.

Jonathan's hearty laughter was contagious. He ran his hand over Michael's thigh. "Just kidding, my love, though you are quite sweet and delicious."

"But forget the fruity, thank you," Michael said, holding Jonathan's hand in place on his thigh. "Okay, where was I before all of that."

"Successful soul catching."

"Right…" He started to read again. "'*One of the great experimenters in the supernatural was Sir Arthur Conan Doyle, the author of the famed Sherlock Holmes mysteries.*'" Michael looked at Jonathan with surprise. "I didn't know that."

"Oh yes." Jonathan nodded. "He and a friend of his kept published accounts of dabbling with ghost hunting and so on."

"Wow… anyway—'*While it is not exactly documented that Conan Doyle conducted soul capture experiments, it seems fairly likely he would have, given his interest in the life beyond.*'"

"That's a bit of a stretch," Jonathan muttered.

"'*One of the most famous documented cases was undertaken by Professor Lloyd Baker. He, and some students at Cambridge University, confirmed that they had successfully captured the soul of a deceased teacher, who had apparently given permission for the experiment prior to his death.*'"

"Well, that's a no-brainer. Couldn't do it after, now could he?"

"Be serious."

Jonathan sighed. "There you go again, being Mr. Serious. But, Cambridge University… I can certainly check that out, and see if there ever was a Professor Lloyd Baker."

"So, if it's possible to capture someone's soul," Michael murmured, "what do you do with it once you've got it? I mean, where would you keep it? Or do you just let it go at some point?"

"Very good questions, for which I have no good answers, I'm afraid." Jonathan grimaced. "Until I met you, and all that's subsequently happened, I didn't have a clue about any of this. Never gave it two seconds thought. Perhaps the book will explain that part to us, later…" He pulled up outside *The Hand in Hand* pub. "Right now, let's enjoy our lunch."

"Are you going to kiss me again in there?' Michael teased.

Jonathan grinned at him. "I'm certain everyone will expect it."

The *Hand in Hand* was just as welcoming as Michael remembered, but he found he couldn't quite relax despite the pint of excellent ale Jonathan bought him, along with a delicious concoction of sausages and mashed potatoes covered in thick gravy.

"I really do need to find a gym," Michael complained, tucking into the mash.

"You can use mine this afternoon if you like." Jonathan squinted at Michael "You all right? You look a little tense."

"I'm okay... Just a bit antsy since we seem to be getting closer to finding out what happened to the *other* Jonathan and Michael. I'm anxious to put this to rest—put *them* to rest, if only we can. I dreamed about them again last night."

"Just for a change," Jonathan said with a smile.

"Yeah, really; but this time it was different. I didn't feel involved in the dream. It was more like I was the onlooker. They were walking through the orchard, hand in hand, smiling at one another. They were so in love, Jonathan. Every time I think about what happened to them, I'd like to kill Henry Bryant, if he were still alive."

"Right. Like, 'I say, get up out of your grave, you blighter, so I can kill you.'"

"Be serious."

"*Michael.*"

"I know, I know. I'm being a pain. It's just that... jeez, I don't know what's wrong with me today. I'm uptight, I guess, about everything that's been happening."

Jonathan took Michael's hand and kissed his palm. "I think you need some of Doctor Jonathan's expert care." He winked at Michael. "My flat has a lovely view, you know."

Michael leaned forward and kissed Jonathan's lips. "From where I'm sitting, there is no lovelier view," he said, his voice husky with emotion.

"Flattery will get you everywhere, my love. Come on, let's go. There's a view waiting to be admired."

CHAPTER TWENTY-FIVE

Looking out the window of Jonathan's flat at the spires of Cambridge, Michael said, "Last time I was here you crept up behind me and kissed the back of my neck, then you stripped me nekkid right in front of this window."

"And I'll do it all again if you don't get your arse into the bedroom," Jonathan chuckled.

"Ah, the romance of it…" Michael turned away from the window and walked slowly to where his lover stood, unbuttoning his shirt and grinning at him. "Last time, you seduced me with a tongue of silver, with words that left me breathless and completely enthralled by your eloquence. Now it's 'get your arse into the bedroom.'" He sighed for dramatic effect, then yelped as Jonathan grabbed him and hoisted him over his shoulder in a fireman's lift. "Bully!" Michael cried through his laughter.

Jonathan threw him down onto the bed and climbed on top of him, tickling him unmercifully. "You are far too serious today, Michael Ballantyne. You need to lighten up, be the bubbly, adorable elf I met a week ago."

"Elf?" Michael squeaked between gales of laughter. "Argh! Stop already! You're killing me.'

"You'll stop being all morose?"

"Yes, yes… It's kinda hard to be morose when you're being tickled to death."

Jonathan lay over Michael, kissing his lips, his jaw, his neck. "Mmm, delicious…"

Michael wrapped his arms around his lover and sighed happily. "Elf, eh? Suppose that's better than a gnome."

"Much better." Jonathan slipped his hands under Michael's T-shirt and caressed his warm flesh. "So smooth," he murmured. Michael raised his arms so Jonathan could pull the shirt off him. They fumbled with each other's belt buckles, pulling them free, unzipping each other's jeans, sliding them over their hips then throwing them to one side. Michael gazed up into Jonathan's face and was enveloped in a sudden surge of emotion; desire and lust and need and love all bound up into one blazing sensation that had him reaching for Jonathan and crushing him to his body, wrapping his arms and legs around him, binding their bodies together.

"God, but I love you, Jonathan," Michael whispered, his lips on his lover's ear. "Love you with all my heart and soul." He rolled Jonathan onto his back, covering his chest with kisses, lingering over both nipples, laving them with his tongue, teasing them with his teeth. He kissed his way over Jonathan's hard torso to his cock, taking the head between his lips, then sliding down its length with one long, gliding movement that had Jonathan writhing under him, moaning with ecstasy. Michael's teeth closed around the base of Jonathan's erection, nibbling gently at the hard flesh. He backed up little by little, his tongue swirling round and round the hot, rigid length until he reached the head. Gripping Jonathan's cock at the base, he gulped at the precum oozing from the slit, then licked it from base to tip in long, pleasure-filled strokes.

Releasing Jonathan from his mouth, he sat astride his hips, pushing the head of his lover's throbbing erection into the cleft between his buttocks.

"Wait," Jonathan whispered, scarcely able to speak. He reached behind him and grabbed a condom and lube, handing the condom to Michael. "Put it on me." He watched through lust filled eyes as Michael stretched the latex sheath over his pulsing flesh. Then he hoisted Michael forward and slipped his lube-coated fingers into Michael's opening. Michael smiled as he eased himself down onto the length of Jonathan's hard shaft. Their eyes locked on one another; their bodies began to rock together, gently at first, then as passion and sensation took over with a fervor that had them both moaning out loud.

"Oh yes, Jonathan… feels wonderful. Fuck me hard."

Jonathan thrust upward again and again, pounding Michael's ass relentlessly. Michael leaned back, supporting himself with his hands flat on the mattress while he moved rhythmically up and down on the hard length of Jonathan's cock. Michael's eyes rolled back in his head, the pressure on his prostate bringing him tiny electric shocks of pleasure. He felt his erection being taken into Jonathan's warm hand, and at the same time his orgasm churned in his balls. It was too good to resist, and as he thrust through Jonathan's fist, he climaxed with a joyful shout, splattering cum all over Jonathan's chest and face. Jonathan grasped Michael's hips, thrusting hard and fast. His body stiffened between Michael's thighs, and a guttural cry was torn from his lips as he came, his body rearing up, his arms enfolding Michael in an embrace born of both passion and fulfillment. The men clung to one another until their breathing returned to normal. Then Jonathan fell back on the bed, taking Michael with him, holding him pressed tight against him, his lips finding Michael's in a searing kiss that threatened to leave them breathless again.

Michael woke from his doze and stretched like a contented cat. Beside him, Jonathan slept on, his deep breathing telling Michael he'd be out for some time. Michael rose from the bed and threw on his jeans and T-shirt, then ambled into the living room. He headed for the kitchen for a glass of water. *All that lovin' makes a man thirsty*, he thought, smiling. After getting his water, he walked over to the table where he'd left the copy of *Captive Souls*.

Need to know more about this... He sat on the couch and took a long swig of water, then settled back to read. Turning the page from where he'd last read, his eyes widened with shock as he stared at the black and white illustration in front of him.

He jumped to his feet and hurried back into the bedroom. "Jonathan, wake up! You won't believe this!"

Jonathan opened one eye, grimaced at Michael's agitation, and sat up. "What is it?" he asked, rubbing the sleep from his eyes.

"Look at this drawing."

Jonathan took the book from Michael and stared at the picture. "My God," he whispered. "The medallion…"

"Yes." Michael sat on the bed. "And see what it's called."

"The Key of Aristonas."

"Right—a key. We were on the right track earlier, so why wouldn't it open the stone circle? What do you suppose we were doing wrong?"

"Nothing. Look at what it says here. '*The key can only be used in the presence of the chosen Trinity, and when the words are spoken three times.*'"

"What words?"

"It doesn't say." Jonathan looked a Michael with concern. "A chosen Trinity. Why does that sound really ominous? If Trenton is involved in this, then he has to have two others to help him do whatever the hell it is he's up to."

"Jonathan, in your vision of your grandfather in the orchard, you said there were two other guys with Bryant."

"Right, wearing robes in preparation for some kind of ritual, using the ancient power he mentioned in your vision."

"But they didn't capture your grandfather's soul," Michael said.

"No, but I bet they took your Uncle Michael's soul to stop them from being reunited in death. Somewhere, your uncle's soul is being held captive."

Michael shuddered. "Under that stone circle?"

"That would be my guess."

"And the medallion can open it. If we only knew the words…"

"But we're not part of the chosen Trinity," Jonathan said. "Somehow we have to get them to meet. Finish what it is they're after."

"How on earth can we do that?"

"What if we find Trenton and tell him you'll drop the charges if he tells us all he knows? If he's not part of the

Trinity, he must know who is. Why else would he be meeting someone in the passages under the estate if he wasn't in this up to his ears?"

"But how do we find Trenton? He's out on bail. He might be in Timbuktu by this time."

Jonathan shook his head. "I doubt that. He's too involved in this. My other guess is that whoever paid his bail is also part of it."

"Two out of three," Michael murmured. "But do you really think Trenton would confess to his involvement? And even if he did, why would he help us? His actions so far don't point to him giving us a helping hand. The guy's a maniac."

Jonathan frowned. "You're right; he's not likely to be much help. We should talk to Arthur when we get back. Maybe he's got some ideas."

"Maybe." Michael looked at the illustration again. "Well, at the risk of being a spoil sport, I think we'd better get back to the house—unless you have to stay?"

"No. God no." Jonathan said firmly, getting out of bed. "I'm not leaving you alone at a time like this. I'll phone the college and take the rest of the week off. I'll probably have to phone my mother, too, and tell her not to expect us after all."

"Oh, she'll be disappointed."

"I know, but I have this feeling things are developing around us." Jonathan stared at him intently. "Don't you get the impression that we're on the verge of finding out what this is all about?"

Michael nodded. "I've had that feeling on and off all day. I think that's what was wrong with me earlier, when you said I was morose."

Jonathan drew him into his arms. "At least we had a sweet afternoon."

"Here's to a lot more of them," Michael murmured, running his hands over Jonathan's bare butt. "Lots and lots more."

§§§§

On the way back to Abingdon, Jonathan called Arthur on his mobile phone. "Hello Arthur," he greeted the constable when he picked up. "Any word on Trenton?"

"Bugger's disappeared," Arthur said shortly.

"Too bad. We really wanted to talk to him about what he knows regarding the chamber we showed you."

"Oh, yes?"

"We found a stone medallion, or rather Michael found it among Trenton's things in the lodge. We also found out from a library book that the medallion is a key of some kind. Could be a key to that stone circle in the chamber."

"Crikey. This sounds exciting."

"Glad you think so," Jonathan chuckled. "Anyway, it can't be used unless some kind of incantation is said by the Chosen Trinity."

"The *what*?"

"Yes. I know it sounds a bit over the top, but that's what the book calls them—the Chosen Trinity."

"Even more exciting," Arthur exclaimed. "But what makes you think Trenton would cough up any information?"

"Well, if Michael said he'd drop the charges against him, and you were there to put some pressure on him...'

Arthur's chuckle interrupted him. "You mean put the cosh to him?"

"Well, not exactly. Just some friendly but official persuasion."

"Hmm, might work. Worth a try anyway. I'll see if the Super knows where he went. You'll be at Bedford Park tonight?"

"Yes, we're on our way back right now."

"I'll be in touch then."

"Thanks Arthur." Jonathan closed his mobile and shoved it into his back pocket. "Trenton's disappeared," he told Michael. "But Arthur's going to talk to his superintendent, see if he knows Trenton's whereabouts."

"It still makes me mad when I think of how little bail that judge set," Michael said bitterly. "If Trenton ever goes to trial, I'll be amazed. I told that Handley guy I was going to hire an attorney, and I still might. They all just seemed so cavalier about the whole situation."

"They certainly were less than helpful," Jonathan agreed. "And I'm not sure why—unless Trenton's a friend of someone in the police force."

"He *was* a private investigator," Michael remarked. "Could be he knows who to call for help."

§ § § §

Jack Trenton was nervous. More than that—he was scared. Things were suddenly not going at all well, and he knew that if he did not succeed in this undertaking, he would suffer dire consequences—he and the others—although in his heart of hearts he didn't give a toss for the others. They had already failed him. The medallion had not been recovered, and it was obvious that Michael Ballantyne must have found it, most probably still had it in his possession—might even have tried to discover its secret.

Well, Michael and his *friend* wouldn't have much luck with it. Without the incantation, it was just another piece of stone. Only when the words were spoken could it unlock the door to the Soul Keeper and set the captured souls free—and that could only happen when he and the others were present. The Trinity... that was how it had always been, and how it must always be. It took the Trinity, three of them to say the words, three times over...

Trenton ran the incantation over in his mind. The powerful words that had been passed down through the ages, uttered by the chosen Trinities throughout the centuries. It was considered an honor to be chosen, but time and time again Trenton had cursed the day it had passed to him. His father had reveled in it, gloried in the power it gave him, even though that power could not bring him the one he craved—at least not alive, not the living flesh he had yearned for. Trenton shuddered as he remembered the night his father drunkenly confessed his passion for Michael Thornton, had told him of the time he had fallen on his knees and begged Michael not to spurn him, but to come to him now that Jonathan Harcourt was dead. He had sobbed as he recounted how Michael had struck him across the face and vowed that he would pay for what he had done.

"You must be mad," Michael Thornton had railed at him. "Mad to think I would have anything to do with you. I know it was you who killed Jonathan. I've known it for a long time, but now I have the proof, and I'm taking it to the police. You will pay the ultimate price for murder, *Henry*."

Trenton's father had struggled with Michael, the man he loved above all else, had begged him not to do anything rash and foolish, but when Michael would not relent, he had knocked him unconscious, taken him to the chamber where with the aid of the two others who with him formed the Trinity, had strangled Michael and taken his soul captive. In his madness, he had considered it sweet revenge upon Michael, the man who would not return his love, and upon Jonathan Harcourt who, even in death, would not let Michael go. By capturing Michael's soul, Trenton's father had prevented them from being united in the afterlife.

When Bedford Park was sold and rumor was rife that the new owners had seen the ghost of Jonathan Harcourt, the knowledge that Harcourt was still waiting for his lover and would not pass to the other side without him filled Henry Bryant with a kind of mad pleasure. It was then that he told his son, Jack, what had to be done, and bound him to the promise that no matter what, the son would fulfill the wishes of the father.

Trenton's thoughts were interrupted by the ringing of his mobile. He glanced at the caller ID and grunted. "Yes?"

"Where are you?"

"Over at your house where you told me to stay put."

"Good. Stay there until I pick you up. The meeting is tonight."

"Finally. How do you know they'll be there?"

"They'll be there. Leave that to me. You have everything you need?"

"Yes. You'll both be there?"

"Of course. What good would it be if there were not the three of us? Relax, Jack. It'll soon be over."

Trenton shut off his mobile and sat back, closing his eyes. *Over. It will soon be over, he mused. And when it is, I'm getting as far from Abingdon as I can—and never coming back.*

CHAPTER TWENTY-SIX

Mrs. MacDonald had the dinner's menu on her lips as Michael and Jonathan strolled together into the kitchen. "Roast lamb with roast potatoes, parsnips, and a lovely salad on the side. Hope you brought home a hearty appetite, young sirs."

"You're making my mouth water," Michael told her, smiling at his housekeeper. "We'll just clean up first and be right back."

Jonathan's mobile rang as they went upstairs. "Hello?"

"It's Arthur. Can I see you both later tonight? I have some info you might find interesting."

"Yes, of course. Where?"

"How about the lodge. It affords some privacy. Say about nine?"

"That's fine, Arthur. We'll be there."

"We'll be where?" Michael asked, opening his bedroom door.

"The lodge. Arthur wants to meet us there around nine tonight. Says he has some interesting information for us."

"Oh yeah? Maybe he's had a chance to talk to Trenton. Just hope he doesn't bring that goofball with him." He walked into the bathroom. "Have to pee; won't be a minute."

There was a knock at the door, and Matthew poked his head in. "Excuse me, Mr. Jonathan."

"Come in, Matthew."

"Just wondered if you and Mr. Michael would want us for anything after dinner. The wife and I thought we'd go to the cinema, if that's all right."

Jonathan chuckled. "I'm sure Michael and I can manage for a few hours without you, Matthew. Leave the washing up after dinner. We'll take care of it."

Matthew gave him a horrified look. "Wouldn't dream of it. Annie would have a fit…"

"Well, you two have a nice evening. Michael and I will be fine. We're meeting with PC Bradley later; you know, the constable who came over the other day."

"The rude blighter you mean?"

"Well, he's seen the light, so to speak. Giving us a hand with the mystery we're trying to get to the bottom of."

"Oh, you mean your grandfather's disappearance."

"Yes. We're pretty certain Jack Trenton's involved in it somehow. We found a chamber among those passageways. The walls were carved with secret symbols of some kind. Looks like it could have been used for secret ceremonies or something." Jonathan could tell by the astounded look on Matthew's face that he was probably giving the man too much information.

"A chamber for ceremonies?" Matthew gaped at him. "The wife will have nightmares if I tell her about this."

"Better not tell her then, Matthew."

"Not tell her what?" Michael asked, coming out of the bathroom drying his hands.

"I was just filling Matthew in on what we'd found so far," Jonathan explained. "He doesn't think Mrs. Mac will take kindly to the idea of a secret chamber under the estate."

Michael grimaced. "Can't say I'm thrilled about it either. But don't worry, Matthew, we've got the law helping us out."

"You mean that young copper that was rude to you," Matthew remarked with a disdainful sniff.

"Oh, he's come around to our way of thinking," Michael said.

"Huh." Matthew didn't sound too impressed. "Dinner will be served in twenty minutes." He turned away muttering something about leopards not changing their spots.

After Matthew had closed the door behind him, Michael kissed Jonathan on the cheek. "That gives us time for a sherry—or something stronger if you prefer."

"Sherry?" Jonathan drew him into his arms. "You're being converted to the British way of life rather rapidly."

"Must be all those British infusions I've been getting," Michael said, snuggling against Jonathan's chest.

Jonathan hugged him tight. "Amazing—you said that without blushing! Oh, by the way, Matthew asked if it was all right that they go to the cinema after dinner. I said yes. Hope that was okay."

"Of course it is. Oh good... we'll have the house all to ourselves. I can chase you from room to room—naked!"

"Sounds like fun, but we do have Arthur to meet later."

"Darn. I'd forgotten already."

"Well, we'll just have to send them to the cinema more often, won't we?" He pressed his lips to Michael's nose. "Now come on, let's have that sherry."

§ § § §

Later, after dinner and having packed Matthew and Mrs. Mac off to the cinema, they sat in the lounge watching television while waiting for their appointment with Arthur.

"I suppose we'd better bring the book and the medallion," Michael said at one point, thoroughly bored with the nature program they were watching. "And flashlights. We should check out that chamber again now that we have some more information."

"The medallion still won't work," Jonathan reminded him.

"True, but I guess Arthur will want to see it." He looked at his watch. "Ten to..." he got up and walked over to the French windows. "Jonathan, there's a light on in the lodge. How could Arthur have gotten in?"

"Didn't we lock up the last time we were there? No, wait a minute..."Jonathan joined Michael at the window. "Last time we had to get out through that outside trapdoor, remember? We haven't been back since."

"Right. He must have tried the door and found it open. Okay, let's get over there and find out what he's got for us."

They grabbed the book, the medallion, and the flashlights and slipped out through the French doors, hurrying across the lawn towards the lodge.

"Could it be any darker?" Michael muttered, shining his flashlight ahead of them.

"No pale Queen of the silent night out tonight," Jonathan said, looking up at the dark sky.

"No who?"

"It's from an old poem by Charles Best. The pale Queen refers to the moon."

"Oh."

"Sorry, but I am a teacher. These things just spring into my mind now and then."

"I'd like to hear the rest of it sometime."

They had come abreast of the side of the lodge, and Michael could see clearly inside the lighted room. There was no sign of Arthur.

"Funny, there's no car here," Michael whispered. They rounded the building and ran up the steps to the front door. It was open, and so was the trapdoor in the middle of the room.

Jonathan peered down the steps. "He must have gone exploring."

Michael hesitated at the edge of the trapdoor. His skin was prickling with a sudden instinct that they were in danger.

"I don't like this," he muttered. "Why would he go down there alone?"

"Fearless policeman and all that," Jonathan replied. "Come on. We should let him know we're here." He started down the steps. "Arthur, you down here?"

When they got to the bottom of the steps, there was no sign of Arthur, and no answering call from him.

"I repeat, I don't like this," Michael said, looking down the passageway illuminated only by their flashlights.

"Let's see if he's gone on to the chamber." Jonathan gripped Michael's hand and started walking down the passageway, the beam from his flashlight throwing strange shadows on the walls. They rounded the corner at the end of the long passage and immediately saw that the chamber door was open. An eerie glow emanated from the open door.

"Arthur?" No reply. "Stay here," Jonathan hissed. "I'll take a look inside."

"No way." Michael gripped his hand tighter. "You're not going in there by yourself. What's that light? It wasn't there before."

Cautiously they approached the entrance to the chamber, then stepped inside. Michael gasped as he looked around.

"Someone's been here. Where the hell did that come from?"

In the centre of the room, just to one side of the stone circle, stood a dais of some sort, covered with a black cloth. At each corner of the dais a candle flickered, causing the wall carvings to seem as if they were moving, and giving the chamber an even more sinister appearance.

"An altar," Jonathan said.

Michael backed away. "I told you I didn't like this. Let's go!"

"I'm afraid we can't let you leave, Mr. Ballantyne."

The cold, harsh voice that came from behind them made Michael jump. Both he and Jonathan swung round and stared at the three robed and hooded men who blocked the chamber exit. Metal glinted in the hand of the man who had spoken.

Jonathan stepped forward. "Who the bloody hell…?"

"Stay where you are." The glint of metal in the man's hand proved to be a gun aimed directly at Jonathan's chest.

"Where's Arthur?" Michael asked, although he knew from the sick feeling in his stomach what the answer would be. The armed man let the hood fall back from his head. He smiled viciously at Michael's shocked expression.

"*Shit*… Inspector Paul Handley!"

Handley continued to smile as he said, "Let them see their executioners."

What?

Jack Trenton pulled the hood from his face, his dark, hard eyes reflecting the flicker of the candles' flames.

Jonathan stared back at him. "Well, no surprise there."

The eyes of a madman, Michael thought. But then, anyone who would get involved in something as crazy as this would have to be insane. He looked at the third man removing his hood.

"Oh, brother," Michael sighed. "I kinda had you figured, Arthur. And I bet you're not even gay, are you?"

"You must be joking," Arthur sneered while Handley and Trenton sniggered.

"Thought not."

"So, what's this all about?" Jonathan asked. "The Abingdon Police Department's annual costume party?"

"Bravado will get you nowhere, Mr. Robertson," Handley said in his harsh clipped tones. "Tonight, what was begun by Jack's father and mine, along with Arthur's grandfather, will be finished, once and for all."

"And what exactly was it that they began?"

Michael could tell Jonathan was stalling for time, but looking around the chamber, then at the three men blocking the exit, one carrying a gun, he couldn't quite see what time could bring them.

Boy, if ever we needed some supernatural help, it's now.

"They sacrificed your grandfather to the demon Aristonas," Handley said.

Jonathan shrugged. "Yes, we had already deduced that. But to what purpose?"

"To increase their power."

"Some power," Michael growled. "They're all dead—it didn't get them very far, now did it?"

"The power lasts beyond the grave," Trenton snapped. "Even now, my father's wishes control my actions."

"And that's what you want?" Jonathan looked at the big man in amazement. "To be controlled by what some dead person wanted? Is that what all of you want?"

"We have no choice in the matter," Arthur said, his tone sour and almost petulant.

"Everyone has a choice," Michael said, staring at Arthur. "You chose to make us think of you as a friend—I hope you're proud of yourself, 'cause in my book you're nothing but a creep."

"Enough," Handley barked as Arthur began an angry retort. "We're wasting time here." He gestured at Michael. "Take the medallion from him and tie him to the altar." While he trained his gun on Jonathan, Trenton grabbed the medallion from Michael and threw him down onto the altar. Michael struggled like a wildcat, but Trenton was just too strong, holding him down while Arthur tied his hands and feet together, then linked them with a length of rope.

Jonathan looked on in futile anger. If he could just get the gun from Handley… God, how had they ever got themselves into this mess? He remembered what his grandfather had told Michael's uncle in Michael's vision.

The police officer you spoke to is a friend of Bryant's—he was with Bryant on the night they took me here.

The police officer—and now they had fallen into the same trap Michael's uncle had, all those years ago. Telling Arthur all they knew had brought them here, and he was as powerless to help his lover as his grandfather had been to save his. Damn, but there must be something he could do!

"Just what is it you hope to do?" he yelled at Handley.

"Release our fathers' souls," Handley said, his gun never wavering from Jonathan's chest. "And the soul of Arthur's grandfather. Jack's father struck a bargain with Aristonas—two souls in return for increased power, but he failed to deliver your grandfather's soul."

"Because he didn't want Jonathan Harcourt and Michael Thornton to be together, even as captive souls," Arthur snarled, stepping back from the altar. He glared down at Michael. "Because he was so obsessed with your uncle, he broke the bargain, and Aristonas claimed my grandfather's soul instead. But Jack's father knew of you two, knew you'd come to replace the others one day."

"How the hell could he know that?" Jonathan asked.

"He could communicate with Aristonas," Trenton said. "The only one of the three who could," he added with misplaced pride. "And so he struck another bargain. He told me to watch for you, to be ready. When old man Burroughs hired a detective agency to locate the American, I was working for them. I read the files, figured out the connection, and knew it was only a matter of time before you two showed up."

"You are all fuckin' insane," Michael yelled at them, straining against his ropes.

"In your eyes perhaps," Handley said smoothly. "But now it's time. Your souls will seal the bargain with Aristonas, and our fathers will be free. Jack… the garrote."

"No," Jonathan whispered. "No," he said louder. "Don't do this." He stepped towards Michael, his hands reaching to help him, but Handley pressed the gun to Jonathan's skull.

"Don't make me shoot you," he snickered nastily. "We'd have to find another soul to replace you."

"What do you mean?"

"You must both die by the garrote. That is the way the demon likes it. In the last moments of death, your soul will struggle to free itself from its earthly body, and that's when Aristonas will claim it."

"Michael was right," Jonathan seethed. "You are all fucking insane."

"Arthur," Handley snapped. "Tie this one's hands behind his back." Arthur hurried to do as instructed, then Handley said, "The medallion—it's time."

Arthur took the medallion and inserted it into the centre of the stone circle. Michael's blood froze as the men began to chant in a language that sounded like nothing he'd ever heard before. Strange, barbaric words that had no earthly counterpart. The chanting went on and on, the ugly sounds burrowing into Michael's brain. He gazed at Jonathan's stricken expression and tried to smile.

"I love you," he said, feeling the garrote being fastened around his throat.

"Michael..." Jonathan's voice was hoarse and seemed to come from far away. The chamber became deathly cold, the air hard to breathe. Trenton tightened the garrote around Michael's neck. A grating noise filled the chamber. Jonathan saw the stone circle begin to rotate slowly, then lift itself from the floor before falling over on its side, revealing an open pit.

"Jesus," he whispered. The chanting grew louder. He stared at Michael, his lover's face now contused, his eyes beginning to bulge in his head. In his mind, Jonathan reached out to his grandfather. *Help us, please, don't let him die.* Aloud he screamed, "No!" and launched himself at Handley, knocking the man to the ground, the gun skittering away across the chamber floor.

"Shit!" Trenton stopped strangling Michael and rushed over to where Jonathan and Handley rolled over one another on the ground. He hauled Jonathan to his feet. "You're ruining it! Ruining it!" he bellowed.

"Sorry about that," Jonathan muttered, trying to free himself of the ropes and avoid Trenton's flying spittle at the same time.

Handley struggled to his feet, searching for the gun and failing to find it. "You idiot," he screamed at Jonathan. "You're just delaying the inevitable. Jack, get on with it!"

A high pitched yell had all the men staring at Arthur, who was staggering back from the open pit.

"Look, look," he croaked, pointing at Jonathan.

Michael tried to raise himself up from the altar. His throat ached abominably. He could barely swallow. His searching eyes tried to locate Jonathan. He gasped as he saw what had scared

Arthur. There were two Jonathans in the chamber: one, the man he loved, still trying to free himself from the ropes that bound him; the other, a spectral image that now tore the ropes from Jonathan's wrists. Free, Jonathan landed a punch to Handley's jaw, sending the man reeling back, floundering as his heel caught in the hem of his robe. He went down, and his head smacked with sickening force on the stone wall behind him.

Roaring with rage, Trenton was about to charge at Jonathan when he saw Arthur heading toward the chamber door.

"No!" Trenton grabbed the young policeman. "You can't leave. It needs all of us, you fool." But Arthur was determined to leave, lashing out at the bigger man with his fists. Jonathan took advantage of their struggle to untie Michael and help him off the altar.

The ghostly Jonathan beckoned them to the edge of the opened circle. They peered into the murky shadows below and watched with amazement what appeared to be a shifting of the darkness, a glimmer of light ascending from the depths.

"What's happening?" Michael whispered hoarsely, clutching at Jonathan's arm. Before their incredulous eyes, a wraith-like shape began to take form. A small cry of recognition escaped Michael's lips as the face of his uncle appeared, followed by the outline of his body. "Uncle Michael," he gasped, watching wide-eyed as his uncle's ghost was drawn into the arms of his spectral lover.

From far below came a chorus of spine-chilling shrieks of rage that jolted Michael and Jonathan from their trance-like fascination at seeing the murdered lovers reunited. Trenton threw Arthur to one side and blundered over to the open pit.

"You have angered the demon," he raged at them. "He will not release our father's souls without sacrifice." He lunged for Michael, but the ghosts were suddenly there, standing in front of Jonathan and Michael. Trenton's hands grabbed at them but found no purchase. He teetered on the edge of the open pit, his face etched with terror as he began to fall. His scream echoed back at them until the stone circle slid back into place of its own accord, sealing the pit and silencing his cries forever.

Shaken, Jonathan and Michael stared at the ghostly presences of their dead relatives. Jonathan was the first to speak. "Is it over?" he asked.

His grandfather's ghost nodded and pointed towards the chamber door.

"Let's go," Michael said, his voice still hoarse. Arthur had fled the chamber, but Handley still lay unconscious on the ground. "We can call for an ambulance from the house."

They hurried along the passageway and up the steps into the lodge. Outside they encountered a distraught Matthew and his wife, who were standing by their car looking down at a prone figure wearing a black robe.

"He just came flying out the door," Matthew told them. "Straight in front of me. I had no time to stop. I think it's that young copper."

Jonathan knelt by Arthur's side, feeling for a pulse. He looked up at Michael, shaking his head. "He's dead, I'm afraid."

"Oh, God…" Mrs. MacDonald let out a moan of distress while Matthew wrung his hands in despair.

"Matthew, you have your mobile with you?" Jonathan asked.

Dazed, Matthew handed his phone over to Jonathan, who dialed 9-9-9. "We need the police and an ambulance over here at the Bedford Park lodge straight away," Jonathan told the operator. "Yes, it's an emergency!" He took Matthew's arm. "This was not your fault, Matthew. It was an accident. Just tell the police exactly what happened."

"But what's he doing dressed like that?" Mrs. MacDonald asked, staring at Arthur's body draped in a black cloak. "And you, Mr. Michael, what on earth happened to you? Your neck's all red and raw. Oh, you poor lad."

"It's a long story, Mrs. Mac." Michael's voice was still raspy. "After the police have been, we'll have a drink and tell you all—well, nearly all."

Chapter Twenty-seven

A couple of hours later an exhausted Michael and Jonathan stood together in the shower, holding one another while the hot spray cascaded down on them. Too tired to even take advantage of the fact that their bodies were, of course, responding to each other's nakedness, they simply soaped one another, indulging only in an occasional kiss or caress. Neither man could scarcely believe what they had been through that evening; their only relief being that they were both still alive and the perpetrators either dead or in custody.

They had been amazed at how tightlipped the police were during the statements Michael and Jonathan had given them. Jonathan in particular noticed that neither the paramedics nor the police took notice of the interior of the chamber. They simply loaded Inspector Handley onto a stretcher and carried him up the steps as quickly as they could. Jonathan had taken advantage of their disinterest to pick up the medallion and bring it upstairs. After the police had left, he had smashed it to pieces, then ground it under his heel in front of Michael. "Just to be certain no one can ever use it again."

The paramedics had examined Michael's throat but declared him to be in no danger. A few days and the bruising would be gone, they had told him. Jonathan and Michael had offered to accompany the police to the station, but had been told it would not be necessary. Indeed, the police seemed most anxious to be gone as quickly as possible.

Drying each other after their shower, Michael wondered aloud just why the police had been in such an all-fired hurry to be gone, and why hadn't they even raised an eyebrow during their statements?

"A fear of warlock magic perhaps?" Jonathan suggested, rubbing Michael's hair gently with his towel.

"I don't know," Michael replied. "But I'll bet dollars to doughnuts there won't be anything in the local paper about any of this. Arthur was the victim of a hit and run driver, Inspector Handley is in hospital recovering from something or other—a heart attack maybe—and Trenton, well, he might not even get a mention."

"You should work for MI5—that's the British equivalent of the CIA. Sounds like the perfect cover up story."

"Yeah, well, after eight years of the Bush administration, we Americans have become very cynical about 'official' explanations." Michael wrapped his towel around his hips and walked into the bedroom. "I mean, they didn't even ask Matthew to come down to the station. What does that say?" Picking up the glass of Scotch Matthew had prepared earlier, he took a long and satisfying swig. He smiled, leaned back into Jonathan's arms, and shivered at the touch of his lover's lips on his ear. "Okay, I'll shut up," he murmured. "I have better things for these lips to do anyway."

He turned in Jonathan's arms and kissed him, long and sweet and hard. He rubbed his naked chest against Jonathan's and sighed with a mixture of pleasure and relief that what had been hanging over them ever since they'd met was finally over.

"Oh babe," he murmured, "I love you so much."

"And I love you so much," Jonathan said, holding him crushed to his body. "When you were tied to that altar and you looked at me and said, 'I love you,' I knew I couldn't let them take you from me. I called to my grandfather for help."

"And he came and did something I never knew ghosts could do. He actually freed you of those ropes."

"Yes, that must have taken all his power—power he must have been honing for the years he waited."

"Not all," Michael said, "because he managed to bring my uncle up out of the pit. Love did that, Jonathan. The love they had—*have*—for one another."

"It sounds so corny when it's said out loud, and yet you're exactly right." Jonathan caressed Michael's face and kissed him gently. "Like the love I have for you…" He paused, gazing into Michael's eyes with a sudden wonder. "Did you hear that?"

"Yes." Michael's eyes held the same slightly shocked surprise. "They're calling to us."

Together they walked over to the window and stared out across the moonlit expanse of verdant lawn towards the orchard.

"Look, Jonathan…"

At the edge of the orchard stood two figures, two men, holding hands and looking up at the house, at the window where Michael and Jonathan stood. Michael felt his heart tremble as the men lifted their hands in salute, then turned and walked hand in hand into the orchard. For a long moment neither Michael nor Jonathan moved in the vain hope that they would catch one more glimpse of the lovers reunited at last. Michael leaned his head on Jonathan's shoulder and slipped an arm about his waist.

"Now, it's over," he murmured

§ § § §

Michael's prediction of a police cover up proved to be correct when, the following day, the local newspaper made no mention of what had happened at Bedford Park. A short paragraph informed readers that Detective Inspector Paul Handley had suffered a seizure and had been admitted to Abingdon Hospital where he was stable but still unconscious.

Arthur Bradley merited an even smaller paragraph stating merely that he had been killed in a car accident and that he had been alone at the time.

Michael shook his head sadly. "I can't help feeling a bit sorry for Arthur," he said, putting down the newspaper.

"Why, Mr. Michael?" Mrs. MacDonald asked, putting a cup of coffee in front of him. "You're far too nice. Serves him right, I say. From all accounts he wasn't feeling very sorry for you— ready to do you in, he was." The housekeeper shivered. "I just can't imagine what you boys went through last night."

"It was pretty hairy all right," Michael agreed. "But I had the feeling Arthur had been coerced into joining the other two morons."

His housekeeper tsked. "Fancy the police getting mixed up in those terrible goings-on."

"And their policemen fathers and grandfathers before them, apparently," Jonathan said as he entered the kitchen.

Mrs. MacDonald beamed at him. "Good morning, Mr. Jonathan. Coffee or a nice cuppa?"

"A cuppa, thanks." Jonathan sat opposite Michael. "I've been thinking. You should probably have those tunnels and the chamber sealed off for real. All entrances and exits permanently closed."

Michael nodded. "Yeah, you're right. I don't think the cops will ever let word get out about what happened here, but just to be on the safe side…"

"Only problem is finding someone to do it without them gossiping about it," Jonathan said.

They were interrupted by a knock on the back kitchen door. Mrs. MacDonald frowned. "Who on earth could that be at this time of the day?"

They heard the sound of voices, then the door was pushed open and Matthew appeared accompanied by a tall man in police uniform.

Oh, oh, Michael thought, *what the heck does he want?*

"Good morning." He gave Michael a keen look. "Mr. Ballantyne?"

"That's me."

"I am Superintendent Barclay of the Abingdon Police Department."

"Pleased to meet you. This is my friend Jonathan Robertson, and my housekeeper, Mrs. MacDonald. Looks like you've met her husband, Matthew. Care for some tea or coffee?"

"Uh, no thank you. I wondered if I might have a word with you in private, sir—and uh, Mr. Robertson."

"Sure. We can talk in the study. Excuse us, Mrs. Mac."

"Breakfast will be ready in half an hour," she prompted him with a warning look at Barclay.

"We won't be long," Barclay assured her with a faint smile.

"Hmpf…" Mrs. MacDonald glared at the policeman's back. When the door was closed, she turned to Matthew and said, "He's most likely going to ask them to stay quiet about what happened. I can't believe the police would be mixed up in that kind of thing."

Matthew nodded. "They're worried and no mistake. Told me there'd be no charges against me, but I shouldn't go talking about it in the pub or the like."

Michael offered Barclay a seat, but he declined, saying he'd rather stand.

"Hope you don't mind if we sit down," Michael said, flopping into one of the big leather armchairs. "So what's up, superintendent?"

"Regarding last night, sir…"

"Yes, it was quite a night," Michael exclaimed. "Jonathan and I were lucky to get out of there alive. What do you suppose got into those guys?"

"I'm afraid I have no answer to that, sir." Barclay wiped at the line of sweat above his upper lip. "The whole situation is beyond belief. Hard to believe it happened."

"Yet it did happen," Jonathan said quietly. "Two police officers from your department tried to kill us—to *sacrifice* us, in effect."

Barclay shook his head. "As I said, I can't explain why they tried to do those terrible things. A mental aberration perhaps."

"They were nuts, all right," Michael agreed. "These marks round my neck? They're the result of a garrote—Inspector Handley's idea. So you're saying you knew nothing of this prior to it happening?"

Barclay stiffened. "Of course I didn't. Such a thing has never been heard of before in the whole of the Abingdon police force."

"Well now, that's not exactly true, Superintendent Barclay." Jonathan studied the policeman carefully. "Sixty years ago, the son of the previous owner of this house—my grandfather—disappeared, presumed murdered, as was Michael's uncle, though that was purported to be a suicide. This is a matter of public record. We believe that Henry Bryant, along with two members of the Abingdon police, committed the murders. Bryant denied the accusations and produced two witnesses—stalwart police officers, of course. The case was swept under the mat, but I think you'll find that Inspector Handley and PC Bradley are direct descendants of those men."

"You have proof of this?" Barclay demanded.

"Unfortunately no; at least none that could be presented in court."

Barclay sat down in the chair Michael had offered him earlier, not quite able to hide the sigh of relief that leaked out at Jonathan's last words.

"You must understand, gentlemen," he said, choosing his words carefully, "that a bizarre story such as this would afford considerable embarrassment to the police department. I would ask you, then, that you not broadcast what happened here." He smirked slightly. "Of course, most people would find it hard to believe, would they not?"

Michael and Jonathan exchanged glances and small smiles. Then Michael rose and walked over to the window. "Out there in the orchard, superintendent, there's an entrance to those passages and the chamber. Just before you got here, we were talking about having it permanently sealed, along with all the other ways in and out, and the chamber destroyed. Trouble is, as Jonathan has pointed out, how do we hire someone to do the job without them blabbing about it?" He smiled sweetly at Barclay. "Would you happen to know of anyone who could do the job—and stay quiet about it?"

"I could arrange that, yes. And I might add, the sooner the better."

"Just what we were thinking." Michael widened his smile. "And, of course, our lips are sealed. Passageways? What passageways?"

Barclay rose from his seat. "Thank you, gentlemen. Your cooperation is appreciated, and I will make sure that nothing like this ever happens again."

"Good luck with that," Michael said, chuckling.

Barclay blinked, but held out his hand. "Good day, then, gentlemen."

They saw him to the door and watched as he got into his car and drove off down the driveway.

"Do you think he was being honest when he claimed to know nothing about what happened here before?" Michael asked.

"Not sure." Jonathan put his arm around Michael's shoulder and steered him towards the kitchen. "Better not keep Mrs. Mac waiting to serve breakfast. But I bet Barclay does do some investigating—and then makes sure it doesn't become public knowledge."

§ § § §

Despite Michael's protests that he didn't want to meet Jonathan's mother for the first time looking like he'd been in a boxing match, and lost, Jonathan had insisted they go to Manchester together to visit her.

"She'd be upset if you don't come with me after I've told her how wonderful you are," Jonathan had teased him. "She's even going to make you a special Lancashire Hotpot."

"What on earth is that?"

"A big, sloppy stew—delicious."

"Lord," Michael had groaned. "This English diet is going to make a Jabba the Hut outta me."

"All the more for me to love."

Being with Mrs. Robertson—Margaret, she insisted he call her—in her comfortable cottage on the outskirts of Manchester brought Michael a sense of the normalcy he so badly needed.

After the manic events of the past few days, being beaten up by Trenton, then a near death experience at the hands of the madman, he was ready to revel in the motherly attention Margaret lavished on both him and Jonathan. That, and the down-to-earth common sense and good humour of Jonathan's sister Doreen made him realize just how much he was looking forward to Brad and Miranda's impending visit. He was already planning a grand reunion with both families at Bedford Park, including Jonathan's newly found grandmother.

Lying together in the rather small bed in Jonathan's old room, their quiet lovemaking took on an even more intensely erotic edge—something Michael had thought impossible. He'd considered it perfect before. Was it perhaps because they had faced death together and been presented with the possibility of having their new love affair brought to an abrupt end that they appreciated these moments alone all the more? Every caress, every heart-stopping kiss, every indefinable moment when they embraced each other's nakedness, when they feasted on one another and brought their minds and bodies together in exquisite sensation, all of that acted as a balm and swept away the sinister memories of that terrible night.

Michael had felt an initial sadness when he and Jonathan realized they were not reincarnations of their dead relatives. It had appealed to his romantic nature to think he and Jonathan had lived and loved before. But the greater realization that Jonathan's grandfather had never stopped loving Michael's uncle, that he had waited all these long years to be reunited with his lover was, in Michael's mind, even more romantic. And of one thing he was absolutely sure – it had been no accident, no coincidence that had brought Jonathan and him together. Had it been engineered by Jonathan's grandfather? Had he somehow managed to infuse those dreams into their consciousness? Jonathan said his grandfather had had a long time in which to hone his power – perhaps he'd even been privy to Lionel Burroughs thoughts, had somehow influenced Lionel into leaving his estate to Michael, setting the scene for what he knew was to be inevitable.

All of it sounded fantastic, incredible, unbelievable, and they would probably never know all the answers—but did it really matter? However it had happened, whoever or whatever was responsible, they were together, and *that* was all that mattered.

Michael snuggled into Jonathan's embrace, kissing his lover's slightly parted lips, then laying his head down on his chest.

"What?" Jonathan murmured, stroking Michael's arm.

"I love you."

"I love you too, Michael. I always have."

Michael closed his eyes and smiled. "Sweet dreams," he whispered. "I'll see you there."

ABOUT THE AUTHOR

J.P. BOWIE was born and raised in Aberdeen, Scotland. He wrote his first (unpublished) novel at the age of 14 - a science fiction tale of brawny men and brawnier women that made him a little suspect in the eyes of his family for a while.

J.P. wrote his first gay mystery in 2000, and after having it rejected by every publisher in the universe, he opted to put his money where his mouth is and self published *A Portrait of Phillip*. Now several books, short stories and novellas later, he is writing m/m erotica almost exclusively. J.P.'s favorite singer is Ella Fitzgerald, and his favorite man is Phil, his partner of 15 years. Visit J.P. on the internet at http://www.jpbowie.com.

SERVICEMEMBERS LEGAL DEFENSE NETWORK

Servicemembers Legal Defense Network is a nonpartisan, nonprofit, legal services, watchdog and policy organization dedicated to ending discrimination against and harassment of military personnel affected by "Don't Ask, Don't Tell" (DADT).The SLDN provides free, confidential legal services to all those impacted by DADT and related discrimination. Since 1993, its inhouse legal team has responded to more than 9,000 requests for assistance. In Congress, it leads the fight to repeal DADT and replace it with a law that ensures equal treatment for every servicemember, regardless of sexual orientation. In the courts, it works to challenge the constitutionality of DADT.

SLDN
PO Box 65301
Washington DC 20035-5301
On the Web: http://sldn.org/

Call: (202) 328-3244
or (202) 328-FAIR
e-mail: sldn@sldn.org

THE GLBT NATIONAL HELP CENTER

The GLBT National Help Center is a nonprofit, tax-exempt organization that is dedicated to meeting the needs of the gay, lesbian, bisexual and transgender community and those questioning their sexual orientation and gender identity. It is an outgrowth of the Gay & Lesbian National Hotline, which began in 1996 and now is a primary program of The GLBT National Help Center. It offers several different programs including two national hotlines that help members of the GLBT community talk about the important issues that they are facing in their lives. It helps end the isolation that many people feel, by providing a safe environment on the phone or via the internet to discuss issues that people can't talk about anywhere else. The GLBT National Help Center also helps other organizations build the infrastructure they need to provide strong support to our community at the local level.

National Hotline: 1-888-THE-GLNH (1-888-843-4564)
National Youth Talkline 1-800-246-PRIDE (1-800-246-7743)
On the Web: http://www.glnh.org/
e-mail: info@glbtnationalhelpcenter.org

If you're a GLBT and questioning student heading off to university, should know that there are resources on campus for you. Here's just a sample:

US Local GLBT college campus organizations
        http://dv-8.com/resources/us/local/campus.html
GLBT Scholarship Resources
        http://tinyurl.com/6fx9v6
Syracuse University
        http://lgbt.syr.edu/
Texas A&M
        http://glbt.tamu.edu/
Tulane University
        http://www.oma.tulane.edu/LGBT/Default.htm
University of Alaska
        http://www.uaf.edu/agla/
University of California, Davis
        http://lgbtrc.ucdavis.edu/
University of California, San Francisco
        http://lgbt.ucsf.edu/
University of Colorado
        http://www.colorado.edu/glbtrc/
University of Florida
        http://www.dso.ufl.edu/multicultural/lgbt/
University of Hawai'i, Mānoa
        http://manoa.hawaii.edu/lgbt/
University of Utah
        http://www.sa.utah.edu/lgbt/
University of Virginia
        http://www.virginia.edu/deanofstudents/lgbt/
Vanderbilt University
        http://www.vanderbilt.edu/lgbtqi/

Stimulate yourself. READ.

www.manloveromance.com

THE HOTTEST M/M EROTIC AUTHORS & WEBSITES ON THE NET

LaVergne, TN USA
23 July 2010
190670LV00001B/4/P